YOU'RE
THE
ONE
THAT I
WANT

YOU'RE THE ONE THAT I WANT

SIMON JAMES GREEN

SCHOLASTIC

Published in the UK by Scholastic, 2021
Euston House, 24 Eversholt Street, London, NW1 1DB
Scholastic Ireland, 89E Lagan Road, Dublin Industrial Estate,
Glasnevin, Dublin, D11 HP5F
SCHOLASTIC and associated logos are trademarks and/or
registered trademarks of Scholastic Inc.

ISBN 978 0702 30365 4

A CIP catalogue record for this book
is available from the British Library.

Printed by CPI Group (UK) Ltd, Croydon, CR0 4YY

Paper made from wood grown in sustainable forests
and other controlled sources.

1 3 5 7 9 10 8 6 4 2

This is a work of fiction. Names, characters, places, incidents and
dialogues are products of the author's imagination or are used
fictitiously. Any resemblance to actual people, living or
dead, events or locales is entirely coincidental.

www.scholastic.co.uk

For my nephew, Alfie Green

1

So I'm just standing there, in the doorway of the event space at this private members' club on Greek Street, clutching my bag of Tesco doughnuts (raspberry jam filling), because I'm not sure if there'll be food.

"Dress to impress," Mum told me when I asked if there was a dress code. *Dress to impress.* Instructions only ever given by the most malicious and vindictive of party hosts, knowing damn well it's open to massive interpretation. I've opted for the suit I wore for year eleven prom back in July. Ditched the jacket in the cloakroom because it was too hot, then caught sight of myself in a mirror and realized I looked like I was in my old school uniform. And it turns out everyone else is in jeans and T-shirts anyway. Yay, me!

Mum, meanwhile, is nowhere to be seen, even though she *knows* I don't know anyone here, but OK, this is her night, she's probably busy schmoozing other TV people, and quite honestly, that's for the best. Mum left her job as head of drama at Pink Wafer Productions last summer, setting up her own production company, Purple Smurf, "to produce the sort of telly she loves" (according to the press release that no press were interested in). Several months later, every single one of her projects had been rejected by broadcasters, the house had been remortgaged twice, and my grandparents were paying all our bills.

Then, in what she called "a final roll of the dice", she pitched *Cherries*, an edgy teen drama with a cast of impossibly sexy characters having an impossible amount of very successful sex. OK, I'm basing that "impossible amount" on my own (lack of) experience in the sex department, but still. If that's you, if you're my age and doing it *that much* and *that well*, then goddammit, *how?*

"They're all sixteen, just like you!" Mum told me proudly as I flicked through one of the scripts one day.

"Uh-huh?" I replied. "But played by twenty-six-year-olds, no doubt?"

"Wrong!" Mum trilled. "Part of what the broadcaster loved about our pitch was the fact the cast are all the real deal. Real teenagers. Actual sixteen-year-olds." She grabbed fistfuls of my cheeks in her hands. "Mm! You just can't beat the vulnerability of your real teenager! The gangly awkwardness! The pathetic fuzz on the top lip. The way the hormones just sort of . . . seep out of you and make your face all shiny."

"Ow!" I said, batting her away. "And also, all of that

sounds gross." Then I went upstairs, stared in the bathroom mirror and realized she was right.

Nevertheless, I've scrubbed up as best I could for this "meet and greet" event where they're introducing the cast to the press after a nationwide search. I've shaved my top lip, spent a day eating protein (well, some chicken nuggets – sort of counts?) to try and be less "gangly" and here I am, Billy No-Mates, a knob in half a suit, with every ounce of me screaming to turn back around, get the hell out of there, and go and eat my doughnuts in Soho Square until it's all over, when I'll turn up and tell Mum sorry but the Tube got delayed; *c'est la vie*.

"You!" A very stern, very angry-looking woman with a ponytail so tight it appears to be giving her a facelift is suddenly clicking her fingers at me.

I raise my eyebrows. Does she work for Mum?

"This way!" she barks, pushing me back out through the door and shepherding my compliant arse down a narrow corridor to the left, through a flapping door and into a steam-filled kitchen. Before I know it, a large silver platter is placed in my hands by a harangued young chef.

"Tempura prawns!" he says, in a Polish accent. "Shellfish! Gluten!"

I open my mouth to speak.

"Go, go, go!" the ponytail woman says, turning me around again and pushing me back out of the door.

I glance helplessly over my shoulder as I emerge into

the corridor, juggling the platter with my bag of doughnuts underneath, hoping the ponytail woman will follow me out and I'll have a chance to explain the misunderstanding. Instead, another waitress flaps through the door, holding a platter of smoked salmon blinis. "Sorry, can you move?" she says.

"Yes, but—" I sigh. The corridor is too narrow for her to get by. "Huh, OK."

So I have no choice except to head into the main room, where my plan is to use the extra space to turn around and go back into the kitchen, where I will firmly, but politely, explain the mistake. Unfortunately, no sooner do I enter the room than guests flock around me:

"Ooh, lovely!"

"Cool, food's here!"

"Love prawns!"

On the plus side, at least I have something to do now. And maybe it's better to be the guy handing round the snacks, instead of the one dying of awkwardness in the corner. In fact, never have I felt so popular. These tempura prawns are going down a storm! After the initial flurry of interest, I take the platter further into the room, weaving through the throngs of effortlessly cool, insanely beautiful TV people.

"Tempura prawns!" I announce, waving the platter about. "Shellfish! Gluten!"

A tall, middle-aged woman rocking skinny jeans, a

designer T-shirt and the confidence of being one of the most important people in the room turns towards me, then freezes.

"Freddie? What the fuck are you doing, darling?"

It's my mother.

"I don't know, they gave me these to hand out."

My cheeks start to burn as Mum hoots with laughter (because I'm nothing if not ridiculous to her), shakes her head (because I'm so disappointing she can't even) and beckons the ponytail woman over. "Sorry," Mum says. "This is my son, Freddie, I don't know why he's..." She gestures helplessly at the platter, her words tailing off, giving everyone in the vicinity (and they're already all staring due to Mum making such a fuss) an opportunity to complete the blanks: *I don't know why he's ... so useless! I don't know why he's ... such an utter knob! I don't know why he's ... my son, I seriously think he might have been switched at birth with some other child and clearly doesn't share any of my DNA.*

"Son?" the woman says, squinting at me. "Oh my god!" She extracts the platter from my hands. "Sorry! You're dressed like a waiter and I just thought— Well, because everyone else is so..." She glances across the vista of magnificent people, then looks me up and down, and no further comment is necessary, really. "My apologies." And off she goes to blatantly share the story with another staff member, while pointing at me.

"Why *are* you dressed like a waiter?" Mum asks.

"I'm not."

"I mean, you sort of *are*."

"It's my prom outfit!" I hiss at her. *"Dress to impress, you said!"*

"And why have you got a bag of doughnuts?"

"In case there wasn't food!"

"Which there transparently *is*."

"How could I have known that?" I bow my head to avoid eye contact as two very glamorous girls and a cosmically pretty boy squeeze past us. Who *are* all these kids, and why don't they go to *my* school? Literally, there is one hot boy at my school – Harrison Kane, who is completely epic, beyond gorgeous, and not the slightest bit gay.

I look back up and Mum rolls her eyes at me. "Well, anyway. At least you came. That's a miracle in itself." She blinks at me, then smiles.

I honestly don't see what the problem is if some of us prefer to spend our days in our bedrooms, shut away from society, when the alternative is to commit some awkward atrocity in front of hundreds of people, which is exactly what I've just done. Anyway, I don't bother arguing about any of this because it's impossible to win against my mother, so I just give her a smile back.

"That reminds me," she says, glancing at my mouth. "Laura's son is here and he's had the most brilliant work done on his teeth."

I glare at her.

"I'm happy with my teeth, Mum!" I snap. "They're not that bad!" They're really not, though. One of them is maybe a tad wonky, but you wouldn't really notice.

"OK, but the ones you can get now—"

"Mum!"

She gives me a tight smile. "Well. Come and meet Jasper."

"Who's he? No."

"He's one of the leads." She leans in. "He's gay."

"So?"

Mum straightens my tie a bit, screws up her face, then loosens it again. "He's adorable." She steps back and considers me a moment, then waves her hands vaguely around my head. "What's all this?"

"Um . . . my hair?"

"Yes, but what's it *doing*? Why's it all sticking up? Haven't you got a comb?"

"It's my look, Mum." I'm telling her that, but it's not like I have a choice. My hair won't really do anything except stick up in tufts, despite me trying every hair product under the sun.

Mum looks doubtful. "Maybe Jasper can give you some tips? He's got *great* hair – you just want to run your fingers through it. Come, see!"

I sigh as Mum starts pulling me towards the other side of the room. I'm resigned to yet another one of her

7

attempts to set me up with someone, *anyone*, because she has been insanely excited about me being gay ever since I told her, but insanely disappointed I've never actually kissed a boy, let alone brought one back for her to meet. Literally, she'll be scrolling through Instagram (she has five thousand followers – four thousand nine hundred and fifty-three more than me – another blow to my self-esteem), showing me pictures of random shirtless boys and saying, "What about him?" even though the boy in question is a model, with hundreds of thousands of followers, who lives in Brazil. Or, even worse, I'll be in town with her, and we'll pass some boy between the age of fifteen and twenty, and she'll be nudging me, occasionally also horrifically adding sounds of appreciation, like, "Phwoar!" which are not words anyone ever wants to hear their mother saying about teenage boys. To be clear, it's not that *she* thinks they're attractive, she's just trying to encourage me, I suppose a bit like when parents are trying to get their little kid to eat his food, so they pretend to eat it themselves and say, "Mmm! Yummy!" even though they don't personally find pureed banana appealing.

Mum manoeuvres me around and through assorted groups, all the while providing commentary as though it were a nature documentary: "They're some of the writers' room – Octavia just had a play about working-class lesbians on at the Royal Court, five stars in the *Guardian*, no real surprise there. . . That's Candice O'Connell, head of youth programming at MegaFlix, completely real tits, would you believe? No, don't look, Freddie! Jesus, I don't want her to think I've raised a pervert... *Megan Hurst* – and I'm not saying this to wind you up, Freddie, but the straightest, whitest teeth I've ever seen."

So far, so "classic Mum". Everyone else is amazing. Everyone else is brilliant. It's just gangly, messy-haired, wonky-toothed, wearing-all-the-wrong-stuff *me* who's letting the side down. I should have stayed at home with my doughnuts.

We push through a group of very loud men and emerge into a small patch of open space. "Jasper!" Mum calls as we approach a boy with his back to us, chatting with two women my mum's age.

Jasper turns around.

Honestly, I nearly choke on my tongue.

He's insanely beautiful. *Insanely*.

I grip more firmly on to my bag of doughnuts. Anything to ground myself.

His dark blond hair is short at the back and sides, longer on top, falling over his forehead, perfectly and adorably. And yes, *fine*, I would like to run my hands through it. Perfect (like airbrushed perfect), smooth skin – not a blemish in sight. Skin that doesn't have that pasty hue of too much time spent indoors and not getting up until lunchtime (basically my existence since exams finished), but rather a healthy glow, as if he's the type of person who eats fruit for breakfast, before doing yoga and having a green tea. He's about my height, but not remotely gangly or awkward; rather, he seems... *confident*. Like he doesn't look in the mirror every morning and want to cry. They may have cast *actual* sixteen-year-olds in this show, but I'm not convinced they've cast *real* ones.

"Freddie, this is up-and-coming star of the screen, and teen sensation, Jasper Perry!" Mum beams. She indicates me. "Jasper, this is my son, Freddie. He's a schoolboy."

Schoolboy?! I try not to scream. "Sixth form now, Mum," I say, trying to keep my voice light, like I'm not mortified.

"That's still school, darling," Mum replies.

Jasper holds his hand out for me to shake. "Hey," he says.

"Hey," I reply, a ripple of actual pleasure radiating through my body when I feel his warm, soft hand in mine. Also, he smells *divine*. Something expensive.

"I've got to catch up with Laura at the channel, so I'll leave you boys to ... get to know each other!" Mum smiles, like that pause before "get to know each other" wasn't in any way mortifying, then prises the bag of doughnuts out of my clammy hands. "The canapés were nineteen quid a head, so I think not." She squeezes my shoulder. "He's *hilarious*." And off she goes, leaving Jasper Perry and me staring at one another.

2

After approximately ten years of silence, Jasper speaks. "Hilarious as in . . . funny?" he says, as if he's been waiting for me to crack a joke.

"Funny, *peculiar*." I grin, opting for self-deprecating, because I usually find that's the best way of taking the edge off mortifying situations.

Jasper doesn't return the grin. If anything, he looks alarmed.

"No," I clarify. "I mean, maybe I am a bit, maybe we all are, what even is 'normal', right?"

Jasper stares at me.

"So," I say, deciding just to engage in normal-person conversation because I'm not sure this guy has much of a sense of humour, "you're one of the leads in this thing?"

He shakes his head. "Secondary character, really." He gestures to another handsome boy, older, bigger built, across the room. "Connor's the lead. Connor McCourt.

He was in that Amazon Prime show last year, *The Kill List?*"

I follow his gaze. "Oh, yes, he's very. . ." I swallow and flick my eyes back to Jasper, who has his eyebrows raised. "Very . . . *lead-like*. Very . . . *manly*." I wince at how much cringe I'm managing to spew out, but nevertheless press on. "He's all. . . I mean, you wouldn't say no, would you?"

Jasper frowns. "Wouldn't say no to what?"

"If he. . . I mean, not that he would. . . Not that *I* would. . ." I mean, I probably *would*, if we're talking turkey, but I get the feeling Jasper is already unimpressed and I don't want to make it worse. "It's just a . . . stupid expression . . . So he's the lead? OK, good. Seems like . . . solid, lead material."

"You said."

I nod.

"Do you want me to introduce you?"

"NO!" I clear my throat and adjust my volume back down to normal. I'm only trying to make some small talk since Jasper apparently can't. "God, no." I attempt a laugh and take a honey-and-mustard-glazed sausage from a passing waiter, dipping it in some ketchup. "Love sausage. I mean, *sausages*. Sounds weird singular, doesn't it?"

Jasper just stares at me. All of a sudden, I feel super self-conscious about everything to do with me. Maybe I *could* have done something with my hair? Is my wonky tooth upsetting for him? Is he pitying me? I do my best to finish the sausage, which isn't the easiest thing when Jasper is watching my every move with cold, hard (but, sure, really smouldering, deep blue) eyes.

I mean, I don't know if it's just me, but I'm not getting much love from this guy. And, like, not pulling rank or anything, but I am the son of his actual boss, so how arrogant do you have to be to not even pretend to make an effort? Not that Mum would sack him just because I didn't like him – she literally has zero respect for my opinions in the field of acting after I "massacred the role of Javert" in my primary school's (frankly insane) production of *Les Misérables* – but *he* doesn't know that.

"You have some ketchup on your. . ." he says, gesturing vaguely at my cheek.

I wipe it away with my finger, look at him, then lick it. "Mm!" I say.

Jasper looks. . . Well, he looks *appalled*, quite frankly.

Good. I like to be defiant in the face of haters.

Jasper looks down at his shoes, while I glance around the room, wondering if anyone's gonna save me from this. When the silence is just too much to bear, I do the only sensible thing. "Let's get a pic for Instagram!" I beam, pulling out my phone. "What's your handle, I'll tag you in?"

"I'm not on social media," Jasper says.

"Oh." I should have known he'd be one of *those.* I nod, encouraging him to seal his fate in the Twat Olympics.

"People begging for likes..." he continues, "those stupid little dances people do. The whole concept of 'influencers', it's just all so vacuous and self-obsessed."

I bet he likes vinyl.

"Do you like vinyl at all?" he asks.

Textbook.

"Not especially," I say. "I guess we all like different things. Anyway, OK, no selfie."

Jasper blinks at me.

"Ooh! Mini cottage pie!" I say, grabbing one off a passing waiter's platter, delighted for a distraction. I need to find a way to remove myself from Jasper, and, actually, this whole stupid party. Let's be clear: I do not belong here. I'd rather be anywhere else. I'd rather be in M&M's World, Leicester Square, and that is really saying something. I take a nibble of the cottage pie. "Want one?"

"I ate before I came. It's awkward to eat at these things." He glances at me, my mouth full of cottage pie, goes to speak again, then clearly thinks better of it.

I'm beyond sick of this shit now, so I double down on my awkward, piggy ways. Handily, another waitress comes by with some glasses of fizz – which I obviously help myself to – and another waiter arrives with some roast beef crostini, which I take two of. "Mmm, mm," I say, juggling all my goodies, while sipping fizz and munching away, all of which must be super annoying to Jasper Perry, King of the Knobs. Hopefully, I'll piss him off so much he'll make his excuses and leave. What's the point of being the hottest guy in the room if you're also boring and rude?

"What's this?" I say, alighting on some new delights. The waitress proffers her platter of cream cheese jalapeños and I pick one and bite in enthusiastically . . . with so much enthusiasm, in fact, that the cream cheese filling shoots out the other end and . . . ejaculates all over Jasper's T-shirt.

I freeze, mouth open, jalapeño dangling in one hand, as Jasper gazes down at the cream cheese jizz, then looks back up at me, his face a picture of horror, disbelief and disgust.

"Sorry, obviously got a bit . . . overexcited!" I say, trying to make light of it, although why I decide to do that by making a joke about spaffing over his T-shirt, I've literally no idea. "Um, can we. . ." And I move towards him – sort of thinking I can somehow help scrape the cream cheese off – and I bash into his hand as he's trying to do the same, which causes some of the fizz to splash out of my glass and splatter down his jeans, and some horseradish sauce from the other canapés to also splat on to his lovely T-shirt, which I notice bears a little tricolour fox woven on the breast pocket, and probably means I've just ruined a really expensive top from a designer I've never even heard of.

We lock eyes. He really does *not* like me. And I really do *not* like him.

"You see, this is exactly why I should have stuck with the doughnuts. This is basically all my mum's fault," I say.

"What difference would doughnuts make?" Jasper says incredulously.

I release a slow breath and count to five.

Jasper sighs. "Look, I have publicity photos, so I'll have to go and get cleaned up."

"Again, I'm really sorry."

"Yeah, OK. Enjoy all the food." And he scowls at me. He *scowls*. Then he walks off. *All the food?! All* the food? Oh my actual god! What an utter prick. I head towards the far wall, shovelling breaded halloumi, spiced vegetable pakora bites and macaroons into my mouth from passing waiters as I go because *screw you, Jasper!* You want me to eat all the food? I'll eat all the sodding food!

Would it really have killed him to be pleasant? I look around, frowning at all the happy, successful, popular people, most of whom appear to be kids my age. Who. Do. Any. Of. These. People. Think. They. Are? Swanning around ... all good-looking and socially confident, apparently with their lives glossy and wonderful already and—

It's happening again. Different people. Different situation. Same feeling. I'd brushed it off at prom, queuing to go inside, while two girls next to me (Anisha and Molly) flicked through the yearbook, giggling at the photos and funny entries. They got to me, and Molly said, "Who *is* that?" Anisha squinted at the picture and eventually replied, "No idea, does he even go to this school?" And I just kept quiet and looked down at my shoes out of embarrassment. To be fair, I used to wear glasses and I'd recently changed to contacts, so maybe that was why. "Who the hell is Freddie Bennett?" Molly mused, and, at the time, I'd thought how rude she was. How could she not know me? I'd been at school with her for five years! But, actually, you know what? She's right. Who the hell am I? Because standing in this room right now, I really couldn't tell you. I'm not a young actor about to break into the big time. I haven't just signed a seven-figure book deal after being talent-spotted on Wattpad, like the girls loudly chatting to my right. You know what I have done? I've passed some exams with very average grades, I'm addicted to supermarket doughnuts, and I'm pretty good at wanking. I guess we're not all destined for greatness, but I want to make some sort of impact. I want to be remembered for *something* – even if the thing you're remembered for is being the clown, or snogging lots of boys, at least you're remembered. No one ever said, "Oh, yeah, Freddie Bennett – he was the guy who got some average GCSE results, remember? What a guy! Got a five in maths!"

I suddenly feel like some street urchin with his nose pressed up against the pie shop window, wishing he could taste all the good things that the lucky people have.

Things . . . have to change.

Maybe . . . *I* have to change.

I'm not really sure how to do that, or what this

"change" even looks like, I just know I somehow need to work out who I am and what I want, and I have to embrace some sort of new me and go out there into the big wide world, not just stay in my bedroom . . . and damn well *live*, because this ain't it.

I drain my glass of fizz, immediately feeling a whole load more positive about how excellent this is all going to be.

"Cheers, Sexy!" I tell myself.

Two girls nearby turn around and glare at me.

"Oh god, not you, sorry!" I say, scanning the room for another tray of Proseccos.

3

I tell my best friends, Ruby and Sam, about the plan for the New Me when we go out for pre-start-of-term Italian food. Dinner seemed like a mature, grown-up way to embrace this new chapter. Better than desperately downing cherry brandy at Ella Morris's house party anyway, not that I've been invited, because she probably doesn't know who I am. I'm sketchy with some of the details about the terrible party that inspired me *because reasons*, but the point is clear: I need to change.

Ruby gives me serious side-eye as she sips her Coke, and I know that means she has doubts about my ability to go through with this. Ever since the three of us were thrown together on a year nine PSHE project, Ruby has shown pretty much only despair at my and Sam's every move. She is a large Black girl who literally has no shits left to give. Unlike almost everyone else, Rubes has never shown any interest in "fitting in", is very happy with her own sense of style and music taste, and has a unique ability to spot any kind of nonsense a mile off – and not be afraid to call people out on it. God, I envy her. She is so comfortable with who she is. She gave a fearless presentation about LGBTQ+ rights in that PSHE project, while we (two slightly effeminate, delicate-looking white boys) cowered behind her, looking down at our shoes every time she uttered the word "gay" and messing up our parts of the presentation with wobbly, breaking voices, stuttering embarrassment, and in my case, getting a bit of a boner for no reason. When some of the other kids tried to give me and Sam grief afterwards, Ruby told them not to mask their own insecurities about their sexuality in some homophobic bullying bullshit. Which, to my amazement, worked. We three had lunch together that day, and we've been mates ever since. And even though Sam and I aren't much compared to Ruby's fabulousness, she seems to like us, or we amuse her, or I don't know what.

"So the new you means you're giving up doughnuts and doing a diary?" Ruby says, putting her Coke back down.

I nod. I nod with enthusiasm and vigour. "Uh-huh! Doughnuts are the old me." I glance at Sam, who's squinting at me, like he's trying to work out if I'm actually an impostor, and the real Freddie has been kidnapped, and give him a wink. His eyes widen in either alarm or confusion, which makes me laugh. He's like a teen boy version of a fawn – gentle, delicate, easily scared, an absolute *smol bean* in purest form. *Not gay.* Everyone always thinks he's gay, but he likes girls. He just can't ever ask them out. Well . . . maybe just the once, but now I'm worried it'll never happen again.

"OK," Ruby says. "I kind of get the whole thing with this Jasper guy, all the beautiful people, blah, blah, you're feeling all bad about yourself. But why the doughnuts specifically?"

I swallow. "Well, you know, doughnuts represent failure and weakness. Maybe the doughnuts are some sort of metaphor for my hopeless life . . . like, doughnuts are round, and I'm going round in circles; I crave the doughnut's sweet taste because I'm clearly focused on short-term pleasure; some doughnuts have holes, and I am in one."

Ruby nods. "Stop trying to distract me with your god-awful metaphors, Fred. *What happened?*"

There's no point in trying to fool her. I haven't told them the full story and Ruby knows it. "So, I somehow drank a fair bit of Prosecco at the launch party – BECAUSE IT WAS ALL FREE – but, *bonus*, it made me quite chatty, so I ended up talking to Candice O' Connell, the head of youth programming at MegaFlix, and we were having a *really* great chat, like, I was saying a lot of interesting things about television and what narratives get told. . . I actually used that word. *Narratives*. Made me sound pretty educated, right?"

"Get to the point," Ruby replies. "And no, it made you sound like a bit of a knob."

"OK, so then Mum appeared and dragged me away from her mid-flow – apparently, I'd been 'bending her ear' for over forty minutes, and had accused her of cancelling *Sense8*, even though it wasn't one of their shows – and Mum packed me off home in an Uber as if I was some sort of liability. But then I asked the driver to stop on the way at Tesco Metro and the next thing I remember, Mum was prodding me awake at three a.m., and I was on the floor in our lounge, in just my boxers, with Disney's *Aladdin* – the full performance in 1080p HD – playing on my laptop (honestly, *mortifying*, she already thinks I harbour "unrealistic ambitions" to be on the stage), some half-eaten doughnuts scattered around me and a little bit of sick."

"I do like *Aladdin* though," Sam says.

"I mean, I probably would have chosen *Hamilton* sober," I reply. "But it's super clear. I'm a *mess* and the doughnuts have to go!" I say, way more emphatically than I actually feel.

"Or just don't drink so much?" Ruby suggests.

"Well, sure. That too! That's the old me. See?"

Ruby rolls her eyes.

"And the diary is to chart all this progress," I add. "Because one thing I am determined to see with The Freddie Project – official title – is *progress*."

"I didn't think people actually kept diaries," Ruby continues, absent-mindedly playing with her box braids. "Outside of plot devices in romcoms so the love interest can accidentally read something that upsets them, causing conflict in Act Three."

"You don't want any conflict in Act Three," Sam adds, slurping his milkshake.

"Conflict is fine in Act Three," I say. "Because after conflict comes resolution and then the happy ending."

Thankfully my further interrogation on this whole cobbled together concept is interrupted by the food turning up. Three lasagnes, rocket salad and garlic bread to share.

"Yes, we would all *love* some Parmesan, thank you," Ruby says as the waiter opens his mouth to ask. "And plenty of it," she continues. She fixes the waiter with a stare to make sure he understands the gravity of the situation. "Please bring a big wedge."

"Massive wedge," Sam adds.

The waiter nods. As a friendship group, we like our cheese.

"Soooo," Ruby says, narrowing her eyes at me. "This Jasper Perry, who, I agree, sounds like a total wanker, has clearly made an impact on you."

"I don't fancy him."

"Lies," Ruby says.

"Look, OK, he's hot," I concede, "but he's also a dick. He says dickish things. But, and I cannot emphasize this enough, *this is not about Jasper!* Or at least, not just Jasper. It's everyone who was at that party. It's all the people at school who don't even know my name. I want people to at least know who I am. I want people to see me and say to their mates, 'You know who that is? That's Freddie Bennett, he's. . .'"

"He's. . ." Ruby says, as I search for what exactly I am.

"Yeah, what are you?" Sam asks. "Gay?"

"No," I say. "I mean, *yes*, I am, but I don't want to be known for that particularly."

"Quite tall, then?" Sam offers.

"OK, so, everyone thinks this is funny, OK, that's *fine*."

Ruby rolls her eyes, then smiles at the waiter, who arrives back with the cheese and starts grating it over her lasagne. She nudges her plate to the side, so he has better access.

"All right, Fred." Ruby turns her attention back to me as the waiter continues grating. "So!" She sweeps her hands in front of her, spelling out the words. *"The Freddie Project!"*

"Tagline – *Randomly No Doughnuts!*" Sam adds.

"What exactly does this entail?" Ruby furrows her brow slightly, steepling her fingers to her mouth like an arts critic on a TV review show. "What are the actual nuts and bolts of this scheme?"

I run my tongue over my lips.

"*I see*," Ruby says.

"No, no," I tell her. "I have thoughts. I'm still working them out, but I definitely have thoughts."

"The floor is yours, my friend!" Ruby says.

Sam points his index fingers downwards. "Take the floor."

I swallow. "OK, so these are not necessarily entirely coherent, or in any particular order . . ."

Ruby glances at the pile of cheese on her lasagne, then at the waiter. "Nearly there."

". . . but they're a start. A beginning. Every plan needs a beginning. And a middle. And . . . an end."

Ruby frowns. "You seem to have looped back round to story structure again. OK, I'm going to put you out of your very evident misery. I will help you formulate this Freddie Project. What happens when you open the door, Freddie? What happens when you leave the door wide open?"

"Thieves rush in?"

"No," Ruby says.

"Cold air?"

Ruby sighs. "Opportunity comes knocking." She gives me a slightly-too-pleased-with-herself smile, then looks back up at the waiter. "That's sufficient, thanks."

The waiter sighs and moves on to Sam, whose eyes widen at the sight of the cheese. "*Oh, yes!*" he says, nodding enthusiastically.

The waiter starts grating again.

"Oh! You did a metaphor!" I say to Ruby, clapping my hands together in mock delight. "Oh, clever, clever you! Why would opportunity knock at an already open door, though?

The door would kind of need to be closed for that, really."

"Is that enough Parmesan?" the waiter asks.

Sam looks down at his plate. "Well, I *guess*?"

"He wants a bit more," Ruby says. "Look at him, he needs the protein."

The waiter glances at Sam, seems to clock the fact he's skinny and small, and resumes grating.

"Opportunity is encouraged by the open door," Ruby says, turning back to me. "Opportunity finds the open door welcoming, but wouldn't be so rash or rude as to simply walk in without knocking first. Opportunity wants to give you a chance to throw on a towel. Opportunity isn't a creeper."

"*Fine*," I say. "But outside of the world of this ridiculous metaphor, how do I open the door in the first place?"

"You start saying yes to things," Ruby says.

"OK, say yes. Huh. Like . . . like everything, or just *some* things?"

"I am resplendent with cheese!" Sam announces, which elicits only a confused look from the waiter, so he adds, "That's enough cheese, thank you."

The waiter moves to me. "I'm guessing. . ."

I nod and he starts grating with the air of a condemned man.

"Just say yes when stuff comes up, Fred!" Ruby says. "Your problem, one of them, is that you're always a no person, a let-someone-else-do-it person – and saying no means nothing will ever happen and nothing will ever change. But by saying yes you're opening the door for opportunity – for a new experience, or a chance at something, a wider circle of friends, maybe even romance. *No* shuts the door firmly. *Yes* opens it and welcomes something new in. See?"

I chew my lip. "But surely... I mean, saying yes to everything would be ridiculous. It could even be ... dangerous or get me in trouble with the police." I blink at them. "Oh, not that I care about that, because, you know, I'm fully *cool*, but, huh, ideally, I don't want to be thrown in jail! Ha ha! But, like, if I'm saying yes all the time, how can I be sure where to draw the line?"

Sam clears his throat. "Let's have a practice. Fred, would you like to join the debating society?"

"Yes?" I say.

Sam nods. "Fred, would you like some dirty street heroin?"

"No?" I venture.

"There, you've got it," Sam says, going back to eating.

"You make it sound easy," I grumble.

"It *is* easy," Ruby replies. "You just gotta change your default mindset."

"Is that enough cheese?" the waiter sighs.

"YES?" I reply. I would normally like more cheese, but I'm saying yes to allow something good to happen.

The waiter sighs and walks away. "Ten quid's worth of

Parmesan!" I hear him grumble to a co-worker.

I stare down at my plate. "And now I have less cheese than I would like. I said yes and now this. Where's my opportunity now, hmm?"

"Don't self-sabotage just because it's scary, Fred." Ruby smiles. "Bon appétit!"

We all make a start on our lasagnes, while I mull over the idea that I self-sabotage. I've literally *said* I want things to change, I want to embrace the full richness of life's infinite tapestry (god, I'm poetic!) so why would I then try and actively not do that? I would take this up with Rubes, but the fact is, this lasagne is gorgeously caramelized on top, soft and luscious in the middle, has a rich ragu and soft, creamy white sauce, is complete perfection and I'd rather eat than dissect my alleged personality flaws.

"So," Ruby says, after we've all been silently eating for a bit. "Do you want to hear my Harrison Kane news?"

"YES!" I squeal. "Oh, *yes*! Big yes to this! How *are* Harrison Kane and his very lovely abs?"

"Harrison Kane and his very lovely abs. . ." She fixes me with a stare. "Are going out with Charlotte Stefani."

"*WHAT?*" I hiss. "That ... duplicitous bitch!" Charlotte Stefani is the doyenne of the school theatre scene. President of the Drama Society, possibly because she creates so damn much of it herself (although in reality, more because her super-rich father basically paid for the school theatre), she has only ever regarded football boys like Harrison Kane (and his lovely abs) with disdain and a sort of morbid fascination about how rough and primordial they are – "Like cavemen, always grunting and scratching their balls," I heard her say to one of her mates once. Indeed, for most of year ten and eleven, she was dating Calvin Jackson, a tall, athletic boy, who, while also a top sportsman, plays hockey and lacrosse – classy sports, which are more in keeping with Charlotte's aspirations. Top set brilliant academically, Calvin's also *a really nice guy*. Way too nice for Charlotte anyway, and what do you know? With the news at the end of last term that Harrison Kane (plus lovely abs) is to be captain of the football team, Charlotte Stefani has changed her fickle mind, probably hedging her bets in case he gets taken on by Tottenham or something, and would therefore be better placed to keep her in the affluent lifestyle to which she's accustomed. As footie captain and queen bee of the drama scene, she and Harrison will be the celebrity couple of the school.

"You're gonna see them together at school on Monday, so you may as well get over it now," Ruby says.

I nod manically. "Have they had sex? Don't answer. Have they? No, I don't want to know. But have they?"

I hold my breath and wait for Ruby to finish chewing some garlic bread and answer.

"According to the rumour mill, and I did hear this via Ella Morris, who heard it from Priya, so it's not first-hand knowledge, but . . . *yes.*"

I gasp. "We were going to lose our virginities together!"

"Only in your frantic, hot, sticky dreams, my friend," Ruby smiles. "And may I say very hopeful of you that his virginity isn't a distant memory. Apparently he's quite . . . well endowed."

"I know, I've seen it waggling around in his footie shorts—"

"Oh my days, I was joking."

I swallow. "Right. Sure. Yep. Me too. Anyway, that's all fine," I mutter. "Because Harrison is old news and this is my fresh start."

I busy myself tucking in to the lasagne again, but the point is very clear to me. People are moving on, changing, getting their lives together. And I need to do that too. Lusting after Harrison Kane (regardless of loveliness of abs) is stupid, and a distraction from the wider issue. I wonder if some part of me fixed on him because I knew it would never happen? Because maybe Ruby is right, and maybe I've actually been sabotaging myself all this time because I'm *afraid* of living. I'm scared of . . . well, I don't know what, but, if I'm totally honest, even the thought of asking out someone who is *actually* gay or bi and might *actually* say yes scares the shit out of me. Everything scares the shit out of me. Somehow, I'm going to have to be brave.

"You're right," Ruby says after a while. "It's a good moment for fresh starts. For all of us."

I hold my hands out in a gesture of *Yes?! And?!* I would

never have imagined that Ruby would want to change anything about herself.

"A girl can't just be top grades and Oxbridge offers," Ruby says. "Well, a girl *can*, if she so desires, but this girl doesn't want to end up in a tragic *Booksmart*-style scenario, you know, where everyone else gets on to great uni courses too, but they also had a social life and possibly some sex."

I can't even picture Ruby with someone else. She's always seemed . . . *complete*. "You're going to go to a lot of parties, then?" I ask.

Ruby nods. "Maybe a few. Maybe be a little more active on the dating scene. I like the idea of a relationship." She turns to Sam and smiles. "What about you, Sam?"

Sam takes a deep breath, then exhales. "I'm just gonna keep my head down, focus on my studies, nothing else. To be honest, it'll be a win if I just get through the term without crying."

I give Sam's shoulder a sympathetic squeeze. He had his heart broken last year by Ella Morris (who he'd fancied since year nine) when he asked her out on a date. After she said, "I thought you were gay?" and he'd said he understood the possible confusion, but he wasn't, and she then said, "Are you sure though?" and he'd said he was sure, he just liked musical theatre and hated PE, but that didn't mean anything, she bluntly rejected poor Sam citing her need to find, "A guy who can really look after me." Sam didn't know what that meant, so he took up karate classes, hoping to impress her, only to get a sprained wrist and then to discover Ella was seeing Jamil anyway – which rubbed salt in the wound because Jamil couldn't look after a stick insect... Like, literally, I was at primary school with him, and he took the class one home over Easter one time, and it never came back. Anyway, after all that, Sam retreated even further into his shell than he was before. It's one of the reasons we're such good mates – we're both very happy just communicating online from the safety of our bedrooms while real life happens outside. But, I guess, at some point, that has to change ... if you ever want anything to be different. I think I'm ready for that. But I'm not sure Sam is.

Ruby smiles, holding her glass up for a little toast. "That's cool, Sam. It's not all about romance. But we're all gonna do *us*, and try to do that well, that's the point. So! Here's to the first day of our futures! Here's to ripping up the rule book, leaving the comfort zone, getting out there and grabbing life by the horns!"

I already feel like Ruby has a better handle on this than me.

4

It's morning break on the first day of sixth form and I'm hurrying along the corridor, gingerly holding my scalding-hot plastic cup of vending machine coffee (we have a coffee machine in the sixth form common room – *oh, yes!*), when Mrs Mason, head of sixth form, stops me.

"No coffee in the corridors," she says.

"Sorry, I didn't know."

"There's a sign on the vending machine."

"Oh."

"*Also,*" she continues, "why were you late for the workshop this morning?"

"Right, OK," I say. I take a sip of coffee.

"No coffee!" she says.

"OK, but what shall I—"

"You might scald a year seven."

"Honestly, I'll be so careful—"

"If you want the vending machine taken away, that's what'll happen. And you can be the one who tells the other sixth formers why." She stares at me.

"OK, fine, but—" I glance helplessly at the plastic cup. What am I supposed to do with it?

"Why were you late, Patrick?"

OK, it's fine, head of sixth form has nothing to do with the younger years, so she just doesn't know my name yet. "It's Fre—"

"*Why were you late?*"

"There was a dog on the playing field."

Mrs Mason folds her arms across her chest and blinks once.

I nod. "Also, by the way, by name is—"

"And that made you late *why?*" she says. "Did you help catch it?"

"Mm, no, we were just watching."

"Uh-huh?"

"It was funny," I say.

"Was it?" Mrs Mason replies. "I don't think it's particularly 'funny' when it means you're late for a workshop on time management, do you?"

I open my mouth, but Mrs Mason gets right in with, "I'm watching you, Patrick. Don't disappoint me!"

"I won't!" I reply. Aw, heck. I can be Patrick. Maybe that's best? Since Patrick hasn't made the best impression already.

"I'll take that for you." She holds her hand out for the plastic cup.

"OK," I say, handing it over. "It's a cappuccino, if you want it."

"I don't want it, Patrick," she says. And off she goes.

And there we go. Barely two hours into day one of the New Me, and the head of sixth form doesn't even know who I am.

"You summoned me?" I say to Ruby and Sam when I reach the drama noticeboard.

"Voila!" Ruby says, gesturing towards a poster, an excited grin on her face.

The poster, typed in Comic Sans – of all atrocities – is advertising the school musical, although it's tantalizingly clickbaity:

> Come to the drama studio at
> 1:15 p.m., where the title of the
> show will be revealed! All years
> welcome – we need singers, dancers,
> actors, as well as backstage!

I have no idea what we're doing here. Sure, Ruby likes singing, she belongs to a choir outside of school, but she's always eschewed any involvement with the school drama scene because, in her own words: "Theatre kids are a nightmare. Backstabbing bitches, every last one of them."

Which is fair enough. Sam's really shy and way too sensitive to have his soul ripped apart during a rehearsal process, and as for me. . . I mean, I love the theatre, I love the West End, I'm a fully paid-up member of the Stereotypical Gay Club in that respect, but actually being in a show again? A cold shiver ripples through me as a memory flashes before my eyes. I'm alone on the stage . . . in the spotlight . . . blinking away tears . . . people in the audience whispering and pointing. . . I shake myself back to the here and now to put this ridiculous idea in the bin, where it belongs.

"No," I say.

Ruby shakes her head. "We had a very clear conversation about saying yes."

"In certain circumstances! And this isn't one of them!" I drop my voice to more of a hiss, not wanting everyone to overhear. "I am fully committed to this project, I am ready . . . nay, *gagging* –" Ruby grimaces "– to say yes to something, lots of things, today." I look around me, searching for examples. "Jumble sale!" I say, my eyes alighting on a hand-drawn poster.

Ruby screws her face up. "I thought you wanted to make an impact! How is that gonna happen if you're neck-deep in old jumpers?" She taps the school show poster. "Go big or go home!"

"Why, Ruby? *Why?*" I hiss. "You hate theatre kids. Why this? It's madness! *This is the dirty street heroin of which Sam spoke!*"

"Poster was here. I'm taking it as sign from the universe!" Ruby chirps. She leans towards me. "If you analyse everything that comes up, you'll always find reasons to say no and you'll never do any of it. Just gotta take what comes your way, I reckon!"

I turn to Sam, cross my arms and raise my eyebrows. *And what about you?*

Sam shrugs. "Thought I'd try out for it."

"*What?*"

"Just saying yes, that's all." He must clock my expression of disbelief, because he adds, "Feel the fear, do it anyway! Besides, Ella doesn't do theatre, so that means she won't be involved, so I won't have to be reminded of her, or her lovely hair, which smells of coconuts."

"Oh my god. Everyone's changing. I hate it."

"That's the whole point, Fred," Ruby says. "And that's why you're coming too. It's the new you."

"You *know* I don't do performing arts!" She does know this. I have not mounted a stage since the *Les Mis* debacle, and nor will I.

"You have a commemorative anniversary *Phantom of the Opera* mug at home. *I've seen it.* You love a bit of musical theatre merch!"

"I love the merch. I love the shows. I can love those things without loving the act of putting myself on a stage for all to ridicule."

"OK," Ruby says, "so what have you said yes to today?"

"Saw the vending machine, asked myself if I fancied a coffee, *said yes*."

Ruby nods. "What happened next?"

"It was taken off me by Mrs Mason, who thinks I'm called Patrick."

"Ah!" Ruby says. "But that gave you the *opportunity* to correct her, so in a way that's good, and proves the idea works!"

I shrug.

"Oh. You didn't correct her?" Ruby says.

"She was very cross and talking very fast, and there was, like, no space for me to say anything."

Sam looks down at the floor, embarrassed for me, I think.

"Any extracurricular stuff you've signed up for?" Ruby continues.

I blink at her. "Ruby, it's only morning break on the first day back."

"Classic Freddie. Now's never the right time!"

"I'll find something," I tell them both. "I'll find something today. Just not this. Anything but this."

"School musical?" I hear a male voice say, over my shoulder. "Oh, cool."

I turn and come face-to-face with a boy so mesmerizingly gorgeous, if he was for sale on Amazon he would have five solid stars and the reviews would read:

Possibly the most beautiful teenage boy I have ever seen! ★★★★★

With his cheeky smile, cute nose, and excellent hair, which is short at the back and sides, longer and quiffed up on top, this is a fine example of some Freddie boyfriend material which I have no hesitation in recommending. ★★★★★

Arrived on time and with no obvious damage. ★★★★★

"Hey, I'm Zach," the boy says, offering his hand to shake. "I've just started here. You're sixth form too, right?"

"Right. I'm Ruby," Ruby interjects.

"Hey, I'm Sam."

"Zach," I repeat, shaking his hand limply. I mean, I don't think I have drool coming out of my mouth, but honestly, I would not be surprised. I try to pull myself together because "pathetic melted pool of lustful teen boy" is not the impression I want to give the loveliest boy to arrive in school since Harrison Kane.

"You're called Zach too?" Zach says. "Wow, what are the—"

"No, that's . . . that's your name," I say. It's going well.

He stares at me for a moment, then breaks into a wide smile. He has good teeth. Very . . . you know, his folks have paid out for some good orthodontic work and he's a regular at the hygienist. Mum would give him her full approval, that's for sure.

"Riiiight," he says. "That's my name. And you are?"

It's at this point Mrs Mason rounds the corner, probably heading back towards the staffroom. "Ah, Patrick!" she says, nodding. "The school show. That would be a good use of your time."

"Yes, definitely, but also—"

"Exciting to see your name in lights, Patrick!" And she disappears down the corridor, followed by completely unwarranted gales of laughter from my supposed "friends".

Zach smiles at me. "Guess you're Patrick, then. Hi."

"Um . . . no."

"No?" Zach frowns.

I swallow. "FREDdie!" It comes out high, then low, my voice cracking all over the place. But I act like that didn't just happen and give him what feels like a really self-conscious, goofy smile, certainly compared to his perfect gnashers. "Freddie Bennett." And for some awkward reason, I do a salute, like he's some sort of army general, or at least a Cub Scout leader "Mrs Mason has me mistaken for someone else." I nod, like that's fine.

Zach nods too.

OK, some more information about him: he's around my height (all the better for convenient kissing – no need to bend down or reach up – but I'm getting ahead of myself);

dark brown hair, dark brown eyes – totally the sort you could get lost in (his eyes, I mean, not his hair); his white skin has that "spends a lot of time outdoors" glow to it, and that totally tallies with his slightly athletic build, suggesting he might be a sports type. Mm, another football player?

"Freddie?"

"Huh?" I blink at Ruby, who shakes her head at me in despair.

Zach laughs again. "I was just asking, are you guys the theatre kids?"

"What? Oh, um. . ." I glance at Ruby, who raises her eyebrows, and then at Sam, who also raises his eyebrows. They're clearly willing me to do it. Like we agreed. Like I promised. I look back at an expectant Zach. "YES. Yes, we are!"

"Great!" he says. "I found some friends!"

"Ha ha ha! You have!" I say. I glance back at Ruby so she can give me some sort of approving nod, but find she's actually looking at me like I'm a knob. Never mind, it's fair to say Ruby has a "resting you're-a-knob face" anyway. I turn back to Zach. "So, are you gonna audition for this thing?" I ask, tapping the poster.

"Yeah, sure!" Zach says. "You?"

"Of course! YES! Love . . . love the theatre!" I laugh. Oh my actual god, what am I doing?

I can feel Ruby just staring at me.

"What do you reckon it'll be?" Zach asks.

I blow out a breath, mainly to steady my nerves and stop myself from screaming with the anticipated terror of everything I'm apparently now doing. "Let's be real, last year it was *Little Shop of Horrors*, so it's probably gonna be *Grease*."

"Tell me more, tell me more!" Zach grins.

"OK, well, *Little Shop of Horrors* was OK, I saw it, I wasn't in it, because—"

"No, those are lyrics from the show," Zach says.

"Oh!" I say. "Oh, yes! Ha! Sorry."

There's a silence before Zach says, "So, seriously, tell me why it's gonna be *Grease*. There are more than just two musicals in the world."

"Oh!" I say. "Oh, well, it's going to be directed by Ms Pearson and, back in the day, she was actually a real live actress, she's always ... going on about it, I had her for English last year and she talked about it all the time, so she always picks a show that she's been in." I'm giving Zach the kind version of what is basically school legend. The fact is, Ms Pearson has somehow manipulated the head teacher into being allowed to always direct the school show because it's her "thing", even though we actually have a really nice, less self-obsessed drama teacher. The fact we do *Little Shop of Horrors* and *Grease* on a two-yearly rotation is, according to Charlotte Stefani, who researched Ms Pearson online, because those are the only two shows she was ever in. Additionally, and again, according to Charlotte – who is a shit-stirring bitch and might be lying – these weren't in the West End, or even on a UK tour, but in "semi-pro" productions at some dive in Croydon. But telling Zach all that would be a bit negative, I feel, and I'm all about the positivity right now ... or at least, I want Zach to get the sense I'm a nice guy, not some bitchy gossip, so it can wait.

"Hmm." Zach nods. "Well, Freddie, you're gonna have competition for the role of Danny!" he says.

My eyes widen. "Oh! Oh, no, no, I'm not really a Danny ... you are, you're much more Danny, all..." He raises his eyebrows as I look him up and down. God, he's wearing grey sweatpants, which are like catnip to me. I make a very conscious effort not to admire anything below his waist that grey sweatpants are notorious for showing off, settling my eyes instead on the just-gentle-enough-not-to-be-intimidating bulge of his pecs through his white T-shirt and sighing. I totally know you shouldn't go on first impressions, you should let romance grow organically and all that, but this is the first boy who has made my stomach flutter since Harrison-I-don't-even-care-about-saying-his-sexy-surname-any-more and I just ... really, truly, want something nice to happen. I clear my throat. "Aren't you? All Danny-like. I'm more of a ... I'm a..." I look at Ruby for help, but she's just looking at me, slightly blankly, slightly amused. I glance at Sam. He's biting his lip, blatantly stifling hysterics. I smile and look at Zach again. I literally can't think of a single character from *Grease*. "Sandy?" I say finally.

Zach nods. "Whatever you like, mate," he says. "But if you're Sandy and I'm Danny, we're gonna have to practise our stage kissing!" His eyes meet mine and I'm ninety per cent sure in that instant that he's into boys. There's a twinkle in them, a questioning, like he's trying to work out if I am too.

"Ha ha! Yeah!" I say, laughing way too hard.

Zach gives my shoulder a quick squeeze. "Cool, see you there. I've got a free, so I'm gonna go and work out for a bit. Do you guys have free weights and stuff?"

I nod. "Yes, only for sixth form, though. Which is what we are, so yes."

Zach smiles and saunters off.

"*That . . .*" Ruby begins.

"Please don't."

". . . was the most buttock-clenchingly awful bucket of cringe I have ever witnessed," she continues.

"No, no. . ." I begin

"You *hypocrite*," she says.

"No, Ruby, actually far from it!"

"You shallow, boy-chasing *hypocrite!*"

"I said yes! I have literally done the thing I said I would!"

"Only because of a boy!" she snarls. "This is not about boys. Boys can be a happy consequence, but they should not be the cause!"

I chew my lip, then look her in the eye. "It was the universe."

She folds her arms across her chest.

"Just like the universe placed this poster for you to see, according to your own words, the universe devised a way to encourage me to say yes. It's all part of some greater plan. We are but prawns—"

"*Pawns!* Jesus!" Ruby snaps.

"Helpless pawns in a complex game of chess." I smile at her, like I actually believe that. But, truthfully, I am quite pleased with myself. I said yes – OK, maybe for some of the wrong reasons, but I still said it, and now Zach knows who I am, we've chatted, we've possibly flirted. In my world, that's progress. The Freddie Project is on track and firing on all cylinders.

Ruby's face tells me she doesn't agree with that assessment, however. "Well, I'll tell you something for nothing—"

Whatever that thing is, Ruby's face suddenly changes from outrage into something softer and kinder. "Hi!" she says, brushing her box braids off her shoulders and smiling as newly single mega hunk Calvin Jackson strolls towards us.

"Morning!" He smiles at us, then glances at the poster. "Everyone hyped for the school musical?"

"So hyped." I nod, although now the adrenaline has subsided a bit and the reality is setting in, I can't make my voice sound like I am.

"Yeah?" he says. "You're going for it? That's great!"

I shrug. "I mean, I guess I'll audition, I'm really not that good though, so—"

"Hey." He puts his hand up to stop me. "Don't do that. Your mum's a TV producer, isn't she?"

"Yeah, but I'm not sure any showbiz talent has rubbed off on me."

"You'll be great. I'm nervous too," he says.

My eyes widen. "You're auditioning?"

"Looks good for uni applications, right? And like I was saying to Ruby earlier, I reckon it'll be a laugh."

Ruby clears her throat, a flicker of shiftiness passing her face, before she smiles. "Absolutely."

"Mm," I say, maintaining eye contact with Ruby. *"Absolutely."*

"Rubes offered to help with my audition song," Calvin continues.

"Oh!" I say. "How amazingly *kind* of her!"

"It's nothing," Ruby mutters.

"Nah, I really appreciate it, Rubes!" Calvin says. "You're a great singer and it's good of you to offer your time."

I clasp my hands together and nod. "Ruby is the embodiment of selflessness," I agree.

"And so humble!" Calvin continues. "She wasn't even gonna audition for this, and I was like, *Ruby – you have to audition*, this show needs you*! It needs you."*

"Mm, well, thank god you convinced her!" I say. I

look at Ruby, who is doing an excellent job of maintaining a poker face through all this.

"All right," Calvin says. "I'm gonna split. By the way, *loving* this free period shiz. I mean, sure, *study period* or whatever, but still. Freedom!" He laughs. "Catch you later, then!"

We stand in silence for a few moments as he wanders off.

Sam clears his throat. "So, in summary, I'm the only person who's not doing this to try to get laid? That's fine. Just so we're clear."

5

As I open the door, a wall of ripe humidity – the sort that can only be created by a room rammed with teenagers – hits me and makes me recoil. The drama studio is heaving. Everyone has turned up for this meeting. Even Jamil, who has been the class clown since year seven, is here, sitting on a back-to-front chair, legs apart, chewing gum. It's amazing what the imminent threat of uni applications can do.

"Woooow," Calvin whispers, taking in the crowd, as he and Ruby follow behind me. He seems slightly in awe, definitely nervous, I guess since he's not in his natural habitat. Plus Charlotte Stefani is here, and I'm not sure exactly how things are between them now that she's dating Harrison.

I look around but there's nowhere obvious to sit. Charlotte (who is ninety per cent glossy, flowing, long brown hair, and dressed in the finest designer gear), briefly glances up at us, but doesn't deign to come over – she's perched on the edge of some rostra by the far wall, holding court in front of the other theatre kids, who are giving off a distinct air of disdain at all these lesser people who have infiltrated *their* space. Kwame, who is literally in jazz shoes and leg warmers, is busy showing everyone how flexible he is, while loudly chatting with Priya (who is probably Charlotte's closest rival in terms of queen bee status). Gales of laughter waft over from the far wall, and you can occasionally make out comments like, "What would Stanislavski say?!" and, "I heard she got cut in the first round, babe!" Dhruv, meanwhile, who clearly considers himself a serious ac-*tor*, is sitting barefoot in what look like some sort of black tai-chi pyjamas, occasionally running his fingers through his long black hair, while reading a collection of Harold Pinter plays, like that's in any way normal, while Charlotte is transparently making snide remarks about people she finds despicable, while pretending *not* to point at them, to Alice, who is basically Charlotte's sidekick and basks in her occasional attention, so long as she remains loyal and doesn't displease the queen.

Ruby sighs heavily at my side. "God, I hate them all," she says, following my gaze.

"Oh, come on, Rubes!" I grin. "Say yes to the theatre kids! Extend the hand of friendship! Look at them. . ." We both look as Dhruv stands and starts doing a series of loud vocal warm-ups, which Kwame and Priya delightedly join. "They're just shy."

Sam walks through the door, takes one look at the theatre kids chanting, "Red LORRY, yellow LOLLY!" then mutters, "I can't, I can't," turns, and starts to walk back out again.

"Sam!" Ruby shouts. "Get your arse in here!"

He resignedly shuffles over to us and flops down on the floor at our feet. "Kill me now."

"You were keen on this before," Ruby tells him.

"Yeah, but reality's hit," he replies.

I know what he means. Just the sight of the rostra sends shivers through me, before I even get to contemplating what spending a whole term rehearsing with some of these kids will actually be like. And then the horror of the actual show – something I already know I'll hate, almost certainly mess up, so why am I here? I take a deep breath of the horribly warm, sweaty air. I'm here because things have to get better. I'm here because I want to feel like I'm part of something. I'm here because I want that.

"Hey, fancy seeing you here!"

I turn, and there's Zach. Gorgeous Zach. Eyes alive and sparkling, seemingly not the least bit intimidated about walking into a studio full of people he doesn't even know. He tosses me a small bottle of mineral water. "Two fell out of the machine. I thought you might like one."

I catch it. "Oh, thanks."

Zach takes a swig of his, stuffs it in his back pocket, then surveys the drama studio, hands on his hips, nodding.

"Nice space. Good acoustics." He looks up at the lighting rig. "Hmm, nice collection of Fresnels and profiles, pretty good kit you've got up there."

I nod, holding the bottle with both hands, like I have the remotest clue what he's talking about. "Oh, mmm," I say. "Yes. *Lights*." Good, Freddie. Good contribution.

Zach chuckles, thank god. "You're funny." And he gives me a cheeky little grin that makes my heart skip and my breath catch.

All of Zach's confident surveying of the space is picked up by Charlotte's antennae, which clearly sense the presence of someone who knows what they're doing, and she's over like a shot. "Lottie Stefani, president of the Drama Society," she says, completely blanking all of us, including her poor ex, Calvin, who's just standing awkwardly barely a metre from her, and extending a manicured hand towards Zach.

Huh. She's going by *Lottie* now? Looks like everyone's going for something new this term.

"Zach Cooper." He shakes her hand.

Charlotte, or Lottie, nods, sizing Zach up, presumably assessing whether he's a threat or a potential ally. "Saw you looking at our lights," she ventures.

"Yeah, pretty good," Zach replies.

"Is lighting your thing?" she asks.

"Nah, I'm an actor." Zach smiles at her.

Lottie smiles back, but cautiously. "Yeah? Have you done much?"

"Loads at my old school," Zach says, glancing at the bookcase of plays to his right. He flicks his eyes to Lottie again. "And I was selected for British Youth Theatre this year."

An ice chill suddenly fills the room. Ohhhh! Lottie's face stays way too neutral upon receipt of that information for it to be genuine. She's livid.

"BYT?" she says, her voice unusually light and breezy. "One of the actual shows, or just the summer course?"

Zach seems to smirk to himself, whips the bottle out of his back pocket and takes a swig, then clears his throat. "The summer course is really competitive. Thousands apply, but they only take around fifty. It was great fun. Learned a lot."

Lottie nods. "Oh, of course, I didn't mean it wasn't good." She rolls her eyes a little. "Sensitive!"

Zach holds her gaze for a few moments, a look of vague amusement playing on his lips. "You never applied yourself?"

"No," she says, too quickly. "I've always believed you learn more from actually doing shows, rather than learning theory. That was something my dad told me, that the artistic director of the National Theatre said to him, at a fundraising dinner."

Zach raises his eyebrows. "Your dad's involved with the National?"

"He's a benefactor." Lottie shrugs. "He just loves the

arts, that's all. He paid for these lights actually. And the school theatre."

"Top guy," Zach says, not sounding remotely impressed.

Lottie gives Zach a tight-lipped smile, clearly vexed that someone's arrived at school who's potentially going to be real competition for her. And I bloody love it. I love that Zach isn't the least bit perturbed by Charlotte Stefani and all her perfect good looks, money and influence, and I love that he's playing her at her own game, like an absolute pro. There's every chance Zach is going shake things up around here – and that can only be a good thing.

"Hi, Charlotte," Calvin says.

"Babe!" Lottie calls over Zach's shoulder, ignoring Calvin, as a confused-looking Harrison Kane bumbles in, wearing his football kit. He's got muddy shins, messy blond hair falling over his forehead, socks gathered around his ankles and ruddy cheeks, having clearly just been playing a match – freakin' gorgeous (if there's one thing I love more than boys in grey sweatpants, it's boys in football shorts), and I feel a pang of sadness and jealousy as he slides his arm around Lottie's waist, that nothing will ever happen between us.

"Babe, did you have to come in your football kit?" Lottie frowns.

"Ah, you didn't *come* in your football kit, did you, Harrison?" Jamil calls over from his chair, smirking as he watches this unfold.

Various deeply inappropriate images fill my mind.

"I came straight from playing," Harrison says to Lottie. "You wanted me to come, I *came*."

Jamil cheers.

"Shut up!" Lottie and Harrison both chorus at him.

Jamil holds a hand up in submission.

"This is my boyfriend, Harrison," Lottie says to Zach, without so much as a flicker of embarrassment that she's saying this right in front of Calvin, who may as well be invisible for all the attention she's paying him.

"Hey." Zach nods.

"All right, mate?"

Harrison casts his eye over Sam, Ruby, Calvin and finally me, nodding slightly at each of us. I manage a small, tight smile and sort of nod back, but I'm not sure he even really knows who I am. So weird how someone can be such a large part of *your* life, albeit in your head, how you can think about them a stupid amount, create elaborate fantasies where you're doing all sorts with them, and yet they barely know you exist. Harrison simply doesn't know how much kissing the pair of us have done, how we ended up in a hotel room together on a field trip, just the two of us, how we got a bit drunk and Things Happened, including particularly awesome things, in the shower, which was surprisingly roomy, for the sort of budget hotel that you'd get on a school field trip.

"Well!" Harrison says, clapping his hands together. "I am *horny* for this musical!"

"Babe, what are you like?" Lottie laughs. "Come on. Come and sit with the theatre kids," she says, flicking her eyes, just quickly, at Zach, then pulling Harrison away by his football top like a small child. "Excuse us. Nice to meet you, Zach."

I watch them go, or more accurately, I watch Harrison go, then turn to Zach, who's also watching them, smiling to himself.

"Theatre kids?" he says to me, with a frown. "I thought you said *you* were the theatre kids?"

"Yeah, um, I guess they're the A-list theatre kids?" I say, in a moment of marvellous quick thinking.

Zach nods and I worry he's disappointed. He's the real deal. British Youth Theatre! Fair enough if he wants to hang out with his people. "I mean, no worries if you want to join them," I add. "That's cool."

He looks at me and smiles. "Nah. Think I'll sit with the A-*star* listers right here." And he does, he sits right down on the floor, and honestly I'm so happy I could scream.

I casually sit next to Zach, stupidly delighted to be in such close proximity to him. Calvin and Ruby are opposite, Calvin still bizarrely nervous and asking Ruby things like, "They're not going to make us do anything today, are they?" and Sam just looking down at the floor, drawing little circles with his finger, and I'm guessing trying to block the whole thing out.

"So, I'm gonna just say it since you're all too polite," Zach says. "Lottie's a total bitch, then?"

"I, um . . . used to date her," Calvin says, almost apologetically. "Until last week."

Zach blushes. "Ohh. Oh, god. Sorry."

Calvin puts his hand up. "No, no, don't be. You're. . ." He cracks a smile. "You're absolutely right!"

That really breaks the tension. We all laugh, even Sam looks up and smirks, and Ruby says, "Zach, I think you're going to fit in very well here!" and I know it's true. Also, no doubt about it, Lottie thought she'd bagged the hottest guy in the year, but I think that crown's just been stolen by Zach. I don't want to get ahead of myself, and maybe nothing will even happen, but at the very least, Zach's arrival has shown me that there *is* life after Harrison Kane. There are other boys. *Better* boys. And that is a very marvellous thought indeed.

Ms Pearson bursts through the door, all wild hair and chiffon. "OK, drama-nauts! Who's ready to blast off and explore new worlds?!"

Zach turns to me, eyes twinkling. "Ohh! You didn't say she was totally off her rocker!"

"Like you said, I'm too polite," I reply, grinning.

He rubs his hands together. "So hyped for this!" And he gives my knee a little squeeze, which I'm sure he doesn't mean anything by other than a friendly gesture, but is something I'm *thrilled* about.

Ms Pearson flicks off the main lights, and there's a collective "Oooh!" as we're all plunged into total darkness, and then another "Ooooh!" as she powers up the lighting rig and stands in a single beam in the centre of the room. In spite of myself, a little ripple of excitement prickles through me. Something about the stage lights, maybe, although I might have mistaken fear for excitement. "Drama-nauts! Let me take you back to the February of 1992. A plucky young actress had graduated from drama school the previous summer and was now spending her days at the open calls of all the major West End musicals, determined to fulfil her dream. This February day was, in many ways, a day like any other – the air was crisp and cold, and our hero was wrapped up against the bitter chill as she stood in line, waiting for her chance to show the creative team of an exciting new musical just what she was capable of. But it wasn't a day like any other. It was a day that changed everything. Fast-forward five months, and that actress was making her debut on the London stage in a life-changing role, in a production which was the talk of the town. Drama-nauts! That production was *Grease*. The role was Sandy. And that plucky young actress. . ."

"Wait for it!" I whisper to Zach, who is all eyes and ears at this insanity, literally, he is *grinning* in sheer delight.

"WAS MEEEE!" Ms Pearson shouts, extending her arms and striking what I assume is a Sandy from *Grease* pose – although it looks worryingly similar to things I've seen pole dancers do in movies.

It's at this point, which is presumably some sort of prearranged cue, that Kwame fires up the music system and the backing track to "You're the One That I Want" starts playing, and Ms Pearson . . . is performing it, gyrating and thrusting around, like a teenage Sandy, who is sadly the wrong side of fifty.

"Horrific!" Zach whispers, clapping his hands together in glee.

I can't help but laugh.

Ruby is staring at her blankly. Calvin just looks confused. Sam – scared. But to be fair, other folk are getting into it – Jamil especially, grooving along to the beat in his chair, and getting some group clapping going, which Ms Pearson seems to appreciate. And, of course, the theatre kids are deadly serious, watching and nodding, with Kwame actually marking some of the routine as he stands in the corner next to the sound system.

Fortunately, she only does one verse and chorus, and then the main lights are back on and she quietens everyone down. "For our daring new production of this classic musical, I will be drawing on my extensive experience of the London stage, but we'll also be adding our own unique elements. Theatre is a live art form. *It lives*. Evolves. So while we should celebrate everything that is wonderful about the original, even if I didn't personally agree with all of the director's choices at the time, we will very much be adapting and growing our interpretation for this new age."

The theatre kids all like this very much, and there is a lot of nodding and some "Mmms" of agreement.

Ms Pearson starts parading around the room, gesticulating as she talks. "Theatre is hard work. Theatre demands commitment, trust, bravery and sacrifice. Theatre demands that you give every atom of yourself, completely, totally, unreservedly to the struggle as it unfolds in the space. Theatre will chew you up, destroy you, break you, and then, if you allow it, rebuild you, as something new, stronger, but forever changed."

I glance at Sam, who looks totally aghast. "Did we sign up for the army?" he whispers.

I shake my head. *God knows.*

"And ultimately," Ms Pearson continues, "you *will* need talent. And lots of it." She looks at Jamil, who has his hand up. "Yes, Jamil?"

"Just saying, miss, I have lots of talent. My talent, miss, it's *large*. My talent is *big*, you get me, miss?"

"I do, sadly, 'get you', Jamil, yes," Ms Pearson sighs.

Jamil sits back, satisfied. "Oh, yeah," he says.

"Ugh," Sam whispers. "Is that why Ella dated him? Because his 'talent' is bigger than mine?"

"Has she even seen your talent?" I whisper back.

"Nobody has seen my talent," Sam replies.

"OK, logistics," Ms Pearson continues. "I will need to hear you sing, so prepare a short section of a contemporary musical theatre or pop song..." She glances at Zach, who now has his hand raised. "Um, yes?"

"Zach Cooper, year twelve."

Ms Pearson gives a weak smile. "OK?"

"Sorry, miss, and congratulations on the performance just now. . ."

Ms Pearson flicks her hair back and a small smile plays on her lips.

"Re the song – how many bars?"

"Good question. Sixteen bars will be fine."

Zach nods. "Cool." I watch him glance towards Lottie, then back at Ms Pearson.

Ms Pearson considers him for a moment, then resumes talking. "The rest of the audition will be done workshop format – a mixture of trust exercises, imagination games, and improvisation to really see who's a team player and who can bring that extra special *je ne sais quoi* to the production. Charlotte?"

"Sorry, Ms Pearson – and totally loved the performance just now, so can I just say, on behalf of everyone in this room, irregardless of if we get casted, how lucky we all feel to be directed by someone with your experience?"

"Thank you, Charlotte."

Lottie glances towards Zach, then back at Ms Pearson. "Also, miss, and sorry to be, like, a total bore, but I'm going by Lottie now? It's just, Equity, which just in case anyone doesn't know, is the *professional* actors' union, already have a Charlotte Stefani on their books, so I needed to change my stage name." She glances at

Zach again and shakes her flowing hair like a shampoo commercial. "And re the improvisation – are we talking prepared or spontaneous?"

"Good question, um, *Lottie* – it'll be spontaneous. I want to see what you're like in the moment." Ms Pearson sighs. "Zach Cooper again?"

"Sorry, miss. And just to echo professional actress Lottie, really grateful that you're here working with us on this, so excited, I really feel we will all learn so much from you, and like my tutor at British Youth Theatre said this summer, you just gotta soak it all up like a sponge, taking all this knowledge from people, like yourself, who have been there, done it, got the T-shirt, right?"

"Right. . ."

"Also," Zach says, "can I just check, because I gather you're an English teacher as well as a West End actress, but is 'irregardless' actually a real word?" He winks at Lottie, who crosses her arms.

Ms Pearson clears her throat. "There are examples of its usage, but most dictionaries would tell you it's . . . non-standard."

"Huh," Zach says. "And should it be 'casted' or, in fact, 'cast'?" he continues. "Sorry, it's just I hear people say these things, and I sometimes wonder." He glances at Lottie again, who is red with fury now, glaring at Zach like she wants to murder him.

"'Cast' would be correct for both past, present and

future use in this context. *I was cast in the play. I've been cast in the play. I hope to be cast in the play.*"

"Gotcha!" Zach grins. "Much appreciated, sorry to interrupt."

I just, honestly, I can't even. This is all too brilliant. For Lottie to finally be getting as good as she gives is the best thing. Zach's a hero. Even Calvin's stifling a grin.

Ms Pearson wraps up by saying that we'll be working in small groups for the workshop, mostly partners, and we can pick who we want to work with, and that this whole thing is going to happen on Thursday – just two days' time! – because she's keen to see who can cope under pressure.

As we're all told we can leave, Zach turns to me. "Workshop buddies?" he says, a hopeful expression on his face.

The way this has all worked out is quite incredible. I've made one small change. I've opened one little door into possibly doing one thing and look what's happened. I give him a big smile.

"Yes!" I say.

6

As if the day couldn't get any better, I walk into my first
English class of the new school year and Zach is already there,
reaching into his rucksack to retrieve a notepad. He sits up,
sees me, then glances at the spare seat next to him. Normally
I would sit next to Ruby (Sam is doing sciences and maths at
A level, so we don't have any classes together any more), but
she's popped herself by Calvin on the table adjacent to Zach's.

"Anyone sitting here?" I ask Zach as I approach.

"It's reserved," Zach says.

"Oh."

"For a Mr Freddie Bennett?"

I crack a smile. "That would be me." I sit myself down,
fish my pen and a pad from my bag, and try not to grin
like an absolute loon. I don't want to get ahead of myself,
but can't help feeling the omens look quite good here. Zach
seems to like me. I tell myself not to overanalyse it, not to
ruin everything by reading too much into anything and

everything Zach does, and then go right ahead and spend the entire lesson doing just that:

- Miss Harper announces we'll be studying
  Pride and Prejudice. "Ooh, bonnets!"
  whispers Zach. He's trying to make me laugh.
  A good thing? Is it because he loves my smile?
- Miss Harper tells us another one of our texts will
  be *Wuthering Heights*. "The novel based on that
  song by Kate Bush," Zach says under his breath,
  glancing at me and *winking*. A little private
  aside. I laugh, to make sure he understands that
  I definitely get the joke and we share the same
  sense of humour. This causes Miss Harper to
  ask, "What's funny?" and, "Would you care to
  share the joke with the class?"
- Forced into sharing the joke with the class
  (but being careful not to implicate Zach,
  because I don't think anyone ever got laid by
  telling miss on them), I manage to make it
  sound not remotely amusing. No one laughs,
  or even really knows who Kate Bush is. I sit
  down again and Zach nudges my leg with his
  under the desk. This nudge speaks volumes,
  it's a nudge of support, of thanks, and of "It's
  OK no one laughed and you look like a dick, I
  get it, and that's all that matters."

- Possible that's all in my head and the nudge was accidental. Unclear.

What *is* pretty clear to me by the end of the lesson, however, is that I'm already spiralling out of control when it comes to Zach, which is bad because this will make me act like a knob around him, instead of a relaxed, cool gay boy, who could take it or leave it.

Due to my immature outburst over *Wuthering Heights*, Miss Harper tells me I'm to carry a stack of *Romeo and Juliet*s that the year nines were using in the class before back to the store cupboard, which is highly annoying because I really wanted to leave with Zach. Our school is located on the outskirts of Beckenham (technically Kent), but most of us live all over south-east London, so there's a high chance Zach will be bussing it like me and we'll get a chance to talk more. Then, as I'm picking up one pile from Miss Harper's desk, Zach's by my side, and he doesn't say anything, just picks up the other pile. "Where are these going?" he asks.

"Store cupboard," I manage to squeak.

OK, he's kind, he's thoughtful, he's the whole package this guy, and I try really hard to make casual small talk as we head down the corridor towards the English store. He's already established his quick wit in class, so I worry that asking "How are you finding the school?" would sound really lame, and I certainly don't want to wade in with anything too heavy like "Any views on the climate emergency?"

because why bring down a fun afternoon with thoughts of our imminent demise? I don't want him to think I'm a killjoy.

And that's the main reason we walk to the store in excruciating silence, which is actually a far worse outcome than any of the speaking options would have been.

I flick the light on in the store and we walk in. It's a small cupboard, really. Shelving on three sides, all piled high with various class texts. I put my pile on an empty shelf to my left, take his pile, give him a little nod, and place that next to it.

"So, um . . . is there an LGBTQ+ club at school or anything?" he asks.

My breath catches, and I turn to face him. He's looking at me, eyebrows raised. So he's gay. Or maybe bi. Or maybe one of the other letters, it doesn't really matter, my chances have probably just increased significantly.

I'm suddenly really aware of his breathing.

And my breathing.

And that I should really say something.

"Um, ah, *no*, actually, we don't have one," I say.

He gives a little disappointed nod.

And I realize I need to say more, because maybe he's not actually so bothered about the club, maybe this was just an opener for a chat about the fact he isn't straight. "But it would be cool if there was," I add. I clear my throat, and glance at some of the books over to the right. "By which I mean, I would go to it." I look back at him again.

He chuckles. "Yeah, I mean, I kind of . . . that's why I asked you about it."

"Oh, right. Sure."

I smile. As a gay kid, I've never thought that I'm particularly obvious. I have the fashion sense and grooming ability of the most hopeless type of straight boy. I don't say things like, "YAAAAAS, girl!" or even watch *Drag Race*. And yet, somehow, Zach *knew*. I really hope he didn't catch me looking at his crotch or anything.

"Sooo," Zach says. "Are we staying here, or shall we go?" He chews his lip a bit.

"Ha! No, sure, let's go," I say.

He smiles, turns and heads out, me following, as it suddenly dawns on me that maybe that was a suggestion that we stay in the cupboard and make out, although it's equally possible it was also a suggestion that we leave and go home. Love and romance is confusing. It's a miracle anyone gets together at all, when you consider how hard it is to establish if someone likes you or not.

"You looking forward to the *Grease* audition?" he asks as we stroll along the now-empty corridor on our way out.

"Hyped," I lie. (I'm terrified.) "Can't wait!" (I really can. I could wait for literal eternity.)

"Any ideas for your song choice?"

"Maybe a few. Gonna . . . mull it over."

"You've got some favourites?"

"Definitely!" (The lies!)

"And the improv workshops sound cool!"

"Love a bit of improv!"

"Have you got a boyfriend?"

I go to answer, but no words come out. "What?" I heard him perfectly well, I just can't believe he simply came out and asked me that. I shake myself. We're still walking along, he isn't looking at me, just acting like he's asked me if I like chocolate milkshake or something. "Boyfriend?" I say. "Um, no. No, I haven't."

He nods.

My throat's so tight it's like I'm being strangled. "Um . . . have . . . you?"

"No," he says. Then he looks at me and smiles. "What bus do you get?"

"194."

"Ah. I'm the 354."

The 354. To Bromley North. Well-groomed, slightly cheeky, gift of the gab? Of course he's a Bromley boy.

"Amazing," I say. "I . . . love the . . . 354." I nearly groan out loud at my social ineptitude. "Great bus."

He nods seriously. "Fantastic bus."

And then he bursts out laughing, and I do too.

"Cool," he says, when we've contained our mirth at my terrible chat. "Today's been awesome." He gives me a sweet smile. "Thanks, mate."

*

Of course Zach's use of the word "mate" consumes my entire mind for the whole of my journey home. Did he use that word just to make it clear he only saw us as friends? Was he sensing that I liked him a bit too much and wanted to firmly but kindly tell me it wasn't going to happen? Or was it just a throwaway word, friendly, him not wanting to presume too much, too soon?

Or shall I just stop ruining everything by overthinking it and let the universe do its thing?

Mum's not in when I get back (I can't remember, I think she's on set all week), so I grab some snacks from the kitchen, whack some cat food in Barry's bowl, give him an arm's-length head pat, to avoid my fur allergy kicking off, and head up to my room. I should really make a start on *Pride and Prejudice*, but the only thing I can think about is Zach. I close the book and open Instagram instead, finding Zach pretty quickly. He has the word "actor" under his name, an email address for "enquiries" and a feed that is almost exclusively pictures of himself, in various what I can only describe as *provocative* poses: Zach in bed, with smouldering eyes, looking directly down the lens; Zach with his top off working out; Zach reflected in the mirror, in just some, um, *bulging* shorts; a close-up of Zach's face, an expression somewhere between ecstasy and pain that looks like he's probably . . . he's . . . I swallow. Oh my god. Oh, wow. Oh, Zach.

Well, I'm home alone, so I pull my blind closed, and I think you probably know how this ends.

7

I am beyond desperate to dissect this Zach business in a lot of fine detail with Ruby and Sam. I need their unbiased, objective opinion. I really don't want another Harrison Kane situation, in which I obsess for several years, getting precisely nowhere. Old Freddie pined for Harrison on the sidelines while Harrison never even noticed. New Freddie will not be such a victim. He will say "Yes!" to this new opportunity. I just need to know (a) if they think I'm in with a chance and, if so, (b) how the hell do I move things on?

Frustratingly, there is no time to talk during registration, then there seem to be endless people around during morning classes and in the common room, and I don't want to air all my business in front of the rest of year twelve, for obvious reasons.

Unable to stand it any longer, I end up sending them a message to our group WhatsApp:

ME: Major news.

So exciting, can't wait to tell you guys.

You are not gonna believe it.

Meet in cafeteria at lunch. Gonna need our own table as it's CLASSIFIED.

See? Performing arts may not be my forte, but I know how to work a cliffhanger. I mean, neither of them has messaged back, but that's just because they're trying to play me at my own game. They're *dying* to know.

I arrive at our table with my disappointing pasta bake, which the school promotes as "healthy" presumably on account of the fact there's a tiny bit of broccoli in it, because otherwise it's carbs and cheese in a sugary tomato sauce, with a side of garlic bread. (It has already crossed my mind about whether eating the garlic bread is a good idea. Suppose a miracle occurs and Zach wants to kiss me? I don't want to be off-putting. Maybe I'll see if Ruby or Sam wants it.) "Major news!" I announce, sitting down. I do a dramatic pause. "Me –" I lean towards them and lower my voice "– and *Zach*!"

There's a deeply appropriate stunned silence.

"Oh. My. *God*. Freddie!" Ruby says, with a wide smile. "You actually... You... You did it? You asked him out? You're a *thing*?"

Sam snaps his fingers. "Boom!"

"No, wait—"

"I'm really proud of you!" Ruby says. "This is the new you! New Freddie grabs life by the horns, sees opportunities—"

"Well, see—"

"And says a big fat *yes* to them!"

"OK, so, *no*, that's not a completely accurate description of what's happening here."

Ruby furrows her brow. "Go on."

I launch into a detailed description of the events of yesterday afternoon, at the end of which Ruby thoughtfully chews a forkful of coleslaw, then says, "So basically you walked out of school together?"

I glower at her. "*Ruby.* I told you – there was electricity!"

"Are you sure that wasn't just static from that nylon carpet they've got down in the corridors?" She spends another few seconds looking deadly serious, while I start to panic that maybe I've completely misinterpreted everything, then she smirks and laughs. "Aw, Fred, I'm messing with you. Yeah, it sounds positive."

I nod. "Right." I fix her with a stare. "*How* positive?"

"He's clearly enjoying hanging out with you," Ruby says.

"He sacrificed an extra few minutes at home to help you carry books," Sam adds.

"He very deliberately opened up a conversation about being gay," Ruby continues. "And he asked if you had a boyfriend – I mean, he's testing the water, isn't he?"

I nod, thinking it through. "Maybe. He called me 'mate'."

Ruby holds her hands out, like, *And?* "What do you want him to call you? That's all you are at the moment. Until you . . ." She lowers her voice. ". . . take things to the next level."

Sam makes an "Oooooooh" sound and I swallow down the lump that's suddenly lodged in my throat. "And how . . . how do I do that?"

"Ask him out," Ruby says, all matter-of-fact and breezy. She takes another forkful of coleslaw and happily pops it in her mouth, like she hasn't just told me to do something completely impossible.

"It's that simple," she continues.

"Easier *said* than *done*," I retort.

"Well, I just did it," Ruby says, smiling.

I glance at Sam, who is already glancing at me. We both turn to Ruby in unison and I cock my head.

"I asked Calvin on a date last night," Ruby says. And then she carries on eating coleslaw. I swear to god, we could be seconds away from a nuclear apocalypse, and Ruby would just be nonchalantly eating coleslaw.

Eventually she looks up at us and frowns. "What?"

"*How* have you done this?" I say. "It's only day two!"

Ruby shrugs. "I like him, we walked home together after school, chatted, then I messaged him later and asked if he fancied going on a date sometime, and he said that sounded lovely. That's how."

That's how . . . *if you're brave.* That's how . . . *if you don't have a massive fear of rejection.* I don't know what it is

73

about me that the idea of *that*, of someone I really like telling me no, would paralyse me to the extent that I can't even ask in the first place.

"And that's exactly what you need to do with Zach," Ruby tells me.

I shake my head.

"This is about saying yes, Freddie!" she says.

"Yeah, *me* saying yes – this requires *him* to say yes. Totally different. Not relevant. That isn't part of this."

"Yes, it is," Ruby says.

"I think it might be, mate," Sam adds.

"No!" I insist.

"Do it!" says Sam.

"Do it!" says Ruby.

"I'm not going to do it!" I snap.

"Not gonna do what?" a voice behind me says. I turn. Of course it's *him*. Zach. A cheeky smile plays on his lips. He pulls out a chair and sits next to me with his lunch of jerk chicken, rice and salad. "What are you not gonna do, Fred?"

I swallow. "I am . . . *not* gonna do the song choice that we were just discussing for the audition tomorrow!" Again, my improv ability was pretty good there. I can't actually believe I managed it.

"No?" Zach says, slicing into his chicken. "What was it?"

I look at Ruby in panic, every song in the world having just left my head. She must see the fear in my eyes, because

74

she sighs and says, "'The Git Up' by Blanco Brown", and I immediately wish she hadn't bothered.

Zach screws his face up. "Great tune... Not sure it's right for a *Grease* audition."

"No, right? Totally!" I say. "Ridiculous. Great tune, but ridiculous." I glare at Ruby, who mouths back, *That's why I said it!* and rolls her eyes.

"Were you gonna do the dance with it too?" Zach grins. "Like it's summer 2019?"

"Ha ha ha!" I say. "No, and no, I wasn't going to do any of it."

Zach nods. "So what *are* you gonna do?"

"Still mulling it over," I lie. "Got a few ... reliable standbys, you know?"

Zach nods. "Yeah, same, haven't decided yet. What's on the shortlist?" He raises his eyebrows expectantly.

Ruby clears her throat. "I'm doing 'When We Were Young' by Adele. Love that song."

"'Where Did That Little Dog Go?' from *Snoopy*," Sam says.

I'm wide-eyed at them both. I really wish I'd spent some actual time thinking about this last night, rather than thinking about Zach in such fine, exquisite detail. And another, very real, panic is filling my body. Zach's going to see whatever I do. And I've told him I'm a theatre kid! I can't mess up, he'll think I'm weird and deluded. Oh god, oh god, oh god.

"Cool choices," Zach says. "Fred?"

"So, yes, so I'm a really big *Grease* fan, so maybe I'll just sing a song from *Grease*? So, like, the one that Ms Pearson sang at the meeting. . ." And I attempt to sing a small section.

I have no idea if it's any good.

Nobody screams. No glass shatters. I suppose that's a good sign.

When I'm done, Zach's face isn't giving anything away, and Ruby says, "'You're the One That I Want'?"

"That's the one! That's the . . . audition song *that I want*! Hahaha!"

She winces slightly. "Fred, why are you singing '*meditate mad erection*'?"

I blink at her. "Because those are the words?"

"They're not the words," she says.

"They're the words." I glance at Zach, hoping he might agree. "Literally, Ms Pearson sang it yesterday! That's what she sings!"

Ruby takes a deep breath, and I sense her patience with me is waning. "Freddie. Darling, dear Freddie. When you sing, you have to feel the lyrics. You have to understand them. You have to find meaning in them. . ."

"I mean, of course! Sure!" I bluster, hoping Zach thinks I already know all this basic stuff.

"Even if those were the lyrics, which they are not, what the hell is a 'mad erection'?"

I think this over. "It means. . ."

Ruby's eyes widen.

"Yeah, Fred," Zach says, smirking. "What exactly *is* a 'mad erection'?" He nudges my leg with his under the table and I spill my glass of apple juice. "You're funny, Freddie," he says.

"Yes, because OF COURSE I'M JOKING!" I reply, trying to keep the blind panic out of my voice. "I'm not doing that song. It's gonna be a . . . big ole surprise!"

I give as big a smile as I can muster before seeing a purple devil horns emoji expression on Ruby's face.

My eyes widen and I shake my head.

"So, *Zach*!" Ruby says. "Freddie had something he wanted to ask you!"

I am going to murder her so badly.

"What's up?" Zach grins.

I swallow and take an unsteady breath. "Um, only, I just. . ." I'm not going to do it *now*! No way! In front of everyone? Even if I do end up doing it, which I doubt I will, I don't want an audience. Why increase the inevitable humiliation? "I wanted to check if you still wanted to be my partner for the improv workshop tomorrow. . ." I glance at Ruby, who is rolling her eyes. "That's all."

"'Course!" Zach replies. "I'm hyped for it. Can't wait to weave some improvisation magic with you, Fred! I've got a good feeling – I bet you're fantastic, you're so funny and sparky. I just hope I don't let you down!"

He's worried *he's* going to let *me* down?

Oh god. That boy has no idea.

8

It comes as a relief when I realize my nerves aren't just about not wanting to make a fool of myself in front of Zach. I really want to do this show. Since saying yes, good things have started to happen – I can't deny it. And for the first time at school, I feel like I'm actually involved, I'm in the middle of it. The auditions are the thing everyone's talking about. The real theatre kids are going crazy, gossiping and bitching about who might be cast as what, already making predictions and slagging off the hypothetical choices ("Jamil as Roger? Oh god, imagine! He'll never learn his lines. Just hope you don't have any scenes with him because you'll be carrying that dead weight for the entire show!"). But everyone else is really into it too, and for the whole morning, wherever you turn, you see someone practising their song, or doing a bit of improv under the stairwell, sharpening themselves up, ready for the workshop. And I'm part of that. I'm part of the buzz, and I like it, and I really, really want it to carry on.

I'm going to do "Footloose" from *Footloose*. I spent all of last night going over it, and happily since Mum is still away on a location shoot, I had the house to myself. The Deliveroo driver said it sounded "very good" when he called to drop off my burger and fries. I hope he didn't say that just so I would tip him. I heard Mum talk once about how, while you shouldn't dress as the character you are auditioning for, a little hint of it, in your clothing choices, can be a subtle way of suggesting to the panel you're the right "look" for the part. So, today I'm in blue jeans and a white T-shirt – a nod to the fifties look that *Grease* requires, and I've even got some product in my hair, to make it look a bit less like I've just crawled out of bed, and more slick. I've practised, I've run through the song lyrics *so* many times. I even googled "top tips for great improvisations" and made a mental note of the "Yes And" rule: to "accept" any "offers" my partner makes during the improv, while "adding" something of my own. I've done my homework. I'm prepped.

And I'm totally bricking it.

We're sitting in the drama studio in rows, forming an audience in front of the rostra, where we're each to sing our song. Ruby is first, smashing "When We Were Young" out of the park and setting the bar ludicrously high. Sam follows with his *Snoopy* song, which maybe isn't as vocally impressive at Ruby's, but certainly makes up for it in cute factor, as the "Ahhhh!'s" and "Awwww!'s" from the audience attest. A year ten girl does a Little Mix song,

Calvin performs an incredible "Somebody to Love" by Queen (I mean, he's an absolute natural, as it turns out, so there really is nothing that boy can't do), and then it's Zach. He confidently saunters up to the rostra, hops on to it, and pulls out an acoustic guitar from behind the black curtain at the back. Huh. Points for dramatic effect and preparing that little surprise. He sits down on a chair in the middle. "This is a song some of you may know, and it's dedicated to someone in the audience who I think will enjoy it," he says.

Everyone's holding their breath. Well, I am.

And then he begins this dreamy ballad version of "The Git Up" by Blanco Brown.

I'm entranced. I just stare at him. It's beautiful. His voice is beautiful. He's beautiful.

"He's singing our song!" I whisper to Ruby.

"It's not your song," she replies.

I make a vague groaning sound as I watch Zach's performance, and then literally hold my breath again as he turns and sings the chorus entirely to me.

"Ohhh," Ruby murmurs. "It's gonna happen. I would place money on it."

"Ohhhh god. Ohhhhh, boy," I mutter.

Sam leans forward from the row behind. "He wants you," he whispers in my ear.

I am beside myself. I can't stop looking straight into his eyes. Zach sings the final note with his eyes closed, before the entire room erupts in rapturous applause and whooping. Led by me, admittedly. And apparently I'm also standing up while I do the whooping, but I think it's an attractive quality, to be enthusiastic. The world is too full of cynics. Like what you like with passion, I say.

Ruby tugs my T-shirt. "Sit down, you muppet!"

"He was good!" I say, still clapping like a demented seal. "Encore! Bravo!"

Zach does a humble little nod towards the audience and then I see his face change, and follow his gaze to where Lottie is very obviously bitching about his performance to Kwame. *How dare she?* I sit back down and cross my arms, giving it all the negative body language I can because now it's *her* turn and I'm going to pump out all the bad vibes that girl deserves, but then forget everything when Zach takes the spare seat to my left and I cannot help myself. "Oh my god, that was *sensational*!" I tell him, doing a chef's kiss with my fingers.

"You liked it?" Zach smiles.

"Zach, I *loved* it!"

"That makes me happy," he says. And I pretty much melt into a puddle right there because something I said *made him happy*.

Lottie sings "All That Jazz" from *Chicago*, but even I can tell her voice lacks both power and any real connection with the words, and she's a long way from making it in any way sexy. I watch, stony-faced, and during the applause at the end (led entirely by the other theatre kids, complete with standing ovation and wolf whistles), Zach turns to me and whispers, "Shocking. Why do that number if you can't pull it off?"

"Oh, totally!" I agree.

Lottie is still onstage, only now she's smiling maliciously in our direction, clearly having clocked we were talking about her. I glance worriedly at Zach, but he's giving her a very confident, equally malicious smile right back.

"She cracked on the final note," Zach says, not taking his eyes off Lottie. He smirks, then gives her a thumbs up. "Congratulations, Lottie! Such a brave choice!"

Lottie scowls as she leaves the rostra and heads back to the theatre kids, who immediately form a witch-like huddle around her, complete with scheming whispers, hissed accusations, and occasional poisoned glances thrown towards Zach.

"Up next – Freddie Bennett!" Ms Pearson says.

Having an icy atmosphere was not the start I was hoping for, but maybe my upbeat song will cheer everyone up. I make a real effort to shut everyone out, and start singing. I can feel I'm a little tentative at first, my throat constricted and voice fragile and wobbly, but within a couple of lines I'm more into it, and even feeling it with my body a bit more, loosening up and maybe not exactly "owning" the stage, but certainly renting a little a bit of it.

Until I make the mistake of looking into the crowd, and there's Lottie, whispering with Kwame, eyes flicking to me, laughing, and I'm back there. I'm onstage for *Les Mis* at primary school and I'm freezing up and the audience . . . talking . . . and this fog envelops me, I can't shake it off, like I'm lost underwater. I can't even hear myself singing any more, just this fuzzy ringing in my ears, and *why? Why? She promised me!*

"Freddie? Fred?"

I blink and Ms Pearson is standing up. I don't know when I stopped singing. Did I do the whole thing? Did I do enough? It's a blur.

"OK, Freddie, well done, you can sit back down," she says.

I nod. "OK. Thanks," I mutter.

There's a moment of horrifying silence from the audience, and then Ruby starts the clapping. Others join in, but it doesn't feel like it's in admiration, more commiseration.

I flop into my seat and glance at Ruby. "You were fine, you just went a bit quiet halfway through," she says.

I nod. That does not sound good.

I don't even want to look at Zach, but he nudges my leg. "Well done," he says.

Oh Christ. "Well done"? I'd rather hear I was "totally shocking" than being told "well done" in a really neutral voice that someone can't even bring themselves to sound slightly genuine with, due to your utter shitness.

I should have known this would happen.

Knowing that I now *really* have to make an impact in the workshop, I throw myself into the initial "warm-up" exercises. The first game involves sitting in a circle, and one person drops a rubber chicken behind someone's back, who then has to grab the chicken, stand up, and chase the person who dropped it round the circle, trying to tag them before they do a complete circuit and sit back down in your original spot. It's very silly and very fun, made more so by the fact Ms Pearson calls the game "Choke the Chicken" – which you have to shout once you've dropped the chicken, and causes insane amounts of hilarity, it being unclear if Ms Pearson knows the true meaning of the phrase.

"I love choking the chicken!" Zach chuckles in my ear.

"Me too," I say.

He gives me a wolfish grin.

After we've all spent ten minutes choking the chicken, it's time to "walk around the space" and "start to think about a character" and "think about how that character might walk" and "what might their physicality be?" and then "freeze!" Ms Pearson walks around, tapping us randomly on the shoulder.

"What's your name?" Ms Pearson asks Zach.

"Quentin Devere!" Zach replies.

"Hmm," Ms Pearson says. "And what do you *do*, Quentin Devere?"

"I'm a teenage tech entrepreneur, I'm seventeen, I created an app in my bedroom while my parents were busy arguing downstairs. I'm the product of a broken home, but I put all my energy into the app, rather than addressing my own deep-seated insecurities and sadness at my parents' divorce. I'm reclusive. I don't have many friends at all. Everyone thinks I've got it all, because I've made millions, but all I really want is something money can't buy – *love.*"

My mouth hangs open. How is he coming up with all this?

"Impressive," Ms Pearson says, moving on from him and tapping Lottie on the shoulder.

"Macy Dupont," Lottie announces, without missing a beat. "Model, influencer and campaigner. I'm in demand at all the major fashion shows – London, Paris, New York, and I use the money from that to fund my real passion, which is environmental activism. I recently chained myself to the gates of a coal-fired power station and spray painted 'Murderers' on the side of Shell's London HQ. I give half my money to fund school meals for poor children and buy blankets for refugees. But no amount of charity work or good deeds can save me from the truth: that my father is the CEO of a company that has caused huge deforestation in the Amazon. I hate him and will probably kill him. I sometimes take drugs, to escape the pain of a world consumed with hate. I am anorexic." She gives Zach a very smug smile.

"Fascinating *and* excellent," Ms Pearson muses. "This is good stuff, folks!"

Ms Pearson taps me on the shoulder.

Horror.

I swallow down the panic.

She taps me again, like maybe I didn't feel it the first time.

I can't even think of a name!

Oh god!

"Freddie?" Ms Pearson says.

"Brenda!" I blurt out, instantly regretting it, even before the sniggers.

"OK, Brenda," Ms Pearson replies. "Tell me about yourself. What are you all about? What are your passions? What makes you tick?"

I think for a moment. "Bread?" I reply.

"OK!" Ms Pearson says. "Let's move on to the next exercise!"

9

An entire week later, the cast list still isn't up and the tension is insane – not helped by the unsubstantiated gossip the theatre kids are spreading:

"I heard Ms Pearson wanted to cast Jamil, but Mrs Mason vetoed it because of his shocking GCSE grades!" (Dhruv.)

"Apparently Ms Pearson nodded at Lottie in a meaningful way in the corridor – she's got Sandy in the bag, babes!" (Kwame.)

"Sonny's a baritone, though – and there's no one who can sing it! None of the boys have deep enough voices!" (Priya.)

Literally, I haven't seen hysteria like this since the year nine "teenage booster" vaccinations. I'm trying to stay cool about it, but it's impossible. I'm obviously not going to be cast as Danny, or one of the major boy parts, but there's loads of smaller ones (even just one of the ensemble "Burger

Palace Boys") that might be right for me – I know, because I downloaded a copy of the character descriptions and have been obsessively studying it, trying to see where I might fit, and who might be my competition, and then trying to compare my audition with theirs to reach my probability of success.

The news that the cast list has finally gone up tears through the common room like wildfire, and I'm lost in the throng that's hurtling down the stairs and along the corridor towards the drama noticeboard, desperate to know if we'll be dancing the hand jive, and if so, who with.

It's a scrum, everyone jostling for position, trying to read the small type on the single-side A4 cast list.

"Oh my god, I'm Vince Fontaine!" Calvin Jackson says, to whoops of appreciation.

"Rizzo!" Ruby nearly squeals. *"Damn!"*

Calvin and Ruby high-five.

Sam's looking ashen. "Oh wow, I'm Eugene," he mutters. "Eugene. I'm gonna have lines. It's happening. Wow."

"Sam, you were *born* to play that part," I tell him as I squeeze to the front and scan the list.

"Patty Simcox!" Alice squeals. "Oh my god!" She turns to Sam. "I think that means we'll be dancing together!"

Sam blushes.

"Let's rehearse our lines!" Alice tells him. "Get a head start – impress Ms Pearson!"

"Um … OK?" Sam says as she starts pulling him

away. He glances over his shoulder at me. "Help!" he mouths, as he's swallowed up into the mass of bodies.

Zach is Danny, because of course he is. And Sandy . . . is Lottie. A stroke of genius, or utterly insane? They certainly have chemistry – albeit the potassium in water type of chemistry.

Harrison Kane as Doody? OK. Jamil as Sonny, Kwame as Roger, Priya as Marty, Dhruv as Kenickie. And. . .

I swallow, then scan the list again, from bottom to top this time.

And then again.

I'm not there.

I'm not on it.

OK, I know my audition was bad, the possibility of this had occurred to me, but couldn't I at least have played some kind of extra? Something in the ensemble? Am I really *so bad* that I can't be on the stage *at all*?

It's like all those years of being picked a reluctant last for any sports team all over again. It's Harrison Kane not liking me. It's every boy, ever, not liking me. And it weighs heavy in my stomach and tight in my throat, and it sucks. It sucks. All my trying, all my putting myself out there, it's all been slapped back in my face. *What were you thinking, Freddie? Who do you think you are? Some people just aren't meant to be anything. You're ordinary, so be ordinary, learn to be happy with that. The forgotten, insignificant kid people don't even recognize in the yearbook.*

"Hey, Fred."

Ruby puts a hand on my shoulder and squeezes, her voice and touch all gentle, because she *knows*, which somehow just makes this worse.

"Congratulations," I say, managing a tight smile. "You'll be brilliant. Can't wait to see it."

"Thank you." She smiles sadly. "Look. . ."

"Ahh, it's OK," I interrupt. "It would have been nice, fun, you know, but I guess I just wasn't good enough."

"You were really good," Ruby tells me. "Maybe you got missed off by accident, or—"

I laugh, not quite managing to hide my bitterness. "I think I just have to face the fact I wasn't good enough."

And it's hardly a surprise. I've never been any good at performing arts – my own mother made that perfectly clear, so I don't know why I didn't just listen to her. Instead, entirely focused on trying to get it on with Zach, I've humiliated myself and only succeeded in making myself feel like shit. Zach probably thinks I'm a total joke, or worse, feels sorry for me, and meanwhile, literally every single person I know and like in this school will be doing the show together, while I. . .

"I have to go," I manage to croak at Ruby, my throat tight. "Well done again. You deserve this. You'll blow everyone away."

"Freddie. . ."

"It's OK," I say, batting her away as I back off. "I'm

OK. I'm an idiot anyway, I definitely shouldn't be anywhere near a stage."

I hurry off down the corridor, losing myself in the throngs of kids heading to the cafeteria before she has a chance to catch up, and take a left out of the double doors into the fresh air. I walk around the side of the building, eventually finding a vacant bench, and sit with my head in my hands, simultaneously beating myself up for letting Zach believe I was a real theatre kid, and also for not being able to bring myself to be happier for Ruby and Sam, because I'm too selfish, so wrapped up in my own failure, I can't celebrate their success.

I can trace it all back, all this "yes" stupidity, all this thinking things could be better. And all lines lead back to one place: *Jasper Perry*. Him and his obnoxious TV friends, making me feel like a loser. If I'd never gone to that party, if I'd never met him, if I hadn't ended up feeling so utterly inadequate, none of this would have happened. What's wrong with being on the sidelines, anyway? Spectating can be just as much fun … more so, when it means you don't risk getting a ball smacked in your face or breaking your leg on the rugby pitch of life.

Someone flops down next to me.

"You were robbed." Zach's voice. And then his arm slides across my shoulders. "I'm sorry, Freddie. I mean, the casting is *laughable*. But I know that's no consolation."

I smile in spite of myself. The fact he came. The fact he's not totally blanking me. The fact he seems to care.

"It's OK. Congratulations on getting Danny. You were brilliant; you totally deserve it."

"Thanks." He shakes his head. "Jeez, though, I know how it feels. I've had my fair share of rejection. Doesn't get any easier."

He's right about that, more right than he knows, but I'm not going to go there.

Zach moves his arm from my shoulders to the back of the bench as he settles, legs apart, relaxed and cool against my pathetic, hunched form. "So, I spoke to Ms Pearson, and she's created a role for you."

I look across at him. "*What?*"

"Not onstage," he continues. "But just as important."

"Backstage?"

He nods. "Head of props. I told her how you're a great team player, and that she needs someone for props who's responsible and organized. I know it's not what you wanted, but if you fancy it, the job's yours." He looks at me hopefully. "I think it'd probably be . . . fun?"

Right at that moment, I don't care that it's not what I wanted. Doing it means I can still be part of it, and I know, in my heart, that being part of it is what I need to do. Because, sure, being a spectator may be safer, and by playing you might get hurt. But you might also feel the soaring high of a massive win – and for that, you really have gotta be in it. And, oh, oh, oh, there's also the small matter that Zach has gone out of his way to fix this for me. And I may not be the world's expert on romance, but this has to mean something.

I smile back at him. "Why . . . why would you do this for me?"

"I like you." He shrugs.

I feel myself blush. I don't know what to say. I'm so out-of-this-world ecstatic that he's said that, so desperate not to mess up by saying the wrong thing, and so . . . embarrassed? I think? Because this sort of thing doesn't happen to me. At least, it never has before. "Thank you. Thank you for doing this, and thank you for . . ." I drop my eyes away. ". . . liking me."

He reaches into his pocket and produces a set of keys, which he tosses to me. "Props and costume store is under the stage, apparently. And you get the run of the place. Wanna check it out?" He cocks his head and gives me a hint of that wolfish grin I saw at the auditions when we were discussing our mutual enjoyment of "Choking the Chicken".

"Sounds good." I smile back.

I didn't even know this was here. There's a small, narrow staircase down from the side of the stage to this underground level, which houses loads of stacked-up spare chairs, old scenery from past productions, and flight cases containing lights and sound equipment. In the corner, there's a locked door, which leads to a smaller room housing the props and costumes – it's the best sort of bric-a-brac shop cornucopia – full of random treasures, many of them hilarious: comedy wigs, a string of fake sausages, a gigantic frying pan (I'm assuming that was used in conjunction with the sausages at some point), old-fashioned telephones, a teapot, a unicycle, a stuffed and mounted bird of prey, a replica human skull (I assume it's replica), and ten sets of pom-poms, which, on initial inspection, are the only things in here that'll be useful for a production of *Grease*.

Of course, it's all too much to resist.

Zach finds a shawl to wrap around his head, a wooden staff and a wicker basket to carry in the crook of his arm.

"Spare any change for a poor old woman?" he croaks in a frail voice.

"Why, yes!" I say, grabbing an iron. "I am but a poor boy, so I offer this humble gift."

Zach flings off his shawl and straightens up. "Aha! I am not a poor old woman at all, but a brave, handsome knight in disguise!" He takes a shield and lightsabre out of one of the cupboards.

"Oh! My hero!" I squeal, hand on my forehead, pretending to swoon into his arms, which is interesting, because I actually am then in his arms and he's holding me and suddenly this feels like less of a joke.

There's a moment where we're just looking into each

other's eyes.

Then he puts me upright, gently places the lightsabre back in the cupboard, and hesitates.

And then...

He takes a few steps towards me, and I'm frozen, slightly open-mouthed, waiting, *hoping*, but still not believing.

"I knew the moment I met you by the noticeboard on the first day that you were going to be my little problem." He grabs my hands and pulls me towards him. His breath is unsteady. I think I'm holding mine. "I totally have a thing for boys like you."

I literally have no idea what sort of boy I am, but whatever I am, if Zach likes it, that's good enough for me.

His eyes are searching my face, asking the question. "OK?" he murmurs.

I nod.

And he leans in and kisses me softly on the lips.

He pulls back a little, and we stare into each other's eyes.

And then, like a lightning bolt, we're mouths, lips, tongues, breathless, hot bodies pressed hard against one another, hands everywhere, legs intertwined, and it's so much, I'm gasping for air, like drowning, maybe, but in euphoria.

Eventually he breaks away.

I swallow and catch my breath. I have no words, but

wow, I've actually kissed someone.

And it was amazing.

How did that happen?

Just by saying yes to life? Is that all it was?

If that is the case, then I'm here for more of the same. Yes to it all! Yes to every single thing! I'm on a snog high – is that a thing? It seems like a thing. So, just like Ruby with Calvin, I go for it:

"Do you want to go out with me?"

"Sure," Zach says. "We'll go out sometime."

That isn't what I quite meant, and I go to say more, to clarify, but before I can, he gives me one of his cheeky winks and walks out of the door. I'm just standing here and I'm not sure what just happened and I'm not sure if Zach understood that I meant it'd be nice to go on a date, but you know what? Doesn't matter. Things are actually moving in the right direction. Finally.

10

"I don't know why I let you talk us into this," Ruby grumbles.

"It's about saying yes," I tell her. "I offered an opportunity, and you said yes to it, as per the rules we made. So. Here we are."

"Here" being the side of the football pitch, and the "opportunity" being watching a sixth form football match in the light drizzle and fading light of a brutally cold autumn afternoon. I haven't told Ruby or Sam what happened in the props store yet – I'm waiting for my moment – and besides, there's something I'm really enjoying about having a little secret. It's more special somehow.

"I can't feel my toes," Sam says.

"Stop complaining and enjoy the view!" I tell him.

"What view? It's just a load of muddy, sweaty sixth form boys in football kit shouting at each other."

"Mmmm," I say.

I watch the game with a keen eye. Not that I have any idea what's going on. Despite being forced to play it in PE for five years, I've never managed to pick up the slightest understanding of the rules, but I'm not here for the goals or whatever. I want to show Zach how supportive I am, and would be, if we were to take things to the official boyfriend stage. I want to show him I care. I want to look at him and remember how wonderful it was to kiss him just a few hours ago, and I want to feel that pride that the fittest boy on the pitch likes *me*. I'm here for all those things, but when Harrison Kane slides across the pitch and clips Zach's ankle, sending him tumbling into the mud, I realize I'm also here for something else: to protect Zach!

"Oh! BAD BALL! BAD BALL!" I shout, pointing at the incident. "Ref? C'MON!"

"What are you doing?" Ruby hisses.

"That was a BAD BALL!" I shout again.

"Do you mean a *foul*?" she says.

"YES! FOUL BALL! REF!" I'm not having Harrison attack Zach in this way, doubtless at the behest of Lottie, who also happens to be watching, sitting at the other side of the pitch on one of those portable stick chairs, painting her nails.

Zach staggers to his feet, some blood visible on his knee.

"REF!" I shout again, since no one seems to be doing anything about Harrison Kane's treachery.

.

Zach brushes himself down, then jogs over to me. "Mate? What are you doing?" he asks.

"He got you!" I say. "He did a bad foul!"

Zach shakes his head. "He actually didn't."

"Yes!" I insist. I mean, I *saw* it.

"Thanks and all, but it wasn't deliberate. We just collided." Zach gives me a tight-lipped smile and jogs back to the game.

I glance at Lottie, who's smirking, and then at Harrison, who is looking at me with a screwed-up face and hands held out, like *what the hell are you doing?*

"OK," Ruby begins, once the game has restarted. "What's going on? I know you like Zach, but this is next level."

I can't wait any longer. I'm literally gagging to spill my news. "Huh, well, maybe that's because this *is* the next level," I reply, trying to make my eyes twinkle with mischief.

"That's what I just said."

"No, I mean, maybe I've . . . I've climbed the stairs and reached the next floor? You know? I'm in the lift, I pressed the button, and now I'm . . . I've moved up. *On.* No, not on, I've moved things on. Yes! I have moved things on. With Zach."

"Have you actually, though?" Sam says. "'Cause you said that before and it turned out you'd just walked to the bus stop together."

"We've kissed."

I let that revelation hang in the air for a few moments.

"You've kissed?" Ruby says.

There's a shout from the pitch, and I watch as Harrison kicks the ball and it smacks into Zach's head. "HEAD BALL!" I shout.

"When did you kiss?" Ruby hisses.

"Lunchtime, in the props store," I say, keeping my eye on the pitch for more unwarranted Zach attacks. "Zach was devastated that I was overlooked for a role in the show, so asked Ms Pearson if I could be head of props. I get my own keys in the store, so we went down to have a look, and ended up in each other's arms."

"Was there tongue-age?" Sam asks.

"Mm, uh-huh. Lots of it. He's got a nice tongue."

"Ew." Ruby grimaces.

"Knew this would happen," Sam says. "Knew the moment he basically sang his audition song at you last week."

"I know, right? That voice! Like warm butter gently oozing and bubbling down the willing holes of a crumpet."

"Ugh. Now you've totally ruined crumpets for me," Ruby says. "Why are you like this?"

"FOOT ATTACK!" I shout, gesturing wildly at the pitch, where Harrison has definitely just booted Zach in the shin. "REF?! REF?!"

Zach jogs over again. "Look," he sighs. "It's great

you're enjoying the match, but you're kind of putting some of us off?"

Oh god, I think he's cross with me. "I'm sorry," I say. "Are you hurt?"

"No," Zach says.

"Harrison needs the red card," I tell him.

"No, he doesn't. Also, you keep shouting 'Ref!' but we haven't got a ref, it's a friendly."

I give him a nod that hopefully suggests I understand and will totally shut up, and Zach gives me another tight-lipped smile and jogs on to the pitch again.

"Look at those legs," I say wistfully.

"So, you kissed," Ruby says. "Then what?"

I blow a breath out. "We stopped kissing. And I asked him out!"

Ruby grins. "Fred! That's awesome! Finally!"

"Uh-huh!"

"So, are you a thing now?"

"He said that sure, we could go out sometime."

"Sometime?" Ruby frowns.

"Whoa, hang on," Sam says. "You asked him out, like, do you want to be more than friends, ask him out?"

"Yeah."

Sam frowns. "But his reply made it sound like, maybe we can just go for a Costa."

"Which I'm so cool with. Love one of their gingerbread lattes, which aren't as nice as Starbucks."

"I think you're talking at cross purposes," Ruby says.

"Ugh. We'd just been kissing!" I remind her. "What did he think I meant? It's fine. I was literally in his arms, pressed up against him, moments before. OK?"

"OK." Ruby shrugs.

"OK," I say. Although, the truth is, I do have doubts. I wish Zach had been a bit more definite about us meeting up and making me feel like this whole thing will be more than just one frantic kiss in a props store. I know I shouldn't, but I can't stop thinking about how wonderful our lives together would be – me, contently preparing a gay, nutritious breakfast of fruits, non-dairy yogurt and artisan granola, followed by freshly baked pastries and homemade strawberry jam, while Zach sits in his grey marl loungewear, staring contemplatively out of the window of our warehouse conversion overlooking the Thames, writing poetry. Later that day, after we've been in our huge rainfall shower and had a staggering amount of sex, which I'm great at, we take a spontaneous trip out of town, to the beach, where we enjoy a picnic of artisan charcuterie, sourdough and pickles from a farmers' market that we chanced upon on our way down. We light a small, environmentally friendly campfire from old driftwood and I roast marshmallows while Zach gently strums his guitar and sings the new song he's written about how much we love each other, which he'll release on Spotify to much acclaim and millions of streams, which is how we pay for all this. I know it's stupid to hope, but Zach told me that he likes me. *Me!* That's a one in a million chance that must be worth celebrating, surely? The universe has given me this chance – I just have to not mess it up.

A cheer goes up from the players and some of the crowd. "WOOO! YEAH! GOOD ONE!" I shout, clapping as well.

"That *wasn't* a goal for Zach's team," Ruby tells me.

"BOOO! HISS!" I shout instead. "REMATCH!"

At the end of the game, I hover while Zach slaps the backs of the other players and says various football-boy type things, like, "Nice defending, mate!" and, "That was a brutal second half!" He nods at me as he passes by on his way to the changing rooms. "Thanks for coming, nice to have a bit of a crowd," he says.

I didn't expect him to refer to me as his boyfriend, but surely he could have called me "a friendly face" or something, rather than "a bit of a crowd"?

"Not at all, amazing fun!" I say.

He nods and makes to head off with the others.

"So, what are you doing now?" I continue.

"Get cleaned up, then we're heading to Harrison's for pizza."

I raise my eyebrows. "Harrison? From the opposing team?"

Zach laughs. "Like I said, it was just a friendly. See you tomorrow, yeah?"

And he jogs off.

I watch him go, then glance at Ruby and Sam, who are standing a few metres to my side, taking all this in. I raise an arm towards Zach. "Yep! See you tomorrow!" I chew my lip as he disappears, then paint a big smile on my face and turn back to Ruby and Sam. "Cool! Anyone for some post-match Morley's chicken, 'cause I'm starving?"

It's true there's an ache in my stomach, but it's not from hunger. It's from the nagging feeling that, for whatever reason, Zach doesn't seem quite as invested in whatever happened in the props store as I am. But maybe I just need to slow down, relax a bit and let the course of true love wend its romantic way. The Freddie Project has yielded incredible results in a matter of days. . . I'm sure it's going to come good again very soon; I've just gotta give things a chance.

11

One week later, and I'm super frustrated. A whole week of no progress. I have been to the props store every lunchtime. In fact, I have *loudly* told everyone in the vicinity of Zach that's what I'm doing, hoping that he might come and find me and we can pick up where we left off. But, no. I've been down there all alone, skulking in the under-stage shadows, waiting and longing, to no avail. And as if that didn't make me feel enough like the Phantom of the Opera, a spot has come up on my chin, so now, with this facial disfigurement, the entire look is complete.

Worse, there has been no mention whatsoever of the kiss, or the possibility of a date. I haven't pressed the issue. Like, I asked in the first place, so my feelings are clear. I don't want to go on about it. Did I misinterpret the whole thing? Maybe Zach wanted to kiss me, he told me he liked me, but he didn't mean for us to be any more than that moment. Did he just need to get me out of his system? He knew all along we were ill-matched, that it could never work, him all good-looking and talented, and me all average. Kiss it out and move on. Was that what it was? Or maybe I was bad at the kiss, like, too bitey, or not sensuous enough, and Zach was disappointed and wants to find a boy with more accomplished lips?

I'm not in the best place mentally, but I make a real effort to trust that, by saying yes to life, everything will come up smelling of roses. Zach is impressive. And yes, I can compete with that – I can be impressive too. Maybe if he sees me being impressive, he'll be, er . . . impressed and go back to liking me again. Which is why, at our first rehearsal for *Grease*, I *impressively* arrive with a folder full of lists of all the props we are going to need for the show, complete with pictures of possible items we can buy and rough costings, ready for Ms Pearson's approval. I also have a clipboard, a pencil tucked behind my ear (sign of a true pro in *any* situation), and a bumbag filled with different coloured tape, safety pins, glue, Blu-Tack, scissors, and other stuff a props guy might need.

"This is great, Freddie!" Ms Pearson says. "It's just. . . I like to grow the props list organically, as we explore the show, so let's keep this situation fluid, shall we? Let's embrace the possibilities, not tie ourselves down to. . ." She glances down my lists. "Coleslaw – recommend Sainsbury's Taste the Difference version, as rich creaminess is more in keeping with authentic American food styles."

I nod. "Oh, sure, *yes*! This is really just a working document – a place to start from!" I glance over to Zach, who doesn't even seem to have heard any of this and is now listening to something with his EarPods in, eyes closed, concentrating. I sigh and walk to the back of the drama studio, where I've set up a little desk from which I can watch rehearsals and be ready to jot down props requirements as they come up. "Excuse me," I say to Lottie and Kwame, who are gossiping in hushed bitchy tones by the side of my chair.

"I wonder what *Freddie* thinks!" Lottie says, clapping her hands together.

"About what?" I mutter, flopping down on the chair.

"The casting issues!" Lottie replies.

I glance up at her, an expression of what appears to be genuine concern on her face, and then at Kwame, who has a face of equal concern, but is also in stripy knee-high socks and standing with bevelled legs, which tells me whatever these "issues" are, this is prime theatre kids bitching territory.

"What's the 'issue'?" I ask.

"Zach as Danny," she hisses. "Why would you do that? Ms Pearson can tell we can't stand each other!"

I shrug. "Maybe she thinks you have chemistry?"

"Lottie has chemistry with Harrison," Kwame says.

"Yeah, amazing chemistry!" Lottie adds.

"Makes more sense to cast the two of them as the

leads," Kwame continues, ever the subservient little arse-licker to Lottie. "Like, does Ms Pearson even know what she's doing, babe?"

Lottie shakes her head. "She gives it 'West End' but the fact is, she *failed*!"

"She *failed*, babe," Kwame agrees. "Not even a 'has been', a 'never was'!"

"I heard she never *was* Sandy, she was actually *third cover*! Third!" Lottie says.

Kwame rolls his eyes. "Doesn't surprise me, with *that* voice!"

At this point, Ms Pearson claps her hands for everyone to come and sit down so we can start. Lottie and Kwame immediately put on a front of utter sweetness and light, Lottie doing ballet steps over to the group, and Kwame sitting himself down in the splits.

"Love your earrings!" Kwame tells Ms Pearson.

"Mm, they're *lush*, miss!" Lottie adds.

I watch Zach as he pulls his EarPods out and gets his script out of his rucksack, so serene and above all their crap. He's wearing black Adidas shorts, white socks, and a grey T-shirt – nothing really that special, very boy-next-door really, but he looks so flippin' gorgeous.

Ms Pearson must catch me looking and mistake my lustful glances for wanting to be more involved, because she says, "Freddie? Come and join us! We're all on the same team, *on*- or *off*stage!"

My cheeks flush as everyone turns towards me and I scurry over and put myself next to Ruby and Sam, which is definitely the safest spot.

"OK!" Ms Pearson says. "*Grease* is love story set in a high school, but this show isn't only a romcom, and I really want us to access all those layers and feelings and emotions – the gruesome underbelly of high school life, right?"

I mean, I'm drawing a blank. It's *Grease*. Why does everything need a "gruesome underbelly" these days to be considered worthy? Why can't people just have a laugh and enjoy stuff – is the world not shit enough?

Dhruv seems to like this, though – he's sitting barefoot on the floor, nodding earnestly. "Kenickie's got a heart of darkness," he says. "A cold, uncaring father, a mother hooked on Quaaludes. . ."

"Actually," Alice pipes up, "Quaaludes weren't introduced in America until the sixties. Meprobamate, known primarily by the brand name Miltown, was the popular prescription tranquillizer of the fifties." She smiles at Ms Pearson. "Sam and I have already been exploring what drugs Eugene and Patty's parents would take in an effort to forget their disappointment with their failed American dreams."

I glance at Sam, who grimaces and looks at the floor. "Three hours at her house last night," he hisses. "Like I don't have actual homework to do!"

"Let's do word association!" Ms Pearson announces, sounding a lot more excited than I feel. "Don't judge, don't try to be clever, let's just get some words flowing. Just say whatever comes into your mind when we talk about *high school*." She holds her breath for a moment, as if in some magical trance. "And . . . GO."

"Power," Zach says, getting right in there.

"Mmmm," Ms Pearson nods.

"Insecurities," says Ruby.

"Football!" Harrison adds. (Bless.)

"Jealousy," Zach says.

"Erections," Jamil announces. "Like, miss, seriously, I really strongly associate high school with—"

Ms Pearson raises her hand to silence him and, worryingly, makes a note, like she might actually try to integrate this into our production.

"Homework," says Sam. "Which I'm really behind on!" he adds, under his breath, scowling in Alice's direction.

"Cliques!" (Calvin.)

"Puberty." (Sam.)

"Love." (Alice.)

"Discovering yourself," says Kwame.

"That's two words!" Priya whispers to him.

I've added nothing so far, and am just thinking I probably should, even if it's just "tragedy" or "nightmare", when Lottie, who has also been notably silent until this point, chimes in with "arrogance" and looks directly at Zach.

"Threatened," Zach replies, eyeballing her.

"*Sad*," Lottie replies. "As in, *a tragic person.*"

"Bitches," Zach retorts.

"Especially gay ones!" Lottie comes back.

"Bitter!"

"Player!"

"Total spoiled brat 'cause my dad's really rich and I live in Dulwich but bizarrely still go to a state comprehensive school and not a private one. Why *is* that?" Zach smiles at Lottie.

"Oh! You two!" Ms Pearson says, with an inappropriate amount of glee. "This is exactly why I wanted you both as Danny and Sandy! That spark! That electricity! This whole enemies-to-lovers vibe you two have going on, it's going to send the audience wild!"

The expressions Zach and Lottie have on their faces suggests neither of them believes that.

"But, miss?" Kwame says, raising his hand. "Like, I *totally* get this, and we are, like, learning so much from you, but how are these words gonna help us? Shouldn't we just start staging the scenes or learning the dances?"

There are some tentative nods and murmurs of agreement from some of the other theatre kids – but nothing too adamant (they're essentially all spineless), just the beginnings of some simmering resentment.

Ms Pearson stands up and starts pacing around the room. "Kwame, Kwame, Kwame, when you stand on that stage, when you say your lines, or sing, or dance those steps, I want each of you to be doing more than merely going through the motions. Sure, you can dance the hand jive. But what's really going on behind the smiles in that number? Which of the Pink Ladies hate one another? Who stole whose boyfriend? Who's vying to be top dog in the T-birds?" Ms Pearson chuckles. "Hell, maybe two of the T-Birds actually have the hots for each other? I'm all for mixing this up if you guys are!"

The T-Birds all nervously glance at one another, except Zach, who's just looking down at his script, making a note in the margin.

"I'm going out with Lottie," Harrison pipes up randomly. "Just saying."

"*Harrison* might be," Ms Pearson retorts, "but is *Doody*?"

Harrison opens his mouth, then shuts it again, looking totally confused.

"*Mmm*-kay," Ms Pearson says. "I can see I've given you all a lot of things to think about there, and all I'm asking, as we start to play with this show, is to keep them in mind. Let ideas evolve and take shape. Nothing is ever wrong in my rehearsal room. It's just an idea to explore."

"Is murder wrong, miss?" Jamil asks. "In your rehearsal room?"

Ms Pearson takes a deep breath.

"Just asking, miss. Like, how far can we explore these ideas?"

"Shut up, Jamil," Lottie pipes up. "If you want to play the joker, go back to hanging out round the back of the sports hall and squandering your educational opportunities."

There's a collective "Ooooh!" from the group, while Jamil just smiles at Lottie, clearly amused at her audacity.

"Let's take five and then hot-seat the characters!" Ms Pearson says, ignoring it all. "Can some of you pack the chairs away? Leave one in the middle."

Everyone sets to it, while I walk over to my props desk. Since I don't have a character, I won't be taking part in the hot-seating exercise. I watch Zach as he gets up from the floor and pulls each leg back behind him, stretching. He hasn't even acknowledged me. I don't know what I've done so wrong.

"You need to stop staring at him," Ruby says, arriving by the side of my props desk, chugging from a large bottle of Evian.

"I'm not staring at him," I explain. "I have to look towards the action in case anyone needs any props."

Ruby glances at my notepad, which is covered in incriminating love hearts, and even one of those calculations where you work out what percentage someone fancies you.

Apparently it's eighty-four per cent. An excellent result. But that being the case, why the hell aren't things working out?

"You're making a crucial mistake," Ruby says, stretching her calves.

"Oh, OK, do tell, Miss Love Expert! Miss . . . Sexy Times Counsellor, Miss—"

"Do you want my advice or not?"

I wave at her to do just that.

"Stop acting like Zach is the only thing in your life and that everything depends on going out with him. It's not attractive. Granted, you may not have explicitly told him that, but you're giving off this. . ." She sniffs around me.

"Oh god, am I? I showered this morning, I swear to god!"

"No!" Ruby says. "You have this air of desperation about you. It's not an actual smell, it's a *vibe*."

"Oh, *great*."

"I'm just saying, it's obvious you've entered a sort of despair about Zach. You're melancholy; it's like you've already lost and there's absolutely nothing else good going on in your life. You can't think like that. What would New Freddie say?"

"Yes?" I mutter.

"Exactly!"

"But what am I meant to be saying yes to here?"

"*Yes* to whatever will be, will be! *Yes* to not caring so much! *Yes* to living life, because this is the only life you've got! *Yes* to enjoying yourself. . ."

I raise my hand. "Yeah, OK, I get it. The 'yes' thing can be spun to suit any situation."

"Whatever, you're *busy*. 'Yes' people always are. And if Zach comes through, he comes through—"

"He's coming through now," I hiss, watching as Zach heads our way. "Hush up!"

"See? It works. He's looked over, and rather than been confronted with you staring back like a lovesick puppy, he's seen you're busy and engaged in something else. Psychologically, that's made him want to get your attention back to him, hence his imminent visit."

"Sure, sure."

She pats my back. "Whatever he says, you're not free."

"I thought I was meant to say yes? That's confusing!"

"Yes in certain circumstances, not always, we already established that!"

I don't have time to answer because Zach arrives. "Hey!" He grins.

"Long time no see!" I reply, before remembering I probably should try to lose the hurt-and-wronged-partner tone from my voice. "Guess we've both been mad busy!" I add, grinning too.

Zach raises his eyebrows. "Right?" He sighs. "Look, um. . . I didn't know whether you still wanted to do that coffee, or. . ." He trails off and plunges his hands into the pockets of his shorts, shifting slightly from foot to foot. *Adorable.*

"Oh, ye—" Ruby nudges me and I catch myself. "*Maybe.*"

Zach nods and chews his lip.

"I mean, sure, of course, that sounds nice." It's like that word game where you have to describe a word without saying a list of banned words. "Very *positive*. Aye, Aye, Captain! *Oui!* Definitely the opposite of no, is what I'm thinking."

Zach looks confused. "Uh-huh? OK. It's only... I kind of didn't know if you still wanted to. Like, you mentioned it to begin with. .." He hesitates, flicking his eyes to Ruby.

"It's OK, she knows ... not that I've told her or mentioned it much." I grimace. *Shut up, Freddie – play it cool!*

"Sure," Zach says. "Well, you mentioned it, but then you didn't follow up or say it again, so I wondered if you'd changed your mind, or. .."

I stare at him, open-mouthed. Oh god! Oh, Zach! He'd been thinking the same thing I'd been thinking! He'd convinced himself I wasn't interested, and so he'd withdrawn, just like I'd done. Oh god, we're the same!

"No!" I nearly squeal. "I totally want to! I'm so sorry, I thought *you* were going to come back to me!"

"Huh. Crossed wires!" Zach grins. "What are we like?"

"So dumbass!" I grin back.

"Tomorrow, maybe?"

My eyes widen and I break into a massive smile, before Ruby casually clears her throat and I'm brought back to reality and The Plan.

"*No,*" Ruby says. "You're helping me tomorrow, remember?"

"Oh, yes, I'm helping Ruby tomorrow," I repeat.

A little smile plays on Zach's lips. I can't quite interpret it, but it's almost like he *knows* what game I'm playing here. But that's fine. Love *is* a game. And maybe we're both willing players. "That's cool, we can take a rain check on tomorrow, but let's do something soon – I mean, if you want to?" He gives me that hopeful look which makes me want to cuddle him like a puppy.

"Let's message," I say.

"Let's do that!" He smiles at me, holding my gaze for just a fraction long enough that I catch my breath. "I need to get ready for hot seating. Get in character. Catch you later!"

"In a while, alligator!" I clear my throat. "Um, no, see you later, crocodile! Um. . ."

"See you later, alligator," Ruby says.

I point at her. "What she said!"

Zach gives me a smile and jogs back to where his rucksack is.

"Oh, cool as a cucumber," Ruby tells me.

"Result, though," I say. And it is. There are no windows in this drama studio, but it suddenly feels a whole lot brighter in here.

12

Coming up with a kick-ass message to send Zach turns out to be very difficult, being as it has to fulfil so many purposes:

1. Casual, but not in a couldn't-care-less way.
2. Flirty, but not in a desperate way.
3. Full of factual information, e.g., potential dates, times and ideas.
4. Showing attractive aspects of personality, e.g., sense of humour, kindness, fun-loving and spontaneous approach to life in general, but not so spontaneous that I don't want to discuss items in point 3.
5. With an unmistakable subtext that kissing (and more!) would be welcome, but no tacky and obvious emojis, like winking man or aubergine.

After a great many drafts, and some editorial feedback from Ruby and Sam, I eventually opt for a simple:

ME: Hey, how about Thursday?

I've fully prepared myself for him not replying, and being fine with that, because I've got a Toblerone on standby to eat (distraction), but as it turns out, he fires back a message pretty much straight away:

ZACH: Can't do thurs. Sorry.

"Thurs"? *Thurs?* He couldn't even be bothered to write the full name of the day? Also, just a brief apology but no suggestion of an alternative? I feel a horrible pang of disappointment – he said he wanted to meet, but is he actually still thinking of this more as friends, now he's got the kiss out of his system? Then there's more:

ZACH: I do archery then.

I mean, fine, I suppose, and that does give him a sort of sexy *Hunger Games* vibe, and the attractiveness of that, and the image of Zach being all capable with a bow and arrow as he kills potential assassins fills my heart with joy. I've got to try not to read things into his messages which aren't there. I need to hold my nerve, not get angry because he's abbreviated "Thursday" and clearly keeps his messages short and to the point, rather than being prone to writing multiple lines of waffle, like me.

ZACH: Friday?

Of course, Friday is totally fine. I'm embarrassingly available with literally no other activities on. But maybe that's a problem. Like Ruby said, I'm too free, too needy.

ME: Oh no! I can't do Friday!

Total lie, but a necessary one. I cannot be the one just fitting in with his schedule the whole time. I'm a successful, independent teenage boy who is living life to the absolute max.

ZACH: Ah man, what you doing that's more important, haha!

Huh. That's a very good question. I quickly type the school website into my search bar, click past the home page with its carefully curated photos of attractive kids in pristine uniform sitting on some lawn smiling at a textbook, and check what clubs are on on Fridays. And obviously, there's hardly anything, because it's Friday, and most people just want to go home after school. So I have the grand total of one option:

ME: Meditation

ZACH: Namaste

ME: What?

ZACH: Never mind

I wait to see if there's any more, like, some further suggestion, but minutes pass and there's not. I can't stand it. Eating a triangle of Toblerone does nothing to take my mind off the fact I might have messed up. *Never mind.* What does that mean? Never mind the date? Never mind *us*? I message him back:

ME: I'm free all weekend though!

Then I delete the exclamation mark before I hit send. Too desperate.

ME: I'm free all weekend though

Yeah, much cooler. In the meantime, it's obviously important to cover my lying tracks, so I fire off a quick message to Ruby and Sam:

ME: If anyone (Zach) asks, I'm meditating on Friday

Unfortunately, due to autocorrect, what I actually send is:

ME: If anyone (Zach) asks, I'm masturbating on Friday

What's worse is that neither Ruby or Sam appear to find this either outrageous or funny, and just reply with:

RUBY: OK

SAM:

Worse still, Zach hasn't replied at all. Ugh. Kissed a boy, nearly had a date, told lies, screwed it up, died lonely and bitter. *Because I didn't say yes.*

I sit around miserably for a bit, try to read some *Pride and Prejudice* (manage about a paragraph), get bored, and when Mum walks into my room about twenty minutes later she finds me deep-throating the Toblerone, because I thought it would be interesting to see if I could.

"Don't spoil your dinner," she says, walking out again.

I whip the thing out of my mouth. "Oh, hi? Is this the police? There's a *stranger* in my house!"

"Oh, hi? Is that the police?" she replies, from somewhere in her bedroom. "There's a teenage boy in my house being indecent with a Toblerone!"

I pad on to the landing. "*No*, I was just hungry. Starving. Had no food for days due to a parent not fulfilling her basic responsibility to feed her child."

"That's funny, because the Deliveroo account has been *hammered*," she replies, clattering around inside her room. "Tell me, how were *every single one of the starters* on the menu at Gate of India?"

"I couldn't decide what to have," I tell her.

"So you ordered it all. Seems sensible."

"I was stress eating, since I'm basically an orphan now."

She opens her door and smiles at me. "Are you OK?"

"I suppose." I shrug.

"School all right?"

I shrug again. "Yeah. How's the TV show?"

"Good." She nods. "I got takeout from the Italian. It's on the table."

"Amazing," I say, heading immediately downstairs and through to our kitchen-diner, where I let out a blood-curdling scream.

There, in front of me, is Jasper.

Not actual Jasper.

A life-sized cardboard cut-out of the snooty little knob, standing up with the *Cherries* logo at his feet and the slogan: *Pop yours on MegaFlix this spring!*

"God, you're a drama queen," Mum mutters, walking in behind me.

"What's he doing here?!"

"It's a prototype from the marketing department – I'm going to take it to set once it's signed off and surprise them all."

I glare at it. How dare Jasper be captured in cardboard here, looking so attractive and friendly when that is certainly not an accurate representation of what he's really like? "It's horrible. His eyes follow you round the room. And how does he manage to look so smug?"

"He sends his love."

"No, he doesn't."

"Well, OK, he doesn't, but he did say to tell you he had to take his top to the dry-cleaner."

I stare at her. "Oh, right? Is that him asking me for a tenner or something?"

"It's a shame you don't like him. He's terribly good, Fred. Quite the find!"

Oh, yes, he's "quite the find"! Mum's obviously really proud of Jasper. I mean, she's at the point of bringing back effigies of him, for god's sake! She hasn't even got one of those personalized mugs from Snappy Snaps with a photo of *me* on it! But Jasper?! Oh, yes, recreate him in 450gsm cardboard and gloss lamination!

I try to ignore Jasper and how irritated/jealous/weirdly horny/inadequate he makes me feel and pick the foil containers out of the brown paper bag.

"The school emailed," Mum says, in such a casual way that I know it can't be good. "Apparently cast and crew for

Grease get priority ticket booking for the show."

I unfreeze myself, and slowly put the foil container down on the table. I was not going to tell her about this whole drama thing. What's the point? The fact I didn't get cast will only confirm how much of a disappointment I am.

Mum puts some plates and cutlery down on the table. "You're backstage, I assume?"

I grimace. "Would it be so surprising if they cast me in the show?"

"Yes, it would."

I stare at her. I should have told her the truth about my meltdown during *Les Mis* all those years ago, instead of just babbling incoherently about getting nervous. But I knew she'd just think me pathetic – Dad had only recently left, and Mum kept saying how we both needed to be "strong". I don't know, I just wish she didn't always greet everything I try to do with such scepticism. I get it, it's funny, and we've kind of fallen into this groove of savagely taking the piss out of each other, but sometimes, just sometimes, I wish I did something which genuinely made her proud of me. I don't need her to be one of those parents who's always bragging about their kid, I just want to feel like I'm not a total crushing blow, or a punchline, all the time – even if no one knows that but me.

"Freddie, there's nothing wrong with your talents lying elsewhere. We can't all be good at everything. This whole nonsense in schools these days where everyone is a winner all the time – it does nothing to prepare you for the real world. It's brutal out there." She sits down and lifts the lids off the containers. Some arancini balls, lasagne for me (already piled high with Parmesan, so nice one there, Mother), and linguine with clams, chilli and garlic for her. "So what are you doing, then?"

"Props." I shrug, spooning the lasagne on to my plate.

She nods. "Good. Backstage is underrated, but they're the glue that hold everything together." She twists some linguine around her fork. "What made you do it?"

"Just thought I should get involved with stuff," I say, concentrating on the food. Not a total lie. No need to tell her about The Freddie Project – she'd have a field day with that little nugget of information. And no need to tell her about Zach. Especially now he can't even muster the enthusiasm to message me back. Don't want to raise her hopes that she's about to have the romantically successful, well-adjusted, popular son she's always dreamed of.

Barry strolls into the kitchen, cocks his head at Jasper, then rears up on his hind legs and tries to use him as a scratching post, knocking Jasper face down.

"Someone's got the right idea," I say.

"*Freddie.*"

"Cats are excellent judges of character."

"That's not true, they generally dislike everyone." Mum picks Jasper off the floor and dusts him down. "Now he's got a mark on his face."

"Oh dear, how sad." I grin.

No sooner is Jasper upright than Barry launches what appears to be an actual attack, throwing himself at the stupid life-sized display and knocking it down again. "Right," Mum says, "it'll have to live in your room until I can take it in."

"I don't think so," I reply.

"I don't want it ruined."

"Put it in your office!"

"Have you seen how little space there is in there? The only room in the house where the cat doesn't go is yours, due to your 'allergy'." She actually does air quotes, like I might be making it up.

"Not my problem," I say. "That *thing* is not living in my room." And on this point, I'm going to stand very firm.

I'm in bed, propped up against some pillows, glowering at Cardboard Jasper, who stands in the corner of my bedroom, giving me "I'm so much better than you" eyes.

"What?" I say to him. "You're nothing but a bargaining chip, you smug bastard."

Mum told me that Jasper being stored in my room was essentially my contribution to *Cherries* and if I couldn't do it, then she couldn't guarantee the Deliveroo account wouldn't be suspended. After I reminded her that her legal duties as a mother include feeding me, she announced that either she would batch-cook and freeze a load of her terrible vegetarian chilli, or else I could go to eat at her friends Colin and Yvonne's house. Colin and Yvonne are the sort of people who eat offal because it's "delicious" and "full of nutrients". They are also nudists. As far as I know, they don't do both at the same time, and I don't want to sound ungrateful, but I can't eat internal organs at the best of times, let alone while under the threat of being confronted with middle-aged genitals. In the end, access to Deliveroo was guaranteed, but the trade-off was that I have to house Jasper in my bedroom.

"You're really not all that," I tell him.

The funny thing about Cardboard Jasper is that he's incredibly similar to Real Jasper, in that he doesn't really say much and comes across as quite cold and aloof. He just stares back with smiling, almost taunting eyes. Eyes that are full of confidence because he's so good-looking, so successful, so popular, so everything my life is not. . . "You can't even get a reply from a boy who kissed you!" he seems to be saying. "You can't even get cast in a school production of *Grease*!" And then: "You've still got that spot on your chin, and don't you think you should sort your eyebrows out?"

I don't need his negativity in my life. I hop out of bed and shift him around so he's facing the wall. The problem is, the angle is such that I can still see his eyes in my mirror, which is even more freaky. I adjust him again, so now he's angled away from my bed, but towards the door. At least maybe that will ward off intruders.

I turn the lights out and try to go to sleep.

But I can't.

Even if I can't *see* him, I can still somehow *sense* him.

God, I hate Jasper Perry.

13

My morning starts badly (pad out of the bathroom after my shower, shut my door, drop my towel as usual and find myself stark bollock naked in front of Jasper, who *definitely* makes a snide remark about the size of my boy parts), and continues badly, since I don't see Zach in the common room before registration, and I don't have any classes with him on Wednesdays. With still no messages, I find myself sinking into a pit of failure and despair once again.

I think I need to face reality: it hasn't worked. If Zach was anywhere near as keen for this as I am, he'd have been more proactive. That's just a fact. Maybe he wants it *a bit*, but I want it *loads*. And therein lies the problem. See, you can just tell from Zach's swagger that he's experienced, you know, in the sex department. Whereas I'm not. Even that kiss with Zach was my first. So this is a big deal for me. Maybe for Zach it's just a bit of fun?

These doubts multiply in my head all morning, and by

lunchtime I'm well and truly about to fall off the wagon. I stare through the glass display cabinet at the doughnuts in the cafeteria, contemplating buying a couple then shutting myself away somewhere quiet (maybe the props store) and forgetting the whole thing. I could just go back to before, because it was easier and a whole load less stressful and upsetting.

Then Ruby spots me and pulls me out of the queue.

"No, you don't!" she says.

"I need the comforting embrace of gluten and sugar!" I protest.

"What's happened?"

"Zach hates me."

"Hates you, or just didn't reply to a text?"

She knows me too well. "I dunno." I shrug.

"Let's walk and talk," Ruby says, putting her arm across my shoulders and guiding me towards the exit of the cafeteria, where Sam joins us.

"Have you told him yet?" he asks Ruby.

"Oh god, now what?" I say.

"Sam and I have been plotting, and we have a plan for you," Ruby says as we walk along the main corridor. "A dinner party."

I laugh. "Rubes, I can barely boil an egg. In fact, I can't boil an egg. Not in a way that's satisfactory for dippy soldiers."

"Sure, sure, sure," she says. "That's why we're gonna do this thing, all of us, all together. Dinner with some mates. That's how it's billed. Me, you and Sam with Zach and Calvin—"

"And *Calvin!*" I squeal triumphantly, glad for a bit of distraction from talking about all my awkwardness. "So, what's the deal? Are you two a thing?"

Ruby rolls her eyes. "Yes. We went on our date, had fun, had a little kiss, and now we're official."

I squeal again. "Just like that! All so easy!"

"Well, it is, Freddie. Unless, it seems, you're you. Yesterday, Zach told you he wanted to go for coffee. How have you managed to mess it up?"

I swallow. How *have* I managed it?

"How do you . . . how do you know I've messed it up?" I bluff.

"Oh, mate," Sam says, squeezing my shoulder and shaking his head, as though he just *knows*.

"I've seen you, languishing in the common room like a lovelorn heroine in an Austen novel," Ruby tells me. "And then last night you're in such a fluster you tell me and Sam you're 'masturbating' on Friday, which, although I have no doubt you will be, I'm assuming isn't what you meant to send?"

I chew my lip. She isn't entirely wrong. "Uh-huh?"

"Imagine what it'll be like if you actually go for coffee," she continues as we walk along. "Imagine the . . . horrors! Imagine the awkwardness, the long silences, the fumbled sentences and all the cringe! And then god forbid it goes wrong in any way, because you'll probably lie down weakly on a chaise longue and simply die. You need backup. You need me and Sam, and a nice, relaxed evening where we can all talk, where there's no expectations, but it's a bit more special than just ordering in some pizzas and getting hammered on fruit cider."

"Plus, I'll be there too, so it won't look like a double date either," Sam adds. "And if you guys all start feeling it and start playing footsie, I'm happy just . . . playing with myself."

He looks alarmed, realizing what he's just said.

"Yeah, please don't do that, Sam," Ruby laughs.

"OK, OK, this is all moving too fast," I tell them. "I need to think about this. It feels . . . rash."

Ruby stops dead and turns to me. "You do want it to work out with Zach, don't you?"

"Yes!"

"Good!" she trills. "So, the three of us will cook – we'll do a course each. Round your house if your mum's away on set?"

"We're going to have *courses*?" This all sounds insane.

Sam frowns. "It's a dinner party! I've bagsied dessert. I'm doing cinnamon-bun bread-and-butter pudding."

"I think that's the sexiest thing you've ever said," I tell him.

"OK, you've tried to derail this enough," Ruby tells me. "You have to say yes."

"No, I don't."

"It's The Freddie Project. You *have* to. We agreed."

"Argh!" I wail. "Goddammit! Can I do the starter, then? I really don't think I'm up to a main course."

"No, you're doing the main, and you're going to make a huge splash with your wonderful cooking," Ruby says, guiding me into the sixth form common room.

"Wait!" I say. "What about Calvin? I don't want everyone else there knowing this is all part of some romance plan – it's too much pressure."

"One step ahead of you. I've told him it's a fun evening for some of the *Grease* cast. He doesn't suspect a thing." Ruby narrows her eyes at me. "You know he's a straight boy, right? They're *very* trusting, bless."

"Huh."

"And look! There's Zach, you can ask him now!" Ruby beams.

I glare at her. "You knew he was here, this is all a set-up."

"I cannot tell a lie." Ruby grins. "Always one step ahead of you, Fred."

Sam gives me a quick blast from a can of Lynx Africa he's produced from his bag. "Exquisite!" he tells me, breathing it in, before Ruby gives me a whacking great push and I stumble over to where Zach's playing table football.

"HI!" I blurt, stopping just in time before I crash into him.

"Freddie!" He smiles. At least he smiles. He nods at Harrison Kane, who he's playing against. "Rematch later, yeah?" Harrison nods and Zach turns to me as we sit on some nearby chairs. "You didn't text back."

"I did text back!" *What?* Of course I texted back!

"I said we'd chat at school to arrange things and asked you when's good and you didn't say."

I shake my head. Have I entered some parallel universe? "I didn't get that message."

"Huh." Zach says. He swipes at his phone, then sighs, showing it to me. "Stupid thing failed to send!"

"Ohhhh," I say. I mean, this is the sort of technical detail I would obsessively check, but I suppose we're all different. However, I am *delighted*. He's been the victim of a tech mishap! It's nothing to do with him being indifferent about me. "Oh, well, that's fine." I glance at Ruby and Sam, who are gesticulating at me to get the hell on with it, and suddenly, yeah, this feels like it might be a good thing to do. "So, idea: how do you fancy joining me, Sam, Ruby and Calvin for a . . . sort of informal, relaxed, um . . . dinner party? It's very relaxed and fun." I nod. "On Saturday? At mine. Mum's away. Not that that last point is particularly relevant, I'm just saying, there won't be any dorky parents about, ha ha ha!" Did I just use the word "dorky"? Oh god, I did. "Kind of a welcome to the school, let's celebrate all being involved with the show, but not with any of the cast members we hate, sort of thing. Whatddya say?"

"Sounds cool."

"Does it? Yes! Yes, it will be, because it is!"

Ruby arrives with Sam. "Hey, Fred! Hi, Zach!" she says, doing all-surprised-to-bump-into-you acting. "Has Fred mentioned our dinner idea?"

"I'm in!" Zach replies. "Who's cooking?"

"We're doing a course each," Sam says, indicating me and Ruby.

"Love it!" Zach grins. He looks at me. "You can cook, Freddie? Impressive."

Ruby is giving me an "I told you so!" look, but I do a great job of ignoring her. Yeah, yeah, OK, she was right, being an active person with many talents, interests and lots on turns out to be more appealing than someone who sits around obsessing and pining. Who knew?

I'm feeling buoyed up. "I'm a *great* cook," I say confidently. Saying it makes it true. I hope. I just want him to be finally wowed by how good I am at something. I want him to be blown away by my culinary skills, which will be incredibly sexy and alluring. How badly wrong can it go?

I try not to think about when I claimed to be a "theatre kid". But then, there's no "recipe" for being a theatre kid, whereas there definitely *are* recipes for cooks to follow. So that's what I'll do. I'll simply follow a recipe for something impressive online.

It occurs to me things will go better if I cook something he likes, and also doesn't land him in A&E. I adjust my expression to something a little more grave. "Any food allergies or intolerances? Anything you don't like?"

"Nope." His eyes meet mine and he lowers his voice. "I'll eat anything."

I swallow as he holds my gaze for a moment.

Then he smiles. "Gotta go. I have a horrific Danny and Sandy rehearsal with Lottie – Ms Pearson wants me to shout my lines from the roof of the humanities block, while Lottie shouts hers from the roof of the science block. Apparently it's to highlight how Danny and Sandy find communication difficult. So hyped. *Not.* Catch you all later." And he strolls out of the common room.

"Result," Sam says quietly, wiggling his eyebrows. "He'll eat *anything.*"

"What just happened there?" I ask.

"I'm not sure," Ruby says, "but if you've got such a thing as 'lucky boxers' then I would consider wearing them on Saturday, Freddie Bennett."

14

Actually living life rather than watching from the sidelines turns out to be both brilliant and terrifying. I am *stoked* that everyone in rehearsals knows my name, and they are using it *a lot*: "Freddie! Put down 'cafeteria trays'!" "Freddie! We'll need a car aerial!" "Freddie! Did you get Twinkies?" Funny thing is, even though everyone is *very* demanding, I actually don't mind? There's something nice about being the person people come to. There's even been talk of me having my own headset for technical rehearsals, so other crew can communicate with me easily in the theatre – and I can't adequately express the unfettered joy that idea brings me. My *own* headset! I'm a mover and shaker now. Anyone with any sort of walkie-talkie device is! Same with clipboards.

Another brilliant thing happens on Friday, when the door to the props store creaks open while I'm sorting out a pile of books for one of the scenes and Zach pokes his head in.

"All right?" he says.

I give him a warm smile. "Hey."

He steps into the store, closing the door carefully behind him. "So . . . I didn't know if . . . I know we're doing the dinner thing, but is that because. . ." He swallows. He seems nervous. "Is it because you just want to be mates, or do you still want to. . ." He flicks his eyes tentatively to mine.

"I still want to. . ."

"Kiss?" He chews his lip a bit.

I just about manage to nod. "Yep."

He smiles, looks deep into my eyes, like, seriously, I'm just a mess at this point, and then we're suddenly all over each other, kissing like our lives depend on it. Hot, frantic, horny, desperate kisses, breathless, urgent, barely coming up for air, I mean, it is EPIC. He's so . . . warm and strong. And he smells so . . . comforting. Fabric softener on his clothes, hint of Lynx (natch, be weird if he didn't), and some sort of eau de toilette that I don't know the name of, but it's woody and rich, and I just want to breathe it in as I nuzzle into his neck. He pulls me into him more, we're *pressing against each other* and my stomach is doing flips.

"Sorry," he gasps, eventually breaking off. "I really needed that."

"Oh god, *same!*" I tell him.

And then he starts laughing.

And I start laughing too.

It's not funny, I'm just so pumped with endorphins.

"I like this," he says. "Just me and you, down here . . . it's nice." He looks around the props store. *"Private."*

I nod. And I cannot believe I say it, so let's blame those pesky endorphins again. "Could get up to all sorts." I flick my eyes to his.

"Oh, Freddie." He grins. "You *bad, bad* boy!"

I grin back at him.

We'll never know how that might have ended, because the bell rings for the end of lunch and afternoon registration, but I am *thrilled* that I'm here, living life, and now it feels like there's a real possibility that this bit of fun with Zach might very well become something a little bit more. So yeah, that's good, it's turning into everything I wanted, it's *brilliant*.

But as the days go on and the dinner party looms, the *terror* starts to kick in too. 'Cause there's a difference, isn't there, between the horny kissing and an actual relationship? There's been no mention of us being anything official – neither of us have even said anything about what we've been doing to anyone really (except me to Ruby and Sam, of course), and we certainly haven't been public in any way. I start to worry about how I really want to get this right, how I don't want to say the wrong thing, or put him off, or for him to realize that perhaps we're not that well suited after all, not as boyfriends, anyway.

It gets so bad, I make an actual *comparison chart*, which is the height of paranoia, but here I am:

ZACH	FREDDIE
Confident	Nervous
Sophisticated	Hot mess
Fashionable	Next.co.uk
Toned and athletic	Skinny and weak
Well-groomed	Man up and pluck your eyebrows, for god's sake!
Experienced sex guru	Experienced *self*-sex guru

You know you're in a mess when you start frantically trawling the internet for help, using search terms like "how to make guys like you". An article on how to flirt with men is filled with advice like avoiding generic comments such as, "I like your shirt," and being more specific. For example, "Wow, that shirt really brings out the green in your eyes." Even I, a desperate and fully certified virgin of the highest order, can tell that simply sounds *thirsty* and no one would fall for it in a million years.

There's nothing I can do about my lack of experience, but the other things I'm thinking I can definitely work on ... which basically amounts to me buying a copy of *Men's Health* magazine to leave casually lying about the lounge, sipping a protein drink, and doing five sit-ups. I feel like Zach will approve of all of these things. I want to be the poster boy for happy, successful, well-adjusted, go-getting teenage boy, who could be pictured laughing on the home page of an Outward Bound camp website, or possibly a middle-class clothing catalogue.

My choice of dish for the dinner party is also a challenge. I started off by thinking of aphrodisiacs, because if I can make Zach extra horny, that could play out well for me. But then I worried that was all too obvious and desperate, and maybe I should focus on cooking something delightful that impresses everyone instead – especially since I told Zach I couldn't just cook, I was "great" at it. Like theatre! Cue me combing through all sorts of recipe websites, panicking at terminology like "bain marie" and "confit" before finding a really impressive beetroot risotto recipe with goat's cheese – exactly the sort of fine-dining-sounding dish I require to make Zach fall helplessly in love with me. I spend Saturday morning bouncing around Sydenham High Street, from deli to greengrocer's, in the style of a carefree but discerning hipster, who probably has an ironic long beard and thinks kale is over and we're back to heirloom spinach, returning home and dicing celery and onion in the kitchen before eleven thirty. This astounds my mother, who is busy packing for her weekend on location, but still has time to fire off an assortment of barbed remarks about the fact I'm up this early, along with, "This boy must be really special!" and, "You can have anything else, but don't drink the Sancerre."

"I don't even know what that is," I tell her, turning the hob off since the risotto base is prepared and I can't do the rest until just before the guests arrive.

"Call Colin or Yvonne if you need anything, they're only round the corner," she says. "And be careful not to overcook the rice." She walks out.

With Mum gone and the vegetables prepped, I whip around the house making sure everything is clean and tidy, then get my outfit ready for later. I've given a tremendous amount of thought to the lucky boxers concept that Ruby mentioned and concluded, based on the anecdotal evidence that is my life to date, that luck is not a thing that is generally on my side. What is on my side, though, is Sod's Law, which clearly states that if my trousers have any hope of being pulled down by Zach, I need to be wearing the worst boxers imaginable underneath. And so, behold the novelty Christmas boxers I received last year, red and green, featuring cartoon elves with actual little bells on their hats, bearing the legend, "Don't open till Christmas!" I don't want to get my hopes up, but wearing these feels like a dead cert.

All this said, I know I need to maintain some chill. If I'm anticipating stuff happening, I'll mess it up, so I should just relax and try to have a nice night. I mean, sure, I've found some candles for the table, but that's not about romance, that's about having a sophisticated evening. And, yes, I have put an essential oil diffuser in the room – what of it?

Did you know that clary sage and lavender can really get people in the mood, sex-wise? Interesting fact.

Argh! God, I like him, god, I like him!

By the time Ruby and Sam appear mid-afternoon to help set everything up, I am so het up that Ruby sends me off to my room with her meditation app.

"Better?" she says when I emerge back into the kitchen, having been told to "focus on the breath" for ten minutes by an annoying American woman with the sort of voice that makes you want to scream, "NO ONE IS THIS CALM IN REAL LIFE, ARE YOU ACTUALLY JUST SMOKING A LOT OF WEED?"

I lie and nod, watching as Sam puts the bread-and-butter pudding he's made at home into the fridge and Ruby unpacks an actual disposable barbecue that she's going to cook her chilli-and-lime-marinated king prawns on, complete with her home-made garlic mayo.

"I guess I just want this to go well," I say.

"And it *will*." Ruby smiles. "Just relax and enjoy it. You've opened the door, Fred – now exciting things have the chance to come in! It's worked OK so far, hasn't it?"

"You're right!" I say, more brightly. I clap my hands and walk over to my pan of risotto on the stove. "Just need to start adding stock to this when they arrive."

Ruby frowns. "What's that jingling sound?"

I turn around triumphantly. "That, my friends, is the sweet sound of guaranteed sexual success!"

They look at me blankly.

"Lucky boxers," I explain. "Or rather, unlucky boxers that will turn out to be lucky, taking account of the weird, twisted fun that fate likes to have at my expense."

"Right," Ruby says. "So you're going to spend all evening jingling whenever you move?"

"Nothing wrong with that," I say. "Everyone likes the sound of a bell. That's why they put them in churches. They attract people. I'll be like the Pied Piper, boys following trance-like after my jingling boxers." I look at their exasperated faces. "Worst case scenario, they're a talking point," I say.

"I think you should change them," Ruby tells me.

"No," I say. "I've thought this through. *I know what I'm doing.*"

15

Calvin is first to arrive, looking on edge in skinny chinos, a white shirt and a tie.

"Is this shirt OK? What are you even meant to wear to a dinner party?" he asks Ruby, before clocking Sam's jeans and jumper and adding, "Oh god, should I be in jeans?"

I love how confident and together Calvin is at school, but out of his comfort zone he's got the same insecurities as the rest of us. Spotify's "Dinner with Friends" playlist starts up out of the sound system in the lounge as I head through to the kitchen, sneaking a furtive look at the time on my phone.

"He's not late," Ruby says, following me in. "Stop fretting."

"Yeah, no, of course."

"Also," she says, getting closer, "it's really nice, like, I love it, but if you spray any more of that aftershave on, you're going to asphyxiate him."

I nod. "Noted."

I keep myself busy by getting everyone a drink and making a start on the risotto, which turns out to be a stupid dinner party dish because it requires your almost undivided attention. After five minutes the doorbell goes, and while I'm *meant* to be adding ladles of stock, then waiting for it to be absorbed, I just pour in a whole litre and a half (if the rice is going to soak it up, it's gonna soak it up, why would it matter if I add it in bits or all at once?) and race through to the front door.

"Hey!" I smile at Zach, who's leaning on the door frame, wearing black jeans, white trainers, a white T-shirt and grey hoodie.

He gives me one of his special grins and hands me a wrapped bottle of wine. "Becs in the year above got it for me," he explains. "*Lambrusco.*"

I love that he knows stuff about wine and what's good, and so on.

"Come in!" I say.

He steps inside the hall, looking around to check the coast is clear. "Fred?" he says softly, as I'm about to lead him through into the lounge. I turn to him and he smiles. "I love that shirt. Really brings out the green of your eyes."

Isn't that just the *nicest* thing to say?

Ruby's barbecued prawn starter is sensational. Barbecue anything and you're generally on to a winner, but she really has excelled herself.

I, on the other hand, have *not*.

"So!" Calvin says, looking down at the bowl of red slop I've just presented him with. "What do we have here?"

I must say, he's a very good liar. His face doesn't show a hint of disappointment or horror. Sam and Ruby had one look at their bowls and then one look at each other, which was all it took for me to know their thoughts. Zach, meanwhile, is still staring at his bowl, perhaps trying to will it into being something else through the power of thought.

"It's beetroot and goat's cheese risotto," I say.

Zach looks up at me and blinks.

As "fine dining" goes, this is horribly reminiscent of something you'd find on the floor at three a.m. during a sixth form party. Despite Mum telling me not to overcook the rice, I have managed to overcook the rice, and the beetroot has filtered through the whole dish (I was expecting it to stay as attractive little lumps, a nice pop of colour against the white of the rice), giving it the unmistakable look of lumpy blood.

"It's a gastric experience!" I add, smiling.

"You mean *gastronomic*," Ruby corrects me.

"Do I? Yes, OK, I do."

Calvin nods, looks down again, frowns, and looks back up. "So, do we eat this with a spoon, like soup? Or. . ."

I shrug. "I mean, whatever takes your fancy. . ." I sweep my own spoon through the risotto, which is swimming in rather a lot of (blood-red) liquid, so certainly it *could* be eaten like soup – if it weren't for the more solid lumps of congealed rice and goat's cheese, which appear to warrant a fairly sturdy knife to break apart.

Sam's straight in, taking a confident mouthful, which he chews with enthusiasm, and then more slowly, and then he just stops, having not swallowed, his eyes flicking to Ruby.

"Mmm, lots of . . . interesting flavours," Calvin says, after his first mouthful.

I glance down at my bowl in dismay (it *looks* awful), then take a tentative spoonful and am totally aghast. It's *horrendous*. Everything is wrong – the texture (hard, yet mushy, dry and yet, somehow, too wet), the temperature (tepid – which makes it seem even more like freshly drawn blood), and the taste! Christ alive, whoever thought goat's cheese was a good thing? How did it even come about? Did someone once say, "Oooh, you know what's really nice? Licking between the toes of someone with athlete's foot – is it possible to create a cheese like that?" Honestly, I'm mortified. I hate the idea of letting people down anyway (despite it being a prominent feature of my life, I surprisingly still haven't got used to it), but it's even worse that all this is playing out in front of Zach. Oh, *yes*, Zach, I'm *great* at cooking!

I have to save this situation. I can't let a stupid beetroot risotto ruin my chance of happiness with Zach.

"OK," I say. "We *could* eat this . . . or I could whack

some bags of turkey dinosaurs and potato smiles in the oven, served with baked beans."

There's a beat of silence, which I'm pretty sure is just polite, like anyone's really giving this any serious thought, and then,

"Great idea!" (Ruby.)

"You have turkey dinosaurs? Amazing!" (Calvin.)

"I'll help!" (Zach – and that, is a *result*.)

Half an hour later, we're back on track, and tucking in to the turkey dinosaurs, plus accompaniments, having downed a couple of glasses of something very delicious called "Echo Falls Summer Berries" with Zach while cooking in the kitchen, like a pair of super-sophisticated gay guys, just whipping up some food in their New York apartment. Actually, it was me doing the cooking. Zach just watched and occasionally did things like pinch my bottom while I was putting a tray in the oven. He's so cheeky and cute. I love it.

Calvin glances across at Sam's plate and smiles. "You, er . . . you have a method there, Sam?"

Sam nods. "I behead them all first, before eating the bodies." He glances up at everyone. "I imagine a Jurassic Park situation, and the quickest way of saving humanity is to kill each dinosaur quickly first, hence the method. I've always done it. I was anxious as a kid. Catastrophized a lot of stuff."

"Speaking of catastrophe," Zach says, "do we need to talk about *Grease*?"

There are general murmurs of agreement around the table, and I know exactly where all this is coming from. Ms Pearson's rehearsal technique has been somewhat edgy and unexpected. With the exception of the hand jive number, none of the show has really been blocked or staged yet. Instead, a lot of time has been spent improvising the events of the summer before the action takes place, trying to pass a balloon down a line of actors without anyone using their hands, and deciding very important things like, "If Danny were a vegetable or fruit, what vegetable or fruit would he be?" (An aubergine or massive cucumber was the general consensus.)

"I heard whispers that Lottie's planning to stage a coup," Calvin says.

Ruby rolls her eyes. "She's all talk."

"Plus, I'm not sure the theatre kids are as close-knit as you think," Sam adds. "Just between us, Alice doesn't even like Lottie that much. She's always putting Alice down and giving her acting notes when Ms Pearson isn't looking."

"Ugh, I can't *stand* her," Zach says, scooping up some beans. He glances up at Calvin guiltily. "Sorry, Calvin. I keep forgetting that you and her used to..."

"Dude, it's fine," Calvin says. "I don't have any lingering loyalty to Lottie. She's a player, man! Social climber!"

"Also she's a rich kid who oozes rich kid entitlement everywhere, and that always annoys me," Zach adds.

It's funny, hearing Zach talk like this, because I always tend to assume that good-looking people are also rich, for some reason, but it occurs to me that's idiotic, and that Zach possibly isn't. That makes me like him even more. There's part of me that slightly resents people who seem to have it easy, whether through money, or good looks, or just natural in-built charm that lets them sail through life. The idea that Zach might have struggled, that he might be ordinary in some ways, like me, really delights me. He's so perfect, he sometimes doesn't seem human. But I guess, actually, he is.

"You make the best beans, Freddie," Zach says, winking at me.

"Ha! Thanks."

He smiles at me (a sort of private, special smile, just between us), then switches his attention back to the rest of the table. "How did a nice guy like you, Calvin, end up with Lottie?"

Calvin shrugs. "You know when you're fourteen, and you have this mental image of what your ideal person is, but it's kind of based on porn? Well, that. I'm not proud of it. I guess it takes time to know who you're really looking for." He glances at Ruby, and my heart melts for her.

"And Harrison? Because he seems like an OK guy," Zach continues.

"Harrison is ... huh, how can I put this politely?"

Calvin begins.

"Thick as pig shit," Ruby says.

Zach chuckles, then dips a potato smile in ketchup and pops it in his mouth.

"He's certainly not the brightest bulb in the box," Calvin agrees. "And I guess not everyone can work out who the best person to be with is – he doesn't see that he's just a trophy to her."

I watch as Zach chases his last bit of turkey dinosaur around his plate with his fork – seems like he's focusing really hard, which is kind of adorable. "Trophy, *how*?" Zach finally asks.

There's a moment of silence before Ruby says it. "Captain of the football team, and he's got a big dick." She sniffs. "Sorry, but it's true."

Zach laughs. "How can you be sure about the dick?"

"School legend. All the girls he's slept with will tell you."

A prickle runs up my spine. "*All*? I thought Lottie was the first?"

"Ah, sorry, Fred, no, I didn't tell you because. . ." She stops herself, glances at Zach, then back at me. "Well, no, he slept with Bec, after prom."

"In the year above?" I don't know why I'm so outraged. Part of me still feels weirdly protective about Harrison; I don't like to think of him being seduced by a cougar.

Zach leans towards me. "You like Harrison? Aw."

"No." I shake my head. "I mean, I did a bit, once, it's true, but I've gone off him recently."

Zach doesn't reply, he just looks at me, that little smile still playing at the corners of his mouth.

"How *do* you work that out, though?" Sam says. "If someone's right for you, I mean? It's like, one minute you think you've found someone who you like, you're having a nice time, and the next –" he blows out a breath "– they arrive at your house with a massive dildo even though you specifically told them you didn't think you were into that sort of stuff." He swallows and looks at each of us in turn. "You know?"

I think I need to have a conversation with Sam later, that's what I *know*.

"I think it depends," Ruby finally says, when she's finished giving Sam a lot of side-eye. "I had a date with a guy from that choir camp I went on over the summer. And within minutes of sitting down with him, I knew it wouldn't work. Know why? Guess what his opening gambit was? '*What Hogwarts house are you?*'"

"Ohhhh," I say, as the rest of the table grimace.

"That told me all I needed to know – it would *never* work. We weren't right for each other."

"I'm with you all the way, Rubes," Calvin says.

"What about you, Zach?" Ruby says, with a twinkle in her eye. "How do you know if someone's 'the one'?"

Zach snorts. "I'm really not the best person to ask

about that."

"Elaborate," Ruby says.

"Only if you want to!" I chip in. I don't want him to feel forced into some kind of interrogation. This is meant to be a chilled night – yet I distinctly feel my friends trying to manipulate the conversation into certain suggestive areas. Not subtle, and quite stressful for me.

Zach takes another sip of his wine. "Well, like Sam said, you think you've found someone, but they let you down, don't they?"

"Do they?" I say, eyes wide. I hope he doesn't mean me. My cooking was shit, but surely he can cut me some slack?

Zach's face softens, and he tweaks my knee under the table, which reassures me. A shorthand way of communicating? That's a thing that couples do, isn't it?

"I had a bad break-up with someone over summer," Zach explains. He shakes his head, the smile gone from his face, and he looks down at his empty plate.

My breath catches. Poor Zach. "You don't have to tell us," I say.

He glances up again, his eyes full of pain. "It's OK. It was at BYT. I guess it was just a summer fling, and I was stupid to think it was ever gonna be anything more, but it hurt me pretty bad." He sighs. "I really liked him. I thought he liked me. Guess I was wrong. But what doesn't kill you makes you stronger, right?"

"Right," I agree.

There's a heavy silence around the table, made worse by the fact the playlist appears to have run out.

"Um . . . I might just visit the bathroom," Zach says, pushing his chair back and standing up. "Save me some dessert." He hurries out of the room.

"Ouch, he's hurting *bad*," Calvin says quietly when he's gone.

"Oh god, have we upset him?" Sam asks. "Do you think you should check on him, Fred?"

"Maybe," I say. "I'll give him a couple of minutes."

Truth is, I'm a bit unnerved by this. Zach has always seemed so confident and in control. It's weird to see him affected by stuff like a bad break-up. It's the first time I've seen him emotionally vulnerable, and honestly, it just makes me want to go and give him a huge hug and make it all better for him.

"More to the point, *Sam*, anything you want to tell us?" I ask. "About people turning up to your house with dildos?"

Sam looks blank. "No."

I nod. "Huh."

"It was just an example." He checks his phone. "Dessert needs another five minutes. Looking forward to that." A notification flashes up on his screen and he frowns. "Um . . . just a minute," he mutters as he heads into the hall.

We're all left looking at one another like WTF? and Ruby goes to say something, just as Sam's hushed voice filters through:

"No, I'm not touching myself. I'm at a dinner party!"

My eyes meet Ruby's. "Is he ... *seeing* someone?" I ask.

"Not that I know of." Ruby frowns. "He said never again, after Ella, right?"

"Right."

We all nod, but it's hard to say anything because we're all intrigued, and although we shouldn't be listening, because we should respect his privacy, we all really want to listen.

"OK, I'll FaceTime you later... yes, OK..." His voice goes even quieter, to the merest hiss. *"Baby lotion."*

We're all staring at each other as Sam walks back in, completely normal, like he's just been on the phone to his mum. (Which I really hope he wasn't.) Ruby immediately kicks into action, in an attempt to make it seem like we weren't listening, by exploding into laughter. "Ha ha ha ha ha! Yes, that's what I said!"

To which everyone else's response is just confused silence.

"All right, Sam?" I say.

"All good," he replies, sliding his phone back into his pocket. "Shall we stick some more music on?"

By the time Zach re-emerges, we're enjoying listening

to Enya's "Orinoco Flow", which he amusingly does a little bit of Irish dancing to before he sits down next to me.

"All right?" I ask him.

"Yeah," he says, his hand finding my knee before sliding up to my thigh, leaving me fighting the almost uncontrollable urge to giggle like a maniac. I can't focus on anything. We're not in school now; we're not going to get interrupted by the bell. If Zach decides to stay over, things are gonna happen. I can feel it. I think this is it. My heart quivers and flutters in my chest because this is the moment. I'm going to do it. *With Zach.*

"So, what made you come to sixth form at our school, Zach?" Ruby asks, bringing me back to reality.

"Wanted a change." Zach shrugs. "People do your head in after a bit, don't they? The thought of two more years with some of the wankers I'd done GCSEs with was too much. Fresh starts are good things, I reckon." He swallows and glances down.

I am loving this. He wanted a fresh start too, just like me. How do you know someone's right for you? Well, wanting the same thing, being in the same place, life-wise, that can be a pretty good indicator, right?

"I *so* agree with that, in fact—" My words stick in my throat as Zach slides his hand round to my inner thigh, and I'm frozen, in some sort of beautiful ecstasy, mouth hanging open, staring into the middle distance, like my brain has had to shut down due to an overload of sensation. "Ug," I manage to mutter.

And then there's the unmistakable tinkling of a freakin' bell.

"What was that?" Zach frowns.

I shake my head. "No idea."

Sam smirks. "I think I should get dessert."

On his way out, he gives Ruby a not-so-subtle high five.

16

Ruby stops by the front door on her way out. "You sure you're OK with this?"

"With what? Of course!" I glance back towards the lounge. "Like he said, his bus isn't due for another twenty minutes, so he's just gonna wait here a bit longer."

Ruby smirks. "Sure."

"Right? *Sure.*" I mean, neither of us is buying this crap. I'm playing it down like nothing's happening, when in fact I'm bubbling over with a weird mixture of awesome excitement and utter terror. There's something icky and socially unacceptable about outright saying, "Yes, please leave so we can shag now, thank you." Hence this ridiculous game of nothing's happening, everything is normal, waiting for a bus, blah, blah.

Sam squeezes past me at the door, having retrieved his coat, takes my hand and presses a condom into it. Nothing more is said; he just nods, like this is all fine (what the hell is Sam doing with condoms, literally, I swear he was still building Lego models barely a year ago?!), and heads outside. "We gotta go if we're gonna catch our bus!"

"OK!" Ruby tells him. She fixes me with a proud look. "All right. Message me."

"Get home safe!" I chirp as she hurries out.

"I've just checked Citymapper," Calvin says from outside, looking up from his phone. "Zach's bus is due in five minutes. ZACH! YOUR BUS IS DUE IN FIVE!" he shouts.

"I'm sure Zach can sort his own bus out," Ruby says, rolling her eyes at me and pulling Calvin down the path.

"I'm just gonna finish my drink!" Zach calls from inside.

"Oh, OK!" Calvin shouts back. "There's another one in fifteen minutes too! Or we could wait for you, if you want?"

I lock eyes with Ruby.

"Actually, I really want to get an early night," Ruby tells him, smiling sweetly.

"Oh. No worries, babe. Come on, then," Calvin replies, putting his arm around her waist. "Let's do this again sometime!"

"Oh, yeah!" I shout.

I close the door, take a breath, and return to the lounge.

"Hey." Zach smiles, looking up from his phone, which he slips back into his pocket.

"Hey." It's just me and him. We both know we've both been waiting for this – weird how I can just *sense* that. But I hope *he* knows he's going to have to start this thing. I haven't a bloody clue.

"What's that in your hand?" he asks.

My eyes widen.

"A condom?" he says. "That's . . . subtle."

I go bright red and shove it in my pocket. "Sam wanted me to keep it for him. Long story. Huh! What a lovely evening!" I mutter, immediately realizing I sound exactly like my mother. I dart to the table and manically gather up napkins. "I'll just do a quick tidy and then—"

He steps in front of me and puts a finger to my lips.

I stare into his eyes while the napkins fall from my fingers.

"I really like Ruby, Sam and Calvin," Zach says in a husky low voice.

"Oh, yes, me too!" (I'm sadly more high-pitched due to extreme excitement.)

"But thank god they've gone, because I've been wanting to do this all night."

My eyes widen as he slowly moves in, then soften as his lips touch mine.

It's different this time.

Before, in the props store, it was frantic, quick, grasping, one eye always on the door in case Ms Pearson or anyone else walked in.

Now it's slow, we're taking our time, the moment spinning out and on, just me and him, and the rest of the world, the rest of *anything*, doesn't exist.

We drift apart, and he looks into my eyes, then smiles. "Listen," he says. "I was kind of nervous about this. Over summer ... like I told you, when I was at British Youth Theatre, and this guy and I. . ." He sighs. "I don't know, I guess when you get burned it makes you cautious."

My heart leaps at what sounds like the beginning of him letting me down gently. He's been hurt, he's in a bad place, *he doesn't want another relationship right now*. I manage a nod, my mouth open slightly, feeling like I *should* say something, but so fearful about which way this is going, I can't.

"So, is it OK if we ... I like you, Freddie, I like you a lot, but ... can we keep this fairly casual?"

"You mean ... like ... um ... what do you mean?"

"I mean, can we take it slow, no pressure, no expectations, just have fun? I can't have another BYT situation with a boy again. I'm not saying you would, I think you're a really nice guy, but it's hard for me ... to take that leap. Does that make any sort of sense?" He gives me a hopeful smile.

"Of course," I say.

"Really?"

I nod. It's obviously not what I want ultimately, but I get it. He's had his heart broken – he needs to learn to trust again. And, hey, I guess you don't become boyfriends overnight. It takes time. You have to really get to know each other. That's actually really sensible – unlike my dreams of throwing ourselves together and announcing ourselves to the world, setting everything up for a great big fall if it goes wrong. So, I think I can say "yes" to this. And I think that's the right thing for both of us. "We can just see how things go, right?"

Zach gives me a sweet smile. "Thank you, Freddie," he says, sliding his hand around on to my bottom. "Thanks for being patient and understanding, or whatever."

"It's cool, honestly."

He meets my eyes. "You up for some fun then?" A little smile plays on his lips.

I swallow. Suddenly this is real. It's happening. *Now!* And I'm so ready, and yet, I'm not at all ready. "Now?" And then in an act that must rank pretty highly among my all-time geeky greats, and only because I need to buy myself a little time to let this sink in, I add, "What about your bus?"

Zach doesn't seem to share my concerns about transport. He's suddenly kissing me again, and I'm on the sofa, and he's clambering on top and straddling me. "When's your mum back?" he gasps.

"Not till tomorrow afternoon," I murmur as he gently bites at my neck.

I slide my hands up the back of his shirt to his shoulder blades, then back down, where I run my fingers along under the waistband of his boxers. I want him so badly, but I'm also shaking with . . . with what? Nerves? Fear? Excitement? All that and more. Zach haphazardly unbuttons my shirt, his breathing heavy, and he starts planting kisses, one below my neck, then on my nipples, then down further, on my stomach, and then lower still, just above the waistband of my boxers.

"Comedy boxers?" He smiles. "Nice."

"Christmas elves," I gasp. "With real bells on their . . . WAH! HA!" I squeal as he pops my flies open.

"Don't open till Christmas?" Zach says, observing the writing. "Freddie, I don't think I can wait that long."

"Not here!" I manage to say. I have an inbuilt dread of my mother walking in on something like this, even though I know she's away. But also, I do kind of want this to special, not happen here on the sofa. I mean, it would obviously be fine, and I know we agreed this was "a bit of fun" but this is my first time, so, I dunno, it just seems like we need to make this memorable. And at least do this in my bedroom. Doesn't have to be with rose petals and champagne, but at least with my fairy lights on, you know?

He does a little pout. "Bedroom?"

"Bedroom." He gets off me and I make a half-arsed attempt to stuff my hard-on back in my trousers, at least temporarily.

He smiles at me. "Lead the way!" He holds out his hand, so I take it and show him out of the lounge, across the hall and up the stairs.

We reach my bedroom door, and he turns me around, pushing me back up against it and kissing me again. "You're so gorgeous," he murmurs.

"Oh, um . . . thank you," I say. "You too." Because even now, I still can't help but make everything I say sound geeky and awkward.

"Come on," he says, sliding around me, pushing the door open, flicking the lights and walking into my room.

And then he freezes, staring into the corner. "What the actual hell?!" he gasps.

"Huh?"

He turns to me, wide-eyed. "Why the *fuck* have you got a cardboard cut-out of my ex-boyfriend in your bedroom?"

17

The epic-ness of my sexual failure is so huge, I can't bear to respond in any detail to Ruby's messages on Sunday, except for a:

I'll tell you on Monday :(

Which I think tells her all she needs to know. After coming face to face with a free-standing, full-colour, life-sized digitally printed replica of the boy who broke his heart, Zach was understandably confused and upset, fleeing my house with the immortal words, *"You've got to be kidding me, you fucking weirdo!"* which is, of course, not a sentence anyone wants to hear from a boy they were hoping to lose their virginity to.

"I don't know," I lament to Ruby and Sam at the start of lunch in the common room on Monday. "I know a lot of people have awkward stories about their first time, but why couldn't I be one of the ones who pukes all over their hot date, or gets overexcited and comes in someone's hair?"

Ruby winces. *"Comes in someone's hair?"*

"It's bad enough," I continue, "that Jasper bloody Perry made me feel totally inferior and generally bad about myself, and even when he's not physically present he still manages to taunt me, because my mother brought his effigy home to worship, but he has now *literally* stopped me having actual first-time sex with a ridiculously hot boy who might have become my first boyfriend. *Hate* is too strong a word." I cradle the little plastic cup of vegetable soup I got out of the vending machine. I wanted cappuccino, but it had run out. It was this foul concoction or nothing, which I'm sure is a metaphor for my life.

Ruby sighs. "Have you tried explaining it to him?"

"Of course," I say. "I sent a series of essay-length messages on Saturday night, and all of Sunday. I even punched the Jasper cut-out repeatedly in the head and sent Zach photographic evidence of its stricken form."

"And?" Ruby says.

"Nothing," I tell her. "But then, that's not surprising. It's bunny boiler levels of freaky." I sigh, check my phone for any Zach-related messages (still nothing) and catch sight of the time. "Ugh. We need to get to rehearsals. And now you can all witness Zach being weird around me and me being too awkward to know what to do about it."

"It's not like you've done anything wrong," Sam says

as we walk out. "It's just ... really, really, really, really unfortunate."

I stare at him. *Unfortunate?* "Fate having explosive diarrhoea all over me" might be more accurate, but hey, let's just go with "unfortunate", like it's a button falling off your shirt, or the shop running out of your favourite brand of beans.

Sam sighs and puts his arm across my shoulders. "Come on, Fred. Maybe it can all be sorted out. Don't give up just yet."

But as we walk into the drama studio, all my fears come true. Zach's on the floor, flicking through his script. He glances up when we walk in, sees me, and when I attempt a small smile he just buries his head back in his script. That's when I know everything's messed up. You can say yes to life all you like, but that doesn't mean life is going to say yes back.

I sit at my props desk at the back of the room, pretending to be busy making notes and flicking through my file, but I'm crumbling. I want to speak to him. I just want a chance to explain. Even if he wants nothing more to do with me, at least I would have tried.

Unfortunately, this isn't a normal rehearsal where Zach might get five minutes sitting out while they work on another scene. Instead, Ms Pearson is going through a backstory exercise she tasked all the actors with, which requires them all to listen and react to the diary entries everyone has devised for their character.

"Are we going to actually block some scenes today, miss?" Lottie asks.

"When you're deep in character, the scenes block themselves," Ms Pearson replies.

"Is that a Stanislavski quote, miss?" Dhruv asks.

Zach looks up. "I think you'll find it's a *Ms Pearson* quote."

Ms Pearson laughs, slightly coquettishly. "Oh, Zach! You charmer! That's very kind of you, and it's lovely that you see me on a par with Stanislavski! Whatever next? Maybe I'll bring out my own book on theatre practice, who knows?" She laughs again. "Would anyone buy that, out of interest?"

The cast all nod and murmur various affirmative answers.

This pisses Lottie off massively, and her mouth tightens into a scowl. "You're *really good*, miss," Lottie manages to spit out.

"Mmm, *thank you*." Ms Pearson sighs and smiles. "Why don't you start, Lottie?"

Lottie opens her folder. "Sandra Dee's diary – Monday. God, I hate Danny, he's so full of himself and arrogant." She glances over at Zach, who isn't even looking at her. "Sometimes I ask myself what I even see in him, since he's so horrible all the time. He thinks he's so clever and full of words, but he's actually really shallow and pathetic.

Hope it's corn dogs for dinner, probably gonna go and eat a Twinkie now."

"OK," says Ms Pearson. "Loving the internal angst about Danny there, how Sandy is so torn about him. You love him, but you hate him."

"I mainly hate him," Lottie confirms, looking at Zach again.

"And that will be electric onstage," Ms Pearson adds. "How do you think that could manifest itself in the blocking?"

"Kicking Zach in the balls?" Lottie suggests, to laughter from the rest of the cast.

Zach remains stony-faced (aka *professional*) and I find myself starting to feel protective over him. I am not going to let Lottie's foot anywhere near Zach's balls. Not on my watch!

Ms Pearson isn't laughing either. "I want you to think about your body language when you're in a scene with Danny. Maybe you turn away from him, maybe you're not hanging on his every word, you might not be saying it explicitly, but let the audience see you're angry with him."

Lottie nods.

"Yeah, that might be more subtle," Zach says, looking up from his notes. "Also, 'corn dogs and Twinkies'?" He frowns. "Isn't that a bit ... stereotypical? Next you'll have her 'making out on the bleachers' before heading back to her white picket-fenced house to eat apple pie."

"*Grease* is the epitome of stereotypical Americana," Lottie retorts, a smug look on her face. "That's part of the show's charm?"

"And I thought Ms Pearson made it clear at the start of this process that she wanted this production to delve deeper, to ask, if you like, what darkness lies beneath the cheery facade of the American Dream."

Ms Pearson is nodding slowly, like Zach is the Dalai Lama, imparting nuggets of wisdom. But Lottie's still not having it. "You can't tell *me* about *my* character!" she hisses. "Stop trying to control the entire production!"

Zach shrugs. "Fine." And he looks over to me. "Fred? Make sure you've got Twinkies and corn dogs on the list? Lottie will need them to ensure her performance is consistent."

"Roger that!" I shout, giving him a thumbs up, while joy and hope surge through me that Zach knows I'm here and he's interacting with me, and we're working as a team to bring Lottie down.

"Zach, would you like to read Danny's diary entry for us?" Ms Pearson asks.

"Yes, *Zach*," Lottie says.

Zach clears his throat and picks up his notes. "Notes from my life – by Danny Zuko. Wow, it sure is hard navigating high school life. Even harder when there's someone you really like, but somehow things keep going wrong. It's like, you feel all this pressure – from your peers, from school, from society, and from the weight of your previous defeats, you know? I feel like I'm two different people. Me with him—" He clears his throat again. *"Her.* And me when everyone else gets involved. Wish I could just wipe the slate clean sometimes, start again."

I am entranced, just staring at him.

He's talking about me, right?

This is all about *us*. About how Jasper has complicated everything, about how he doesn't want all that baggage to get in the way of working things out. I glance around the rest of the room – Lottie visibly seething, Calvin nodding, Harrison staring down at the floor, Ruby looking really impressed. Everyone can feel it, the *weight* of what he's just said.

Ms Pearson dabs the corner of her eyes with a tissue. *"That* was truly beautiful, Zach. *Thank you."*

"Thank you for the opportunity," Zach replies, giving a humble nod.

Lottie rolls her eyes.

Ms Pearson decides she's going to hear the rest of the diary entries over the course of the next few days (probably a wise choice, since no one's is gonna top Zach's, so that saves everyone's embarrassment), and that she's decided to work on a Pink Ladies scene – or, more specifically, and much to Lottie's obvious disdain, a "status game exercise" involving which Pink Lady is *really* queen bee.

"Oh, Freddie?" she calls over, just as everyone else is

packing up to leave. "The crate of Coke bottles arrived, so you can take them down to the store, if you like?" She heaves the crate over and plonks it on my table.

"Need a hand?"

I look up. *Zach.* "Oh, er, yeah, thanks."

He nods and picks up the crate, following as I lead the way out. We walk in silence down to the theatre and the props store. It feels like whatever we need to say needs to be said alone. And the minute the door swings shuts behind us, Zach puts down the crate and is straight in with it:

"I'm sorry about Saturday."

"No, *I'm* sorry, I—"

Zach puts his hand up. "Please. It was a shock, that's all. It was. . ."

"Weird."

"*Really* freakin' weird," Zach agrees. "I mean, obviously I did not expect Jasper to be in your room. But I also didn't know what your mum did, or that she was producing *Cherries.*" Zach shakes his head. "That damn casting was all Jasper talked about at BYT, and then when he actually got it. . . I dunno, it's like he . . . we were having a *great* summer. You know? A lot of *fun*, you know?"

I nod. I think I know what he means by "fun" now.

"And then he got the part and he totally changed towards me. Went really . . . cold and . . . superior and . . . and then he just basically dumped me 'cause I wasn't good enough for him any more."

Being on the same page about Jasper like this fills me with hope. I knew I was right about him, I knew I was right to feel he was somehow messing up my life, and now I'm proved right. And it feels good to have that shared experienced with Zach. Feels like it somehow makes us stronger. "None of that surprises me," I say. "I met him at the meet and greet party, and he was a total dick to me."

"Huh," Zach says. "Why do good things never happen to nice guys?"

"Right?" I agree.

"Just really arrogant and staggeringly good-looking ones."

I reply with a small chuckle, but that brings it home. Whatever Zach might have said about liking me, he's had an actual relationship with Jasper – a boy who is basically a model. OK, it's not all about looks, and I hope Zach wouldn't be that shallow, but I am way out of Jasper's league, looks-wise. Jasper's next level. I hate to admit it, I really hate it, but I still think he is so *hot*. Not in an obvious, tacky, "boy with his top off on social media" sort of way. He's all class. He's smouldering. Sophisticated. And this is the boy that Zach was in a relationship with. And then here I am ... and I am *so* not that. I'm so different. Why would Zach even like someone like me?

If me and Zach are ever going to work, in a long-term way, beyond the "casual" thing we talked about, do I need to compete, somehow? I've no idea what I can really do about it; I look the way I look, and I don't think thousands of pounds of plastic surgery are really an option. . .

Zach puts his hands in his pockets and shuffles from foot to foot. "Anyway, I've done a lot of thinking. . ."

I swallow, because that phrase usually augurs ill. Is this why Zach wanted be alone in the props store? To let me down somewhere quiet and private?

"Jasper ruined summer for me," Zach continues. "But I'm not prepared to let him ruin anything else." He looks up at me.

It takes me a moment to compute what he's just said, and that the words are a good thing, a happy thing, that they're *not bad!* "OK!" I say.

Zach bites his lip. "So . . . are we good?"

"Yep!" I nod. "We're good." I try and steady my breathing. "We're good."

His face breaks into a wide smile, and he steps towards me before enveloping my body in his firm, capable arms. He nestles his head into the crook between my neck and shoulder, and we stay like that for a few lovely moments, breathing, being, enjoying each other.

"Let's pick up where we left off," he murmurs into my neck.

"Huh?"

"Where we left off on Saturday. Let's do what we were going to do."

I chuckle. I'm half-scared he means it, but this isn't the place, however much I'd like to.

"I'm serious," he says, still into my neck.

"Here? Now?"

"Here. Now."

I release myself and step back a little, torn between wanting to, glad I haven't messed up after all, still a bit miffed he didn't message me back all weekend, absolutely wanting to lose my virginity, but being definitely less keen on that happening in a bloody props store in the depths of the school theatre, before the bell goes for the end of lunch.

"What if someone comes?" I ask.

"That's kind of the idea." Zach smirks.

I cross my arms and give him unimpressed eyes.

Zach laughs. "Ms Pearson's busy rehearsing, and no one else would come down here, but if you're worried. . ." He clicks his fingers at me. "Keys?"

I take a deep breath, then pull the set of keys out of my trouser pocket, tossing them to Zach. He grins, then locks the props store door from the inside. "Safe and sound," he says.

His eyes meet mine, waiting for my approval. It might not be exactly how I wanted it to happen, but I think I need to get over myself. The Freddie Project means I have to say yes, right? I bet "a lot of *fun*" Jasper would say yes to this. I need to show that *I'm* fun. God knows, there aren't many other selling points.

"Freddie?"

I swallow, then smile and nod.

He grins back, walks over to me, undoes the top button of my trousers, then plants a kiss on my lips as he slides his hand into my boxers.

"*Freddie*," he murmurs.

18

I float into the sixth form common room at the start of our free period very much in the style of a fabulous butterfly, who feels light and free after many years of being a grim caterpillar wrapped up in some sort of rigid cocoon. (The caterpillar being me, in case this metaphor isn't clear, and the rigid cocoon . . . the expectations and constraints of a heteronormative society, crushing my gay soul – *until now!*)

"Ta! La! La!" I trill as I canter up to Ruby and Sam, who are going through their *Grease* scripts.

"Where have you been?" Ruby asks.

"Mmmm!" I sigh contentedly. "Isn't it a *lovely* day? The sun is shining, the air is fresh—"

"I mean, we are literally in London, zone four, so 'fresh' is a stretch, but whatever," Ruby mutters.

"Not a cloud in the sky! Everything today seems more vibrant! The colours so rich! Like in high definition! This room . . . the trees. . ." I extend a hand towards her. "Your face. . ."

She bats me away. "You've sorted things out with Zach, then?"

I laugh. "Mmmm, ha ha. Yeeeeees, you could say that!" And then, setting up a joke I've been wanting to do since *for ever*, I start making a big show of frowning and patting down my pockets and rifling through my bag.

"Lost something?" Sam asks.

I grin at them both. "Why, yes, since you ask! Only my . . ." I glance around to make sure no one is listening, "VIRGINITY!"

I'm high as a kite about all this, barely able to contain my joy. This is what it feels like to finally be one of those *people who have been intimate with others, not just themselves*. And it feels good. It feels amazing. This is cloud nine, and I want to remember every detail of this entire afternoon for the rest of my life.

Ruby pulls me down so I'm sitting opposite her and Sam. "Talk!"

I don't want everyone gossiping about this, mainly because that's one sure-fire way to screw everything up – it's everyone else's opinions and little comments that slowly eat away at anything good – and if Zach knows I've excitedly blabbed about it, I guess that might not seem like I'm keeping my side of the "casual" bargain. So, keeping my voice hushed, and making sure no one is nearby, and switching to talking about schoolwork when anyone passes by, I tell them. It's a little tricky, because a lot of it ends up being like, "And then he reached down and touched my ESSAY ABOUT AUSTEN'S VIEW OF MARRIAGE IN *PRIDE AND PREJUDICE* and then he got out his NOTES ON *WUTHERING HEIGHTS* and we started WORKING ON A PROJECT ABOUT *TWELFTH NIGHT* TOGETHER."

I obviously don't go into *all* the details, or *all* the subtle romantic nuance to this, but I tell them enough.

Ruby looks at me with weirdly unimpressed eyes, and blinks. "So, in summary, you wanked Zach off in the props store?"

I shrug. "I mean, essentially, yes, if you want to be reductionist about this."

"Huh," Ruby says.

"I hope you antibac'd the props afterwards," Sam adds.

"Funny."

Ruby looks at me and squints. "Does that count as losing your virginity?"

My eyes widen. "Oh! I'm sorry, only penetrative things count, do they?" I blow out a breath. "Didn't have you down as a fully paid-up member of the patriarchy, Rubes!"

She rolls her eyes. "All right, *fine.*"

"You're so Victorian in your attitudes!" I continue.

"You need to be more open to what people may like to do, sexually. Everyone's different!"

"Yeah, OK."

"I'm just saying, it's all valid, whether it's a vibrator, or a dildo. . ."

"Some beads," Sam offers.

We all stare at him.

He moistens his lips and turns red. "What?"

"If it's not hurting anyone else, I think it's OK," I say.

Ruby grumbles, pulls a large transparent beaker from her bag and sits back in her chair.

"What in god's name is that?" I frown.

"NutriBullet shake."

"Wow." I nod. "Not even the sweet tropical type – one of the bitter green ones."

"I'm going running with Calvin later, so it's for energy."

"Running." I say it like a word I've never heard before, and to be fair it's really not a word that's had much usage in our friendship group.

"Nice to have shared interests, right?" Ruby says.

I smile, shaking my head. "Look at all of us. Changing, growing up. Me, getting with boys. Ruby and her green protein shakes." I look at Sam. *"Beads."*

I didn't think it possible for Sam to turn any redder, and yet, somehow, he does. "Sam?"

"What? Nothing. I just said it. I don't know," he says.

Ruby downs a large portion of her shake, then glances at me. "So . . . what's the deal exactly with you and Zach?"

"OK, so we're keeping it casual and we're having 'fun'." I nod at Ruby and Sam's confused faces. "We're a . . . fun thing, I suppose. Fun things having fun by doing fun things." I grin. "Fun!"

I've decided it's easiest to present it like this. Ruby and Sam care about me, so if they know I'm desperately hoping this is going to turn into something significant, before I know it, they'll be analysing everything that happens between me and Zach, Ruby will be taking him to one side and "having words", Sam will be threatening to "deck him" if he hurts me (hilarious, because Sam is short and skinny, but it's the thought that counts), and honestly, I think it's better just to be chilled. Like Zach says.

"OK," Ruby says. "So this isn't serious?"

I groan. "Ruby, Ruby, Ruby, Ruby, Ruby! Let's just go with the flow, yeah? Let's be young and carefree and see where the wind blows us."

It's at this point that Zach himself walks in, does one of those "bro handshakes" with Harrison Kane, slams some coins in the Coke machine, grabs a can in a ludicrously macho and deeply sexy fashion, then sees me and nods. "All right?"

"All right?" I nod back.

And then he pops the ring pull on the can and heads out again.

"Wow," Ruby says. "I feel like I'm in *Dirty Dancing*. The sexual tension! The romance!"

"Look, we agreed just to enjoy . . . *things*. I mean, who knows where this may lead. For now, it's strictly fun, and I'm cool with that."

"You are?" Ruby asks.

"Yep. Totally. Fun with Zach is fun for me. It's harmless. And it's fine, because I am totally *not* in love with him."

"Why are you mentioning love, Freddie?"

"Because you did."

"No, I didn't."

"I'm not in love with him," I tell her.

And I'm not. There's lots *about* Zach that I love. I love his cheekiness. I love his face. I love how tender he can be. I love his charisma. I love his easy attitude towards life. I love his nose. I love his ears. I love the way his hair is so perfect. I love how he makes me feel. I love the way he touches me. I love the longing in his eyes when he looks at me. I love his smile. And his naughty grin. I love all those things, and lots more. But I am definitely not *in love* with him.

19

I'm still fizzing with excitement for the next week. Zach's leg continues to press against mine in English, and he catches my eye and smiles when someone else is talking, checking to see if I'm finding a joke funny, or rolling my eyes at some shit Lottie is stirring up in rehearsals. And, of course, he regularly comes to find me in the props store, which I'm probably spending more time in than I really need to. (Although I've made some loud mutterings about "the state of the place" and "needing to tidy up", so I think our secret is safe – I'm not sure what the rules are about doing this sort of thing on school property, but I feel like we're probably in violation of them.)

Things continue to go well as we move into the second week. We're having fun; he's even come to my house after school for some extra fun. I did say I'd be happy to go to his too, but he thought that was a bad idea. I get it. Not everyone has parents who are out all the time, or even accepting of their kids being gay, so I don't push it. I don't know, I think part of me wanted to meet his mum or something. Somehow meeting the folks feels like it would be more official. And as we move into the third week, that's what I'm craving. Everything is nice, I'm enjoying it, I love being with Zach, I have learned a lot of interesting new skills, and all that is *great*, but it's not enough. It's just not enough. Which makes me laugh at myself, because I don't know who I am to be so needy and expecting so much. Seriously, a guy like me should learn to be happy with what he can get, especially when it's a guy like Zach. And I try to be. But, no, instead I let various horrible thoughts divide and multiply until I'm besieged by self-doubt and totally convinced Zach will dump me any day now. I can't shake the nagging doubt in my head that the reason he only wants things to be "casual" and the reason he doesn't want to be public and "official" with me around school is because he's embarrassed. *Because I'm not like Jasper.*

But in the spirit of The Freddie Project, I am going to see this as an opportunity for self-improvement that I can say yes to. This leads me to two rash decisions. First, I text Mum:

ME: Hi. Decided I might try for a brace.

Ten minutes later, she replies, apparently so keen she's already made all the arrangements:

MUM: Finally! 4:30 p.m. Wednesday, Dr Lynch,
104 Wimpole Street. OK?

ME: Sure. Are you coming too?

MUM: Freddie. You're old enough to go to the
dentist by yourself now.

That's just not true – I can't be expected to make
decisions and have injections without an adult present to
hold my hand – and I hope that Sam or Ruby will come
with me instead. Meanwhile, part two of my plan takes
place during my free on Tuesday. Knowing that Zach has
gone to work out in the gym, I swallow all my pride, put on
my PE kit from year eleven (of course I don't have a proper
non-school gym kit, it's literally never crossed my mind as a
thing I would need) and head to the gym too. My thinking
is simple: despite all my lifetime's experience, surely I too
have the potential to have one of those "glow up" moments,
where someone very ordinary suddenly gets hot. See also:
Sandy from *Grease*. Plus, it would give me and Zach another
shared interest – like Ruby and Calvin have. And I want
to talk with him. I want to go out for food, chat and have a
laugh, not just . . . not just the other stuff.

I stroll into the gym as confidently as I can, glance
around at all the equipment and machines that I have no
idea how to use, then seriously consider walking out again,

before I spot Zach, looking over from what I think is called a "bench press". He's standing by the side of it, counting reps for Harrison, and literally does a double take when he sees me.

"Hey," I say, raising my hand. He nods back, finishes counting Harrison's reps, then comes over.

"All right, Fred? Working out?"

"Yeah," I reply.

"Legs? Arms?"

I shrug. "Just doing a few . . . lifts, I guess."

Zach nods. "I'm just spotting Harrison, so. . ."

"Sure," I say, watching him head back to the bench press, where Harrison is lying on his back, ready to go again.

A year thirteen finishes on a machine right next to me – some sort of thing you sit on, and then you have to pull a bar attached to the weights down to your chest. I reckon that seems fairly simple, and I'm literally about to sit down and give it a go when Mr Harries, the head of PE, comes over. "Have you done your gym induction?" he asks.

"Um. . ."

"I'll need to check the list. What's your name?"

He taught me PE for five years, but OK. "Freddie Bennett. I won't be on the list, sir."

"You can't use the equipment until you've done the induction – next one is on Friday. Do some crunches on the mats if you want to work out." He looks at me with disdain. "Are you sixth form?"

I glance towards Zach, hoping he isn't hearing any of this. "Yes!" I hiss.

"Oh. Why are you wearing uniform PE kit?"

"It's all I have."

He rolls his eyes and walks away. This is already humiliating, but I'm not quite ready to give up, so I head to the mats and start doing some approximation of sit-ups.

It surprises me how completely out of shape I am. After five, it's necessary to pause, and I glance over to Zach and Harrison, who have swapped over, so Harrison's doing the counting while Zach pumps the weights. I'm not sure what I was thinking. This was supposed to help make me feel better about myself. It was meant to show Zach I could be like him. I'm gasping for air, unable to even complete five sit-ups. It's a disaster. I get up, do a couple of vague leg stretches and saunter really casually over to the bench press, where Zach and Harrison are now chatting while sipping protein shakes.

"Woooo!" I say, feigning a workout high.

Unfortunately, I've interrupted Zach and Harrison in the middle of a very important conversation about gym stuff.

". . .isolation day tomorrow, and I'm ready to—" Zach stops and looks at me. "Huh?"

"Sorry," I say. And just as I add, "I was just saying—" Zach carries on with, "—get 'em stacked!"

And then we're all silent for a bit.

Zach and Harrison both take a slurp of protein shake in unison.

I don't have a drink. Another rookie error.

"Bro, you look swollen today," Zach tells Harrison.

"Yeah?" Harrison smiles and glances down at himself. "Cheers, mate."

I nod, adding my agreement, but afraid to say anything in case it's wrong. It's clear I should have done some homework before coming here.

Zach flicks his eye to me for a moment, runs his tongue over his lips, then slaps me on the back, really bloody hard. "Freddie, my main dude, we're gonna split and go shower. Have a good workout!"

"Oh, OK, sure, thank you!" I say. "Um. . ."

My words trail off as Zach and Harrison grab their towels and head to the door, chatting about something to do with "gains".

I like it more when I'm with Zach during rehearsals. At least I know what's going on there. This feels like enemy territory. And although it's nothing he actually said, I get the feeling Zach didn't appreciate me being here today.

20

I have two options for how to play it in rehearsals the next day: (a) prepare a batch of rocky roads, lovingly crafted by my own hands and served on a gingham cloth inside a small wicker basket, which I'll present to Zach at the start of lunch. Or (b) chill the hell out.

I decide to opt for (b), although I do in fact have a lovingly handcrafted batch of rocky roads in my bag, by way of a back-up. I arrive in the drama studio, which has now been marked up with tape all over the floor, showing the positions of various pieces of set throughout the show, and set myself up at the back, as usual. I know Zach is here, I *heard* him chatting with Kwame when I came in, but I haven't looked at him. I'm just going to do my thing, go over my props notes, maybe draft another email to our school's outsourced catering company to see if I can get permission to borrow some of the cafeteria trays (something which is proving insanely difficult, and now there's mention of "insurance policies" for some reason, the world's gone mad), and give him some space.

"*Hey.*"

But it seems Zach has other ideas. I look up at him. He smiles and pulls a chair up to sit next to me.

"So, look," Zach says, his tone of voice telling me I'm not going to like this. "What's all this turning up at the gym business?"

I shrug. "Just thought I should try to get fit, I guess."

"Huh." He nods. "OK, well, that's cool, but just so you know, Harrison thought it was odd. He said to me afterwards, 'Do you think Freddie has a crush on you?'"

My eyes widen. "He did?"

"And I haven't told anyone about us, because we agreed casual."

"Totally!" I say.

"I just don't want people chatting about us, you know?"

"One hundred per cent!"

"I guess it's like, *here* it makes sense for us to talk and be seen together. But, like, hanging out in the gym too?" He lowers his voice even more. "I just don't want things to get complicated. I'm loving this. *Us.* Are you?" He looks at me with sweet, hopeful eyes.

"Yeah! I mean, of course I am!" I stutter.

"Good. What me and you have is special, and I want to keep it that way. . ."

I am nodding manically at this point.

He gives me a warm, gentle smile, and I'm ready for him to make my heart sing with some beautifully romantic sweet nothing, maybe about how he loves my eyes, or that the world seems brighter with me in it.

"If you wanna work out, I'd focus on your upper body," he says instead, glancing at my skinny arms and chest. "And maybe try Mondays and Wednesdays? They're my rest days, so we'll give each other some space."

"Oh, right, good idea," I say as brightly as I can.

It obviously doesn't work, because he says, "*Fred*, come on, we don't have to hang out with each other all the time – we've each got our own mates too, what's wrong with that?"

"Yeah, I know, it's just. . ."

"Zach?" Ms Pearson shouts from the other end of the studio. "Let's make a start!"

"Laters, Twinkle," Zach says, winking at me and tickling my back as he leaves, like everything is fine. But it's not fine.

I'm deep in thought as the boys go over the steps for "Greased Lightnin'", or, as Ruby calls it, "The Toxic Masculinity Dance". New Freddie says yes to everything, and I said yes to this whole situation with Zach. Yet I'm still feeling like that's not enough, and that maybe I need to take more control here. You know, set the agenda a bit more? But how?

I don't know whether I've got a guardian angel, or if it's

just an amazing piece of luck (for once) that my mum texts me at this point:

MUM: Fred – do any of your school show mates want to be extras on Cherries? Got some shoots coming up. You and three others please. It's paid. (You can put your fee towards your brace – lol!)

So when Ms Pearson breaks the boys, screaming at everyone about "Why the hell don't you know the lyrics or backing vocals yet?" and sending them all packing to learn them, I seize my chance.

Zach's sitting on the edge of the rostra. Ever the golden boy, he knows the backing vocals, so he's excused from the music rehearsal and is peeling an egg instead, because boys like Zach don't eat crap out of the vending machine. But for once, I don't feel like the inferior person here.

"So, um, Zach, I'm not sure if you're interested, but my mum says there's some background artist work coming up in *Cherries*, so I said I'd ask around at school." I give him a little smile when he stops peeling his egg and looks at me. "No rush, but let me know if you fancy it."

And like a *boss*, and definitely like someone who couldn't be accused of smothering him by anyone watching, I turn and walk away.

21

"Aaaaand . . . ACTION!"

. . .Aaaaand here we are, shooting this godforsaken scene for what must be the thirtieth time. Everyone raves about working in TV and film like it's amazing, but because of Mum I've been on a lot of sets over the years, and I have to tell you, once you get over the minor excitement of being near people you recognize off the telly, it's tedious. A lot of *Cherries* is set in a high school, so the production company have taken over this old site, which was vacated by an actual school last year when they moved into new buildings. A section of the playing field is rammed with trailers, Winnebagos, catering trucks and generators, and inside it's such a mess of cables, random lights, camera tracks and flight cases that you genuinely wonder how this will ever look realistic on-screen. And the people! There are people absolutely everywhere. I still have no real idea what most of them do, but a lot are carrying scripts or clipboards, while others have rolls of electrical tape hanging from their belts. They've all got coffee in cardboard cups, and the other unifying factor is the look of panic on all their faces as they holler into walkie-talkies.

"We need him *out* of make-up and *on* the set!"

"Can someone get sparks to sort this out, please?"

"We're going to have to change the call sheet for tomorrow!"

Not that Zach seems to be finding any of this boring. In fact, from the moment I mentioned it to him, I don't think I've ever seen him quite so excited and hanging on my every word.

"Freddie? Seriously?" he said, scampering (actually *scampering*!) after me out of the drama studio that day. "That would be amazing!"

"What about Jasper, though?" I replied. "I'm not sure if he'll be there or not, it depends on what the schedule is – I don't want you to feel awkward."

I was interested how Zach would deal with this. I know he's ambitious, and I knew he'd want to do this, but I also know how badly Jasper hurt him. So badly, he can't be anything more than "casual" with me, for fear of a repeat. I liked his reply: "Like I told you before, I'm not going to let Jasper ruin any more of my life." He stuffed his hands into his pockets and did the slight shuffling from foot to foot thing that is just the right side of shy to send me crazy. "Besides, if you're there, I think I can face him."

That's what I wanted – right there! Me and him against the world. Well, against Jasper, at least. That's a team. That's a relationship. I didn't exactly feel great when I offered him this chance. It felt a bit like I was trying to buy my way into his favour, but I guess I got there in the end, I got him to realize he needs me in some way; that I can be more to him than maybe what he first thought.

Zach's excitement was evident in the days that followed, bounding up to me and not even trying to play it cool: "Oh my god, I've just had someone from wardrobe call me about my measurements!" and, "My first call sheet! I'm gonna frame it!" It's cute, seeing him so thrilled about it. He tried to keep his excitement in check when we rolled up in a minibus, acting like he'd seen it all before, but he was so wide-eyed at everything, you could tell he hadn't. It feels like I understand Zach a bit more, that I'm closer to him somehow. I kind of know what he's thinking, and I like that.

Cherries is a single-camera shoot, which means it'll look nicer on-screen, but we have to shoot each angle separately, which takes more time. In this particular scene, this jock-type character (played by that handsome Connor McCourt guy I saw at the press party) is humiliated by his (soon-to-be-ex) girlfriend, when, sick of his boasting about having sex with her, she fakes an orgasm in the middle of the packed canteen. Mum told me the scene was a "fresh take" on a well-known eighties movie called *When Harry Met Sally* and as such it was "groundbreaking", "edgy", "bold" and a load of other bullshit words that TV people claim everything is, where the truth would actually be better described as "copied from someone else" and "really not as exciting as you think it is".

Anyway, our job as "supporting artists" is to sit in the background, eating our lunch, chatting away, and then looking up in shock and surprise when this girl starts orgasming in front of us and Connor's character storms out, humiliated. Mum took me to one side before we started this morning (at six a.m., god help me). "Freddie, it's fine, I don't mind you doing this, but please don't look at the camera or do your 'acting' face," she said.

I sighed. "Whatever." I wish she wasn't so embarrassed by me all the time. Anyway, there's no way I'm ever going to live up to Jasper levels of talent, so I made sure I was sitting with my back to the camera so she couldn't accuse me later of ruining the show and being the cause of MegaFlix cancelling it after the first season, the platform's subsequent financial collapse and the end of the serialized television industry for ever.

Luckily, Jasper isn't in this scene, so there's been no awkwardness, and Zach, Ruby and Sam have thrown themselves into some serious improvisation, having actual conversations about fictional schoolwork as we continually eat cold pasta bake from the props department. I've mostly done a lot of nodding and also wondering whether there's a way I could steal the trays at the end of the day, because we need them for *Grease*.

"And cut there!" shouts the first assistant director.

There's a hum of activity as the shot is watched back on little monitors, lights are moved, and make-up quickly retouched.

Zach nudges me. "This is so cool, Freddie. Thanks, mate."

I give a little nod and immediately start fretting over his use of the word "mate". But then his foot gently strokes the back of my calf under the table, and I think, maybe it's OK after all, since "mates" don't generally play footsie with each other.

"OK, set back, please, we're getting close-ups!" the first AD announces.

I groan. I'm so over this day.

The day, however, carries on for a further three hours. The same scene. A scene that will ultimately play out on-screen for around forty-five seconds. I swear to god, the best three words you'll ever hear are not "I love you" or even "I brought cake!" They are, "That's a wrap!"

So we're heading around the corner of the set, on our way back to our trailer, Zach's gabbling on about, "Can we legit put this credit in our bios for the *Grease* programme?" and is "accidentally" leaving a few of his headshots on various surfaces as we pass by, and suddenly there he is.

Jasper.

Actually, *double* Jasper because he's standing next to

his cardboard cut-out that Mum has brought in, inspecting it with a frown on his face.

"What happened to my head?" he asks Mum.

"Ugh, Freddie let the cat get to you," she replies. "It's OK, this is just the prototype, we're having more made."

Great. Multiple Jaspers. There's something about the way he looks so relaxed and at home here that really annoys me, with people fussing around him and my mum being all protective. Also, he's in these smart, white, knee-length shorts and a deep blue short-sleeved shirt, and he looks so fresh and breezy and annoyingly *hot*. I'm sure he knows it. Amazing how this oh-so-perfect persona hides what he really is – the type of guy who'll ditch his boyfriend when he no longer matches up to his big-time dreams.

So it happens like this: Jasper looks up first, sees me, kind of smiles, but it's probably more of a grimace, then glances over my shoulder, sees Zach and his mouth falls open.

Zach, meanwhile, sees *him*, stops mid-sentence, and I swear to god, this eerie *chill* passes through the room. I shiver. It already feels like we're about to experience more actual drama than we've seen on set all day.

"Ohh, I feel like I want to make a swift exit," Sam mutters.

"We could, we *so* could," Ruby replies, also under her breath.

"And yet. . ." Sam continues.

"Like bystanders watching a car crash, we just can't tear ourselves away."

"Shut up, both of you!" I hiss.

"Freddie! And Freddie's friends!" Mum beams. "How was it? Just telling Jasper how you let the cat attack his head."

I nod. "Sorry," I mutter. Best not to mention how I also punched it, multiple times.

But Jasper's not listening. He's staring at Zach, and Zach's staring back. I'm worried there might be a fight. Either that, or they're going to snog the tits off each other and have crazy "I hate you" sex. It feels like it could literally go either way, and neither would be a good outcome for me. There's more than just tension between them. It's a sort of electricity that you only get with a deep, shared history and I can't shake the feeling I might have screwed myself over here.

Mum's phone rings. "OK, have to go. Fred, there are some ready meals in the freezer if you're hungry later." And she's gone. The only adult in the immediate vicinity has gone.

"Hey," Zach says to Jasper.

"Hey," Jasper replies. "Why are you here?"

The way he says it makes me prickle. The superiority in his tone. The idea that he's somehow better than us, that lesser mortals like Zach have no place on this set. I can see exactly what Zach means, so I jump in to help him out.

"He's with me," I say. "We were filming today."

Jasper's eyes widen.

Suddenly Zach is behind me, his arm round my waist. This is the first time Zach has acted like we might be a bit of a "thing" in public, and I love it, but I have to try not to smile because I don't want to ruin the gravitas of the situation.

Jasper's eyes widen further.

"Oh," Jasper says. "He's with *you* and he's ... *with* you?" He chews his lip. "Cool."

"How have you been?" Zach asks, still with his arm around me, while I nearly explode with excitement at the fact Zach did not deny he was *with* me, with me!

"OK," Jasper says. He seems to scowl, and then, really forcing himself to speak, adds, "You?"

"Yeah." Zach shrugs.

As if things couldn't get any more awkward, Connor, who's been playing the jock all day, but is apparently as camp as a row of tents in real life, arrives. "Hey, babe," he says to Jasper.

"Connor, this is Freddie, *Sarah's son*, and *Zach*," Jasper says.

Connor's about to go in for handshakes, but stops himself, having interpreted the pointedness in Jasper's voice, looks at Jasper and says, "Zach?"

"*Zach*," Jasper replies.

This must be pretty horrible for Zach, being referred to in the speech equivalent of italics all the time, but then it gets worse because Connor puts his arm around Jasper's waist, mirroring what Zach is doing to me, and staring at us (well, Zach, really), his expression changing to one of contempt.

Huh. So Jasper and Connor are a thing? I don't know why, but this annoys me. I feel Zach tense, clearly hurt not only by seeing Jasper again, but also that he's moved on to some other hot boy so very quickly and easily. I put my arm around Zach's waist, so we form a sort of united front against wicked cad Jasper.

And then Jasper puts his arm around Connor's waist.

There are no more arms and no more waists. God knows where we go from here.

"How have you enjoyed being *extras* today?" Connor says.

Ah. So that's where we go. Passive aggression.

"It was great, thanks, but it did drag, didn't it? I had no idea how long it would take for you guys to get the scene right," Zach replies.

Connor chuckles slightly menacingly, like he's about to punch Zach. "I'm guessing you haven't done any TV before?"

"It was great fun!" Ruby says, smiling and stepping in, like some sort of hostage negotiator. "So interesting to see how it all works. Really looking forward to seeing the final thing!"

Jasper nods. "Sometimes things get edited out." He

glances at Zach. "Just saying, don't get too excited."

"Well, I'm fairly sure that won't happen," I say.

"I'm not being trying to be funny," Jasper replies. "A lot of things are up to MegaFlix; they get the final say on all sorts of stuff."

Annie, the third AD, scoots up to us. "Ah, great, I need your email addresses so I can send you release forms to sign," she says to us. "And, Jasper and Connor, don't go anywhere, I've got some more social media stuff from marketing I need you to put out on your Insta channels."

I glance at Jasper and raise an eyebrow. The boy who thought social media was tacky appears to have changed his tune.

"*What?*" He frowns at me.

"Pretty sure you said you didn't do social media. At the party."

He glares at me. "I didn't. Now I have to. It's contractual. That OK with you?"

I shrug.

Jasper looks away and mutters something, shuffling about on the spot.

"So!" Annie says, brandishing her pen and clipboard. "Ruby?"

Ruby and Sam give Annie their email addresses, while Zach and I stare at Jasper and Connor, in some hideous stand-off.

"Zach?" Annie says.

"Zach Cooper *Actor*, all one word, at icloud dot com,"
he says, without breaking eye contact with Jasper.

"Freddie?"

"Hm?" I say. "Oh, just send it to my mum."

"No, it needs to go to you, and not your school email
either," Annie says.

I run my tongue over my lips. "Well, my personal
one's complicated so let me write it down for you." I put my
hand out to take her clipboard.

"It's OK, just tell me, I don't want to risk not being
able to read your handwriting."

I take a breath. "Right, it's just . . . I'm not even sure it
works any more, it's. . ."

"I'll call you if it bounces back."

"OK, but, like, I made this address when I was
thirteen, so. . ."

Annie glares at me. "I'm really busy."

I take a deep breath. "OK, so . . . I mean, like I say, I
was thirteen, probably *twelve*, actually, I should make a new
one now, but. . ."

"Freddie!" Annie snaps.

"Donkey dong nine inches . . . at outlook dot com."
Silence.

"Is donkey dong all one word?" Annie asks,
straight-faced.

"Yep."

"And the number nine?"

"Uh-huh."

"So that's donkey dong, all one word, and the number nine, inches. . ."

"At outlook dot com," I confirm. "Yep." I don't look at anyone. I don't need to. I can see Ruby and Sam quivering with suppressed laughter in the edge of my vision.

"Great!" Annie says, finishing writing with a flourish. "The minibus is ready to take you home out the front when you're ready! Thanks for today!"

I keep my head down and shuffle towards the exit. Damn karma coming for me so quickly, after I accused Jasper of social media hypocrisy. "Fredster!" Zach smirks, slapping my arse. "I need to get my stuff from the trailer, I'll see you and your . . . *donkey dong* at the minibus."

No sooner has he scooted off than Jasper is at my side.

"Hi," he says.

"Hello."

"So, um . . . what are the chances, huh?"

"Are you talking about Zach? He's at my school."

Jasper nods. "Oh, right. Um. . ."

"I know all about you two, don't worry," I tell him.

Jasper's eyes widen, mortified, I've no doubt. I'm sure Jasper loves to play the honourable, polite guy. What would all his fans think if they knew the *real* him, who dumps boys the moment he gets a sniff of fame?

"You do?"

"Yeah," I say. I stare at him and he swallows.

"Oh. OK." He glances at me, eyes searching my face. "Um, I'm sorry, by the way, if I was a bit . . . when I met you at the press party, you know?"

Ha! An apology? More like a PR exercise to make him look better, now I know the truth about how he treated Zach. I have to smile to myself.

"It's fine. I'm sorry I . . . got stuff all over you."

"I was a bit stressed with everything. There were so many people we had to meet, journalists, people from MegaFlix, it was a bit full-on, and, well, I did try to find you later, but. . ."

I raise my eyebrows.

"Um, you were sort of . . . being carted off by your mum." He nods. "You were pretty animated about how MegaFlix had cancelled *Sense8*, even though—"

"Ah," I say. "Yes, not their show."

We smile at each other, before I remember I really shouldn't be doing that and he is a horrible person.

"Have you considered changing your email address?" he says with a smirk.

I do have to laugh at that. "Yeah, yeah, I *am* going to get on that."

We share another smile, which feels like I'm cheating on Zach, but it's fine, because then Connor barges up to us and says, "I cannot believe you're dating that prick!"

I'm so shocked, I laugh. I'm sure Jasper has spun his version of events to his new boyfriend, but really? It's not

Zach who's been a prick today, it's these two. I shake my head and stare them both down. "I can't believe *you're* dating *this* prick!" I reply, indicating Jasper.

And then I turn and walk the hell out of there.

22

Just as I think things have turned a bit of a corner and maybe Zach is ready for us to be more public in a possible boyfriends way (which he *did* basically admit to Jasper, so it's not like I'm imagining it), I message him to see if he wants to do a double-date thing with Ruby and Calvin on Sunday (a trip to this indoor crazy golf place in West London), and he doesn't:

> ZACH: Throat's a bit scratchy. Need to be
> careful with the show coming up. Think I'll
> have a quiet Sunday with lots of honey and
> lemon. Have fun. X

It's fine, that's fine, and I join Ruby and Calvin anyway, like some hideous spare wheel, because they assured me it's more fun with more people, and Sam couldn't make it because "Alice wants us to use some Stanislavski techniques to really get to the core of Eugene and Patty" and apparently that's going to take the whole day.

It's not Ruby or Calvin's fault, but I *do* end up feeling like a spare wheel. The little glances and smiles they give each other; the shorthand way of talking, the shared jokes; the way Calvin stands behind Ruby and shows her how to putt a golf ball more effectively – it's just sweet, it's cute and nice. It's everything I want with Zach.

I resolve to try to talk with him again, and an opportunity comes via the *Grease* group WhatsApp on Sunday night:

LOTTIE: There ain't no party like a show party! Mine, next Saturday. Y'all are invited. Even you, Zach! Lol! Bring drinks, you know what I mean.

Ignoring the fact she said "Y'all" like she's American, and the fact she's suddenly being nice to Zach (this is probably more about Lottie establishing herself as top dog in the production – the joint lead who also organizes parties is inevitably going to be popular), this has the potential to be the moment Zach and I go public. It's a party. People often turn up to parties with a date. And I'd like to turn up with Zach.

But Monday arrives, and he doesn't make talking easy. I find myself standing next to him at the urinals in the boys' toilets at the start of lunch, and he doesn't even glance at me. Sure, there is an unwritten "urinal code" which forbids such interaction, but since we're alone in there, and since he's already seen it anyway, I'm surprised he keeps his eyes front and his mouth shut.

"How are you?" I venture.

"Does your mum know any agents?" he replies.

"Um . . . I guess, maybe?"

He sniffs, shakes, and buttons up. "Just thinking, maybe it's time to get one, especially with *Grease* coming up – they could come and see me in action."

I nod. "Um, sure. I can ask?"

"Cool," he says, briefly showing his hands some water at the sink.

"So, I was just—" I'm rendered inaudible by the jet engine sound of the hand drier.

It goes on for twenty seconds.

"Sorry, what?" Zach says when he's finished.

"Just about the party on Saturday," I say. "Like, if you wanted, we could do drinks at mine first." I glance at him to gauge his reaction. His face is entirely neutral. "And, if you wanted, like, totally no pressure, but you could . . . crash at mine after?" I try to make it sound as casual as possible, like he likes, but I swear he almost flinches.

"Maybe," he says. "I gotta go – Danny and Sandy rehearsal."

"Right! I'll be along shortly!" I say breezily. Oh god, I recognize that tone in my voice. It's my mother, when she's on the phone to development execs and they're turning down one of her projects.

I smile at him and he looks back at me funny. Maybe he's just one of those guys who doesn't do talking in the toilets.

Zach and Lottie are the only cast members called for today's rehearsal because they're doing a scene at the end where Danny and Sandy kiss, and Ms Pearson wants to spend time "making this the most erotically charged moment ever seen on a high school stage!" I've been asked to be there because I'm basically classed as stage management, but I'm surprised to find Harrison in the drama studio when I arrive, having a hushed (and what looks like *fraught*) conversation with Lottie in the corner. I quietly get on with setting myself up at my usual spot, glancing at Zach as he paces the marked-up stage space, running lines in his head and gesticulating.

"OK, fine!" Harrison snaps. "But I'm staying here, and you can't stop me!" He stomps over to the back towards me, drags a chair off one of the stacks and flops down on it, arms crossed, frowning.

It's not nice to take comfort in other people's pain, but it's reassuring that even the school's golden couple don't have a plain-sailing relationship. Maybe everything I'm feeling about Zach is normal. I'm sure someone a lot wiser than me, probably it was Shakespeare, once said that love is a roller coaster, and sometimes, you've just got to ride it.

"Mmm-kay!" Ms Pearson says. "What I'm looking for in this scene is the sense that you two are totally hot for one another. As an audience member I want to feel the passion, and for me to feel it, *you* have to feel it." She smiles at Zach and Lottie, two people who transparently hate one another.

"That's going to be quite hard," Zach says, not looking at Lottie.

"Ohmigod, *same!*" Lottie retorts.

Ms Pearson nods, clearly expecting this. "My only love, sprung from my only hate. Who said that?"

Harrison puts his hand up. "Was it Little Mix?"

Ms Pearson sighs. "Why are you here, Harrison? You're not called today."

"Lottie's my girlfriend." He looks at Zach pointedly. "Just checking she's going to be OK."

"Babe!" Lottie says. "Seriously!"

"Oh my god, what do you think's gonna happen?" Zach says. "I don't fancy her, Harrison, I'm gay! Besides, I can barely look at her without wanting to hurl."

"Let's start," Ms Pearson says, getting right in, "with an exercise. Take it in turns to say something you like about the other person."

Zach frowns. "In character, or. . .?"

"As *yourselves*," Ms Pearson says, with a wide smile. "As Zach and Lottie."

Lottie rolls her eyes. "I love how conceited you are."

"I love how you probably don't know what that even

means," Zach retorts.

Ms Pearson raises a hand. "OK, so—"

"I love those really naff Instagram posts you do like you think everyone loves you."

"I love that you're looking at those." Zach grins.

"I love that you're so arrogant you think this whole show is about you."

"I love that you recognize Sandy's the secondary lead."

"OK," Ms Pearson interjects, "so this isn't really sounding like—"

"I *really, really, really* love your smarmy, arrogant face!" Lottie snarls.

"And I love that you're nothing more than a spoiled rich kid!"

"*Oooh, I'm Zach, I think I'm a god, kneel before me, worship at the altar of Zach!*"

"*Oh, hi, is that the cloakroom? I'd just like to check my privilege, please.*"

"You know nothing about my life – it's not my fault I'm beautiful and my dad is rich. I fucking hate your guts, Zach Cooper!"

"And now we kiss," Zach says.

And, er . . . they certainly do.

Zach wraps her in his arms, and the kiss is slow, and long, and tender, and—

Harrison stares at them, mouth hanging open, bottom lip trembling. Then he jumps up, throws his chair back and storms out of the drama studio.

And I'm right behind him.

"It's only acting!" Lottie calls after us.

I know that. I know it's acting. That's not the problem.

Everything about how Zach kissed Lottie, the look in his eyes, the movements, the way he broke away and looked in her eyes. . .

Yeah, it was *acting*.

And it's exactly like when Zach kisses me.

23

"OK," Zach says, squatting down opposite me, while I'm slumped on the floor, against the corridor wall. "It was *acting*. You don't need to be upset."

"You kiss her like you kiss me!" I hiss.

Zach grimaces and checks left and right up the corridor.

"Sorry, I know I shouldn't be saying stuff like that while we're being *casual*," I mutter.

"You know why I kissed her like I kiss you?"

I shrug. *Because it's not real. None of this is real. Because you don't really like me. Because I'm essentially unlovable.*

"Have you heard of Uta Hagen?"

"No."

"OK, so she was an acting teacher, and one of her techniques, in essence, was to encourage actors to mentally recreate the conditions of lived experiences to behave authentically onstage through something known as substitution, and—"

"In plain English?"

"It looked like how I kiss you because that's what I was imagining when I was doing it," Zach says. "How else was I going to kiss Lottie? I had to pretend it was you onstage, lose myself in it, *in you*, and hope it would seem realistic. Which," he sighs, "it clearly did."

I look up into his eyes. I feel like an absolute fool. I got it all wrong because I'd convinced myself that there was a problem between us, so I was out looking to prove myself right, because however hard I try, I still, deep down, don't believe someone like Zach wants me.

"I'm sorry," I say.

"Cool, it's OK." He looks up the corridor again. There's no one about. He rubs his face with the palms of his hands. "Argh, I knew this would happen. I knew it wouldn't work. We agreed casual, didn't we?"

"Yes, totally!"

"Like, if you want more than that, I just. . ." He sighs. "Is that what you want?"

I swallow. "No?" I say, in a small voice. "I mean, I don't know."

Zach sighs again and nods, like he's weighing up how to discipline a naughty kid. "OK, but storming out like that just because I'm *acting* kissing someone else, suggests you kinda do."

"Maybe I just felt sick."

"Maybe."

I'm angry with myself. I'm kind of angry at him too. I'm angry that he does and says all the right things when we're in private, but that I'm left feeling insecure because he won't go that extra step which would let me know he really means it. My mind switches to thoughts of the party on Saturday. No way is he going to agree to turning up with me as his date now – I've gone and ruined it. I ask anyway. "Zach, on Saturday. . ."

He doesn't skip a beat. "So, me and some of the other T-Bird lads are planning this thing where we're gonna turn up together. . ."

My heart sinks. "Oh, right? OK."

"It's gonna be awesome, just wait. We only decided it this morning, but obviously it means I can't come to yours first."

"OK. Sure. Sounds . . . great."

He nods. "Yeah. But we'll see each other there."

"Yeah."

Zach quickly stands up as Lottie flaps through the double doors and heads towards us.

"Wow," she says, shaking her head. "Harrison is totally pissed at you."

Zach groans.

"I've just had to spend five minutes reassuring him that it was an acting kiss, and, no, I'm not having a secret affair with you, Zach, and, yes, Harrison, you *are* a better kisser – who knew boys could be so needy?"

Zach laughs and Lottie smiles at him, then looks down at me.

"And why did *you* storm out?" she asks.

"Wanted to check on Harrison," I say, at the same time as Zach says: "He felt sick."

"I felt sick and wanted to see if Harrison was OK," I clarify, as Zach also clarifies: "He was sick with worry about Harrison."

Lottie blinks at us. "Oh *god*, are you two—"

"No!" I yelp, realizing that Lottie blabbing to everyone else about me and Zach will totally not be Zach's idea of *casual*. "Are us two *what*?"

Lottie nods and smiles. "OK, boys. OK. That's fine." She taps her nose, a smile twitching at the corners of her mouth. "Shall we resume rehearsals?" She glances at Zach, then glides off through the door of the drama studio.

"Fuck's sake," Zach mutters.

24

Zach is cross about me wanting more than we agreed, and simultaneously making Lottie think we're a "thing" when we're not a "thing" and he wanted to keep things simple and fun. He doesn't say it explicitly, but I can tell, from the way his leg stops touching mine in English and how he doesn't drop by the props store any day for the rest of that week that I've messed up. I was all set to have "the chat", but I think I just need to let things be for now. Although that doesn't stop me lamenting the situation as Sam and Ruby and I walk over to Lottie's house on Saturday night.

Ruby sighs. "You said you weren't in love with him. 'Bit of fun', you said."

"I know," I say. "I guess it somehow became a bit more. For me, anyway."

"Well, I never saw that coming," Ruby says, rolling her eyes.

"Have you actually told him how you're feeling?" Sam asks. "Like, I totally appreciate that's scary, but have you?"

I shrug. "Not really. Every time we even edge towards talking about anything like that, he gets prickly and cross. It's pretty obvious how he feels."

Sam nods and we walk in silence for a bit, until he adds, "Talking does help, though. Just saying."

"True," Ruby agrees.

"What would you tell him?" Sam continues. "If you weren't scared about how he might react, what would you say?"

I blow out a breath. "I guess, just that . . . I like him . . . a lot . . . and that I love that we have fun and stuff, and it's nice, but that . . . I think the really good stuff is the other stuff, if you get me? Like. . . watching a movie and cuddling? Going into town together? Just being there for each other, really. You know, life gets you down, you're stressed, upset, or whatever, and the other person holds your hand, gives you a hug, just makes your day better." Saying it out loud makes me realize just how much I want that.

Ruby and Sam both put their arms across my shoulders, hugging me close to them as we continue to walk along the pavement.

"What you want is important too," Sam says. "It's not a relationship if it's all about just one of you."

I glance at him. "When did you get so wise?"

A smile plays on his lips, and he looks away.

"You know what you have to do, don't you?" Ruby says.

"Yes," I say.

Ruby squeezes my shoulder. "Are you going to do it?"

I take a deep breath. *"Yes."*

It's very hard to generalize about areas of London because pretty much wherever you are, you can go from crushing poverty to unimaginable wealth in the space of two streets, but if you're going to generalize, then Dulwich is one of the rich areas. And this is where Lottie Stefani lives, in the type of house that could only have been bought with the sort of cash you get from a massive inheritance or laundering Russian money. I've always had a nagging feeling that Lottie's parents are the sort that *could* afford to send her to private school, but they've gone state because they want their daughter to experience a little of how the lower classes live, before she leaves us behind for yachts and private islands.

Anyway. Good house for a party. She's laid on a lot of food and drinks, and she has a massive garden and this integrated music system, and while her parents haven't let us loose with the real glassware, they have provided plastic "glasses" so we're not even drinking out of old random mugs, or those flimsy little plastic white cups that you can only fit one mouthful of drink in. It's pretty swanky, although it won't make any difference. By midnight, if the stories of past parties are to be believed, I imagine it'll be utter carnage. A sweaty, messy, grubby, hormone-addled disaster zone, awash with an assortment of bodily fluids.

I can't wait.

When I arrive with Ruby and Sam, there's already a high percentage of theatre kids singing show tunes in virtually every room, and fair bit of conversation with people screaming things like, "OH MY GOD! I *LOVED* HER ELPHABA!" but I guess this is what it's all about. Kwame gives me a nod and a, "Hey, Freddie," as I squeeze past him, chatting (bitching?) to Priya in the hallway. It makes me smile. I know my benchmark is pretty low, but I really feel like I've made it. I'm at an exclusive theatre kids party with people who know my name, and not just because of my mum.

We get some drinks, have a few canapés (canapés!), and then Alice and Dhruv find us.

"What Ms Pearson is simply *not* getting," Dhruv says, running his fingers through his flowing, theatrical hair, having been holding court for ten minutes now, "is where Kenickie's hard exterior really comes from. He's angry, and that anger comes from pain, and the pain stems from loss. As such, is it really appropriate for him to hand jive at the hop like he's on top of the world? No, it is not."

"What would he do instead?" I ask.

"As a counterpoint to the witless festivities, he should

be alone, in the parking lot outside the school. And maybe we choreograph a piece of contemporary dance for him that really highlights his inner turmoil."

Ruby laughs, then immediately stops when she realizes Dhruv is serious. "Yeah, no," she says, nodding. "That's a really interesting idea."

Dhruv frowns at her. "It's about injecting realism."

We all nod very seriously, and I find myself giving a thoughtful, "Mmmm," like a real theatre kid.

"What about Patty?" Dhruv asks, like he can't be bothered to hear the answer. "I guess she's more . . . straightforward?"

"On the contrary," Alice says, giving him just a hint of a "screw you" smile. "Patty has some very surprising hidden layers. Eugene too. Right, Sam?"

Sam swallows. "Oh, um . . . for sure."

"Remember," Alice says. "*It's always the quiet kids.*"

No one has time to establish what exactly it always is about the quiet kids, as Lottie is shouting for us all to go out into the front garden, where Zach, Calvin, Harrison and Jamil screech to a stop on the driveway in Calvin's ancient Nissan Micra and perform "Greased Lightnin'" all over it, with Calvin occasionally shouting, "Careful of the aerial!" and, "Don't scratch the bonnet!" which definitely adds something to the number.

They freeze in position at the end and we all whoop and applaud (while Dhruv scowls, because Zach sang the number a million times better than he ever has), and the lads high-five and look well pleased with themselves.

Ruby rolls her eyes. "Boys love attention."

"I mean, I don't know if you can say that when you're literally in the school show," I tell her, just as Zach does an actual backflip off the car, landing elegantly on the ground and striking a John Travolta *Saturday Night Fever* pose, to various gasps and rapturous applause. "On second thought, no, you're absolutely right."

Zach strolls past me, winks and slaps my arse on his way inside. "Fredster!"

"Hi, hey—" But he's already gone.

"Why does he call you that?" Ruby asks.

"Like, a pet name, maybe? I guess you could say it's cloyingly romantic?" I wiggle my eyebrows.

Ruby frowns. "You couldn't say that. Would you say that, Sam?"

Sam shakes his head. "It's more ... too-much-testosterone, straight-boy nickname."

I know they're both right. And I hate it that Zach called me that. Like I'm just his buddy.

"When are you going to talk to him?" Ruby asks.

"Soon," I say. "I'll just let him get a drink."

"PIZZA'S HERE!" Harrison Kane shouts from across the drive as he accepts a huge stack of boxes from the Deliveroo guy. "Artisan toppings on sourdough bases 'CAUSE THIS IS DULWICH!"

"Or maybe after pizza," I say.

Ruby rolls her eyes.

Talking to Zach is totally the plan, but he's like me in year eleven PE – either not there whenever I look for him, or armed with excuses.

"Mate, I just gotta chat with Calvin!"

"Helping get some more ice, back in minute!"

"Fredster!"

That last one wasn't even an excuse, he just said it as he hurried past, before I could even open my mouth to speak. After all this trying to get Zach's attention, I manage to lose both Ruby and Sam, so find myself in a rather tragic wallflower situation in the big lounge, holding my drink and trying to low-level groove to the music, like I'm lost in the beat, possibly a bit stoned, happy-with-my-own-company-'cause-I'm-so-zen type of attitude.

"What you doing all by your little self?"

It's Zach. He grins and gives me couple of little jokey jabs in my stomach. I'm so happy to see him. Maybe he was waiting for the right time to come and talk to me, like when he could be sure other people wouldn't interrupt.

"Ah, hi!" I say. "So, look, I was thinking . . . would you like to go and look at the garden with me?"

Zach laughs. "Sounds . . . super-exciting, Fredster! What's your favourite plant?"

"I mean, it's not really about pla—"

"No, but what's your favourite?"

"Um . . . daffodils?"

"There's actually a plant called a Stiffcock," he says.

"No, there isn't."

"Yep! *Diospyros crassenevis*, that's its botanical name. Swear down. *Stiffcock*." He looks over to where Lottie is chatting with some mates. "Hey, Lottie? Got any *Stiffcocks* in your garden?"

"There's about three couples making out behind the summer house, so probably," she says with a shrug.

Zach guffaws.

"OK, so that's great, but what I really wanted—"

"I need a drink," Zach interrupts.

"That's fine, so shall we—"

"And I put your name down for Seven Minutes in Heaven." He winks at me.

I love that wink. It's a wink that's connected to Seven Minutes in Heaven, which means he wants to be locked in a dark cupboard with me and do stuff. I am so up for that. I just wonder if there's a way I could engineer some talking into that seven minutes? Because that could work really well. Me and Zach, and his undivided attention for a whole seven minutes. Job done.

"Starts in the games room in fifteen, so meet you in there, yeah?"

"Huh? Games room? Who even has a games room?"

Zach laughs, stopping when he locks eyes with Harrison Kane, who is standing across the room by himself, glaring.

"Lottie my-dad's-probably-in-a-drugs-cartel Stefani, that's who!" Zach says. "Can't wait!" he whispers, before quickly disappearing into the crowd.

OK. This is going to be my chance. Big talk. And what any big talk needs . . . is a little extra alcohol for a confidence boost.

So. *Tequila*. Why is this a thing? A bunch of people were doing shots in the kitchen. Joined in. Immediately regretted it.

Nevertheless, still joining in.

Why . . . why is . . . phish snark ling me, huh? Think, haps bad choice. . .

Very blurry, and before I know it, am singing "Baby Shark Do Do Do Do Do Do" on the karaoke.

Lots of clapping and cheers.

Am a pop god.

Feeling very sexy and powerful and Ruby is so right, boys love attention, this boy is loving it.

Hip thrust movement gets big reaction.

Everyone wants a piece of me.

Have reached mean-cheerleader-girl levels of popularity and respect.

Zach is here now.

"Ahhhh, ha ha! You're wankered! Excellent!"

"And you are . . . pretty!" I tell him.

"*This guy!*" Zach says, playing to the crowd, as he pulls me off (No! Not like that, *naughty!*) and out of the room.

"Is it time for the sex cupboard game?" I mutter.

"Do you need some water?" Zach asks me. I like Zach. So caring and kind in his humanitarian efforts towards drunk Fredster.

"Tequila!" I announce.

"Ahh, no, no, no," Zach replies.

Next we are in a big room, lots of people, faces, a circle, a bottle, much excitement.

"I'm a pop god!" I whisper in Zach's sexy ear, as he pulls me down to sit next to his sexy self.

"Yes, you *are*," he says.

Squeals and "Ooohs!" as the bottle is spun and it's Ella Morris with some kid, I think a year eleven called Tom, in the cupboard first.

"Wha. . . What d'ya think they are – *hic* – doing in the cupboard?" I giggle in Zach's ear.

"What do *you* think they're doing?"

I giggle again because *funny* and because am liking talking naughty stuff with Sex God Zach. "I fink . . . hm . . . like, m'be he'll and then . . . her . . . in, and . . . then huh, huh, huh, KAPOW! Or-gan-ism."

"Sounds awesome, mate."

"Zach, Zach!" I hiss. He leans towards me. "Zach, if, in the cupboard, it's me and . . . um, you . . . in the cupboard, like, in it, together, can we . . . huh . . . *talk* because . . . I really, really . . . like you a lot and need to . . . talk . . . about that?"

Zach stares in my eyes with his eyes all cross and full of meaning. "Not here, yeah?"

"Ohhhhhh," I say. "Oh, no, not . . . that, I mean, yes, that, but also not that because talking?"

"OK, cool, so save the talking for that, yeah?"

I nod. "No talky now."

"No talky now, that's right."

I nod. "I'll '*put a . . . cock in it.*'"

"Oh, Fredster, I wish I was recording this." He pats my leg with his handsome hand.

Soon Ella and Tom appear again.

Smudged lipstick. (Ella.)

Obvious boner. (Tom.)

"We didn't do nothing!" Ella makes big protest of it.

Tom – shifty. Gives thumbs up to some mates. "Get in!" one of them shouts.

Time for the bottle to go round again and. . .

Time washes by. Can't keep . . . track of who is with who in where.

I reach my hand over at one point . . . on top of Zach's.

I want to hold his hand because *that's what people do*.

He . . . casually moves his hand away.

230

Then Zach is getting up, many cheers.

It. Is. Time.

Try to scramble to feet too, to join him in love nest, but no! Am pushed back down!

"It's Zach with Harrison!" a person tells me.

"No!" I protest. "Me!"

No one cares or listens.

Have to watch as Zach enters cupboard with Harrison.

Really really really want to talk to Zach, say stuff, express feelings and emotions and reach mature understanding so relationship can be fruitful and fulfilling. Also want to have good tonguing with him and lose self in the infinite pleasure palace that is Zach. But have to wait now.

Time passes.

Lottie seems twitchy. Maybe worried that Harrison will punch Zach and party will descend into chaos, fighting, food thrown everywhere and precious vases broken and so on. And perhaps she is right... Harrison's menacing face from earlier replays in my head – staring at Zach ... hating him ... wanting him ... dead?

Some raised voices... And then, a THUD from inside cupboard, like a body hitting the door.

Oh god, has Harrison hit Zach already? Is Zach on the floor, bleeding?

And then some sort of moan, like someone's in pain.

I scramble up, determined. Against the rules, I

approach cupboard as people scream at me, "No!" but don't care. If Zach is hurt, rules can go to hell. They don't know about Harrison. They don't know the danger.

I fling open the cupboard door and bodies tumble out and there is Zach snogging the face off Harrison Kane.

25

I'm lying on my back in bed, staring up at the ceiling. Have I been asleep? I'm not sure. My eyes hurt. Everything hurts. My head's about ready to explode – partly from a tequila hangover, and partly from trying to compute the events of last night.

That kiss. That deep, passionate, horny *snog* is branded on to my brain, seared on to my retinas, I can't stop seeing it.

It wasn't a joke kiss.

It wasn't like how Zach kissed Lottie onstage.

And it wasn't like how he ever kissed me.

This kiss was . . . *real*.

When I opened the cupboard door and the pair of them fell out, there were cheers and whoops, there were scandalized and excited-for-the-gossip "Ooooooh!'s", there was a scream from Lottie, followed by shouted accusations, but from me. . . I couldn't even speak. I was staring, dead inside, totally lost, I didn't understand.

"Zach? What are you doing?" I finally managed to say.

Zach didn't even clock I'd spoken.

And then I ran out.

I lie here, trying to rationalize it in the cold light of day. Zach was drunk. Harrison was drunk. Sometimes people do stuff they don't mean when they're drunk. Or maybe it was a big joke, something to get people talking? But I don't remember Zach or Harrison being that drunk at the party, and nobody was laughing afterwards.

What I do remember, before I ran out, was Zach giving Harrison a "look". It was so brief, just a quick moment of connection and shared understanding. It's a look I've wanted Zach to give me since this whole thing with him started. He never has, of course. His looks have always been loaded – horny looks, dirty looks, "let's meet in the props store for some fun" looks. Zach's look to Harrison was different. It was gentle. *Caring*.

The "look" niggles at me.

It means something.

And then it hits me.

Zach and Harrison didn't get together for the first time last night.

They've been seeing each other for a while.

Tender, caring "looks" don't just happen quickly – they develop over time. *Because they're about feelings*.

When Harrison stormed out of the drama studio after seeing Zach kiss Lottie, it wasn't because he was jealous of

Zach kissing his girlfriend; it left him feeling insecure *about* Zach, just like me. When Zach was reading Danny's diary in rehearsals, talking about how hard it was to be himself and how much he liked someone, I thought he was talking about us. But he wasn't; he was talking about him and Harrison.

So, what was I? Does Harrison even know about me and Zach? When he was staring menacingly at Zach, was he actually just angry with me, for flirting with *his* boyfriend?

How is Harrison even gay anyway? *Is* he gay? WHAT IS GOING ON?!

I groan. I'm such an idiot. I honestly believed someone like *me* could end up with someone like *Zach*. But that's not how life really works, is it? Screw Hollywood for making normal people like me believe wonderful stuff like that can happen to us.

My phone has hundreds of notifications, but I don't look at any of them. I want to shut myself away. The one saving grace is that it's half-term next week, so I don't have to be in school facing it all any time soon. I pull on some joggers and a hoodie and head to the kitchen to find some paracetamol. I wish Mum was here. She might be slightly unorthodox in lots of ways, but she makes good tea and bacon butties when I'm feeling like shit. When I find out there isn't even any bread in the house for toast, I sit on the kitchen floor, head in my hands, and I cry.

Ruby arrives an hour and a half later with a carrier bag which I'm assuming contains McMuffins and hash browns and I'm so pleased to see her that I throw my arms around her.

And then I start sobbing again.

She holds me until I've calmed down, but when I peel myself away from her, I notice that she looks wrecked too.

"What happened after I left?" I mutter.

She sighs and glances at the floor. "Can we sit down?"

My stomach immediately knots. Whatever it is requires us to "sit down" – the sure sign of something serious. I lead her through to the lounge and we perch on the edge of the sofa. There's a weird stillness in the air, like life is happening somewhere else right now.

"First off, Zach started off claiming that in kissing Harrison he was merely rehearsing for the kiss in *Grease*."

I frown. "The scene where . . . Danny kisses Doody?"

"I know, right? Absolute joke. Claimed he was nervous about getting the kiss with Lottie right because he'd never kissed anyone before, so Harrison offered to help him practise, I mean, *the level of bullshit*."

"But . . . he's kissed me," I say in a small voice. "Quite a lot."

Ruby nods. "Yeah, well, he's saying that didn't happen."

"What didn't happen?"

"Lottie started going on about how she thought you two were dating – apparently that much was clear when you stormed out of the rehearsal the other day?"

I close my eyes and sigh.

"Then Harrison got all funny, and started saying stuff like, 'So, you've been seeing Freddie?' and, 'You two sure looked cosy chatting earlier on!' Seriously, Fred, he went from straightest straight boy to neurotic homosexual in five seconds flat, and Zach was all, 'He's a bit obsessed with me. He's got a thing, maybe I lead him on a bit, but we're definitely not seeing each other.'"

I stare at her and swallow.

"Obsessed?"

Ruby shrugs. "Also, and. . . Look, I'm just going to say all this because you need to know and I think a short, sharp shock is best, OK?"

I nod weakly, mouth open, as a chill prickles through me.

"Harrison told Lottie he likes Zach, and apparently can't stop thinking about him and thinks he needs to, and I quote, 'explore his sexuality'."

"WHAT?" I can't believe what I'm hearing. Harrison! Exploring his sexuality! I feel another sharp pang of rejection – that he didn't want to ever do that exploring with me in all the years we've been at school together.

"Meanwhile, he and Lottie have split up, and Harrison went back to Zach's house to 'talk about things'."

My throat is so tight. Harrison is allowed back to Zach's house. I never was.

"Stop," I manage to croak.

Ruby sighs. "I'm sorry, Fred." She puts an arm across my shoulders.

I try to hold them back, but tears spring from my eyes again. "They spent the night together and Zach was happy for everyone to know that?"

Ruby nods. "Yeah," she murmurs. "They left with their arms around each other."

Everything I wanted. Everything I hoped me and Zach would do. Did he not like me enough? Does he just like Harrison more? Doesn't matter. This is how it works, isn't it? When you're not in the same league. You can be getting to know a guy, it can be going OK, but when a better-looking boy suddenly wants what you've got, you're always gonna lose out.

"OK," I mutter. "OK, then."

"I was looking for you at this point, Freddie, searching everywhere. I didn't realize you'd gone home," Ruby continues. "Meanwhile, Lottie's all upset and crying and getting comforted by Calvin—"

"Your Calvin?"

"He's the only Calvin, Freddie. But, yes. He comforts her, you know, like a good, honourable ex would, and at some point after I've been looking for you for ages, I walk in and they're snogging on the floor of the kitchen."

"WHAT?"

"'Oh, Lottie, I've missed you!' That's Calvin. And Lottie's all, 'I just need you back, Calvin, I should never have dumped you!'"

"WHAT?"

Ruby swallows and nods. And now it's her turn to cry, and my turn to hug her.

"But . . . Calvin's such a nice guy! He adores you!" I mutter. "How could this happen?"

"I don't know, Freddie."

"I'm sorry, Rubes."

She nods. "I know. I'm sorry too, Fred."

It's so much I can't get my head around it. I said yes to life, but life has not said yes to me.

"Don't descend into a pit of despair, Fred," Ruby says after a bit.

"How . . . how do you know I'm descending into a pit?"

"Because you're bouncing your knee up and down and breathing really hard. We can get through this."

I swallow.

"We have to push through. This setback can't destroy the plan."

"Screw the plan!" I blurt out. "I want doughnuts and McDonald's and to go back to being a slightly weird recluse and just seeing you and Sam and I don't want a boyfriend anyway. Sex is overrated. . ." Sure, things *had* been good. I'd been enjoying myself. I was doing stuff. I *was* someone. Or so I thought. But what's the point if you're only setting yourself up to be humiliated and hurt? All I want is for someone to like me. I don't even have to be the *most* important thing in someone's life, I just want to be *an* important thing. Why is that so hard? I push all that back down where it belongs, buried, and turn to Ruby, forcing myself to play the melodramatic clown because, honestly, that's easier. "Please tell me there's a tub of Ben and Jerry's in that bag so we can just hole ourselves up here, watch bad movies and weep until it's time for us to die."

Ruby opens the bag.

"What the hell is that?"

"It's sauerkraut," Ruby says, in a voice which suggests that's totally reasonable. "Live, raw, unpasteurized sauerkraut." She prises off the lid. "Got a couple of spoons?"

"No. I mean, yes, I have spoons, but why in god's name have you brought this stuff? Where's the Ben and Jerry's? Where are the sausage McMuffins? Cokes? Apple pie?" It's all I can do not to cry again at this point, quite frankly.

"All problems start in the gut—" Ruby begins, by way of some ludicrous explanation for this travesty.

"What?" I howl. "Zach dumping me and claiming nothing ever happened is not a problem that started in my gut! What ridiculous website did you get this shit off?"

"High-quality gut bacteria help to maintain your general health. We are not going back to school after half-term looking like losers, Freddie. We are going back in glowing. We will be radiant with health, we will have great skin . . . energy. Those boys will see we're not broken; we're better than ever before!"

She smiles at me pleadingly.

"I'm not eating fermented cabbage," I tell her.

"So, totally, I was like you to begin with. I was all ready to just grab us a ton of McDonald's, loads of those so-called 'sharing' bags of Wispa and Twirls, ice cream, crisps, caramel popcorn and some cans of San Pellegrino because—"

"We're nothing if not classy."

She nods. "But I didn't."

"Well, *why not*, Ruby? If there was ever a time to stuff ourselves with crap, it's now!"

"Because that's how the downward spiral starts. We've come too far to fail now."

I shake my head. "I mean, it literally feels like we've come about ten centimetres."

"Strong. Determined. Successful," Ruby says.

I blink at her.

"Affirmations. I downloaded another meditation app thing. Say it."

"Weak. Sad. Disastrous."

Ruby stares at me.

"Just give in to it, Rubes," I say. "What's the point?"

"The point," she says, "is that no project is ever straightforward. There are always ups and downs. So, what are you going to do? Give up the moment things get rough?"

"*Yes*?!" I suggest. "I am emphatically saying 'yes' to giving up right now."

"Go and get some spoons," she insists.

*

By the time Sam arrives half an hour later, he finds us both with tears in our eyes, taking alternate spoonfuls of the fermented cabbage while trying to "manifest" good fortune by burning wishes we've written on scraps of paper in the flame of a candle.

"I don't know what's happening here," he says, holding up two carrier bags, "but I brought cookie-dough ice cream, full-fat Coke, Kettle chips and there are two meat feast Domino's on their way, with stuffed crusts and some sides of garlic bread and barbecue chicken wings." He shakes his head. "Put that cabbage stuff away, and let's find a gruesome serial killer documentary to settle down and enjoy on Netflix."

"Oh, thank god!" I mutter.

Having Sam and Ruby here helps a bit. But however hard I try to lose myself in re-enactments of dead bodies being chopped up and dissolved in vats of acid, I can't shake the image of Zach and Harrison kissing, and I can't stop the dull, nagging ache in my heart.

It's when Sam gets a series of notifications on his phone (which make him grin in a way that makes me think not all of them are messages about the imminent arrival of the pizza) that I remember to finally check *my* phone. I whizz past the ones from Ruby asking where I am and head to Instagram, because I think I'd rather just know and see what I'm dreading seeing, to get it over and done with.

And there it is.

A picture of Zach and Harrison, their arms around

each other, looking very much in love.

And something about the photo isn't right.

It wasn't taken today. Or even yesterday.

Zach's got a fresh scar on his leg. The one he got that afternoon I dragged Ruby and Sam to see him play football.

That's when the truth that has been right in front of me this whole time finally hits me.

Whatever Zach and Harrison have been doing, they've been doing since the day of that football match. The same day I kissed Zach for the first time. I know he said "casual". I know we agreed "fun". I guess I just didn't think that meant seeing other people because Zach said it was only because of his fear of having his heart broken again – we just weren't rushing into anything, that was all. That's what I thought.

But, no. All the crap Zach and Harrison were both apparently spouting after being discovered at the party was just a front, because, all this time, Zach was doing with Harrison what he was doing with me. Hedging his bets? Trying us both out? Whatever it was, he was playing me, and possibly both of us.

Only it looks like Harrison won.

If I was ever really in the game at all.

26

According to Ruby, "silence is the most powerful weapon", so we both agree on a policy of no communication with Zach or Calvin during half-term. Ruby says this will drive them crazy as they try to work out what is going on in our minds, thereby giving us the upper hand when we return to school.

Two days in and it's *me* who's being driven crazy. I can't stop thinking about Zach and Harrison, replaying over and over every little detail since September, trying to work out what was real (if anything) and what wasn't; trying to establish when the exact moment was that Zach and Harrison first got together – something which still makes my stomach churn when I think about it, it's so wild to me. Burying myself in *Pride and Prejudice* only fuels my anxiety about what guys are really like, so I jack it all in and decide I might as well try to get the last few props for *Grease*. One of the main things that still eludes me is the cafeteria trays and, remembering there are definitely plenty on the set of *Cherries* (and after Mum refuses to bring some home, claiming, "I have enough to do, get your arse down here yourself!"), I decide to get my arse down there myself.

They're shooting some classroom scenes when I get there, so the cafeteria set is blissfully deserted, meaning I can help myself to six trays with no bother, which I shove into my Tesco Bag for Life. I bump into Mum on my way out.

"Go and get some food from the catering truck," she says.

"I thought you were home tonight?"

"Yes, but I'm out with Yvette. Colin's had a meltdown and now he's insisting they sell the house and move to Cornwall so he can write one of those novels about high flyers who have a breakdown and move to the country to make chutney, which accidentally becomes a viable business. Yvette's beside herself. She has to be within half a mile of a Gail's Bakery at all times."

"I'll get Deliveroo." I shrug.

"*No*," Mum says. "I see what you're ordering, Freddie, and it's a miracle you haven't come down with scurvy. Catering have lasagne on today, so at least that has tomatoes in it. Let me see?" She does a goofy face.

"Do you mean my brace?" I frown.

"Show me."

I bare my wired-up teeth at her. I had them fitted yesterday. I wasn't going to bother, now that Zach has dumped me, and the improved teeth were meant to be for his benefit, but the wheels were already in motion, no refunds, and I couldn't back out. I wish Mum would have paid for the "invisible" ones, like she kind of suggested she might, but it is what it is.

"Reminds me of that James Bond film, you know. . ."

"Don't say it, Mum."

"The villain in *The Spy Who Loved Me*."

"OK, you're actually doing this?"

"Jaws."

"God, you're hilarious."

"I have to run. Go and get food." And she disappears.

I head to the catering truck, get myself a portion of lasagne with a side of garlic bread and some salad (because *scurvy*) and mooch into the double-decker bus that's had all the normal seats removed and replaced with tables and chairs you can eat around. I'd like to eat by myself, since I don't know anyone here, but the tables downstairs are packed with laughing, gossiping cast and crew members, so I head upstairs, only to find more of the same. I'm about to head down again, probably to eat on my lap outside, when Jasper looks up from a table at the far end and we lock eyes. He swallows. I follow his gaze as his eyes flick to the spare seats opposite him, then back to me. Seats may well be available, but I have zero intention of sitting there trying to eat my food as Jasper scowls at me and we both recall how I called him a "prick" not so long ago. I turn round to pursue my original plan of going outside when I'm met with six people all trying to come up the stairs as I descend. It's no good, there's no space, and I'm forced to reverse, not only back up the stairs but halfway along the aisle, as they all stream up and sit with some friends at two of the tables in the middle.

By now, I'm basically next to Jasper, but trying to ignore that fact, when he says, "These seats are free."

I pretend I haven't heard (there's lots of chatter up here) and act like I'm waiting for the aisle to clear again.

"Freddie? Do you want to sit here?"

So then I have to act all surprised to see him, even though I've already seen him, and we both know that.

Anyway, I end up sitting down at the table.

"Hey," he says.

"Hey," I say.

"How are you?" he says.

"Fine," I say.

"Good," he says.

"Good," I say.

I start eating my lasagne, but I can feel him watching me and it puts me off. "Look," I say. "I'm sorry about calling you a prick. It was rude of me. Especially in front of your boyfriend."

Jasper flinches slightly.

"I mean, I shouldn't have called you that anyway. The boyfriend bit is irrelevant."

His eyes meet mine.

"I was in a place where I was feeling protective about Zach." I break his stare and bite into the garlic bread.

"How is Zach?"

"Yep. Fine." We are *not* going to talk about *this*. I bet Jasper would absolutely revel in karma coming for me so damn quickly.

"Say hi from me."

"Huh. *Sure*."

"Not that he'll care, since he's such a dick."

I snap my eyes up from my food and glare at Jasper. I don't know why I don't just agree, since he's entirely right, but instead I find myself feeling all protective again. "That's a bit rich coming from the guy who dumped him when you got your big part."

Jasper holds my gaze for a few moments. "I didn't dump him, though."

I blink, once. "What?"

"I walked in on him in the costume store at BYT with another boy," Jasper continues. "So I think that was him dumping me, really."

I swallow the garlic bread. "He told me you dumped him. After you got the part in *Cherries*. Because he was small fry, and you were big time now."

Jasper raises his eyebrows. "Wow. And you believed him?"

"Well, yeah, I believed him."

"Because you think that's the sort of thing I'd do? Because I'm a prick."

I sigh. "I mean, I do, *did*, think that, a bit, I suppose, so the MO fitted."

Jasper nods again, clearly unimpressed.

I look down and try to focus on my food. I hate this. Now Jasper thinks I'm a dick, and quite honestly, he's the one being a dick about the fact that I, with good reason, thought he was a prick. Unless I'm actually being a total knob and need to apologize more?

"Again, I'm sorry," I offer.

"You said. It's fine. I don't care. Maybe you're right, anyway," Jasper mutters.

I look up at him. There's a self-deprecating tone in his voice I recognize from my own. I do it when I'm feeling bad about myself, but why on earth would Jasper be feeling bad about himself? With those looks! And that career! At sixteen!

"Do you want some Parmesan with that?" he asks, pushing a glass shaker of pre-grated cheese towards me.

"Oh, I thought that was sugar for some reason."

He almost smiles. "I know, so much better grated fresh, but beggars can't be choosers, and lasagne without Parmesan is like a cupcake without icing."

I almost smile in return. At least we have one thing in common that we're not going to fight about. I give my food a heavy dusting of cheese.

"You've been 'Zached', then?" he says.

I freeze, swallow, then replace the Parmesan shaker carefully on the table.

"I saw the pic of him and ... Harrison, is it? On his public account," Jasper explains. "So I assumed you finally knew?"

I grit my teeth. Jasper already knows that Zach's dumped me, and yet he still played innocent and asked how he was when I arrived. So manipulative. That's totally Jasper – he's positively Machiavellian in his power moves. I make a vague grunting noise. It's also great to know that Zach's antics are so common they've become a verb. *Zached. To be led on and royally screwed over by a boy you really like.* "Wait," I say. "What do you mean 'finally' knew?"

Jasper's mouth opens a little, but no words come out.

"What do you mean?" I repeat.

"Zach has an alt account. He's got pics of him with Harrison all over it. None of them say they're together or anything, but it's pretty obvious. That's why when I saw you together at the shoot, I was surprised, but then, that's Zach all over. Different week, different boy."

"An alt account?"

"It's not in his name, and it's private. You won't find it unless you know what to look for."

I'm suddenly not hungry. Jasper *knew*. Who else knew? Has everyone just been laughing at me the whole time? Getting the popcorn out and sitting back, ready for the show?

I throw my serviette down and stand up abruptly.

"Freddie?"

I'm sick of this. I'm sick of feeling like the collateral damage for everyone else's happy, carefree lives. Freddie gets hurt, doesn't matter, it's only Freddie.

I grab my bag, hurry out and don't look back.

Jasper emails me that evening:

To: donkeydong9inches@outlook.com
From: sexylover_69@outlook.com
Subject: Sorry

Hi Freddie,
My apologies. I probably didn't handle telling you that in the right way. I didn't mean to upset you.
I'm sorry.
J

Oh, really? He "probably" didn't handle it in the right way? I bet he loved telling me about Zach's alt account. I bet he thinks I got exactly what I deserved after I called him a prick and acted so smug thinking Zach was my boyfriend. I've been pacing about the house since I got home, so damn angry I don't know what to do with myself, and this email is the icing on the shitty cake. How dare he get my email address from production and try to make amends? I don't even want to hear from him, or anyone else connected with Zach. I fire a self-righteous email back, cc'ing in both my mother and Annie, the third AD, who doubtless handed over my private details:

To: sexylover_69@outlook.com
Cc: SBennett@purplesmurf.co.uk,
AnnieC@purplesmurf.co.uk
From: donkeydong9inches@outlook.com
Subject: Re: Sorry

Jasper. And also Mum and Annie.
Can I just remind you that under GDPR
regulations, handing over my email address
without my permission is ILLEGAL.
F

Ten minutes later and my mother emails back:

Hi Donkey Dong 9 Inches,
No one gave Jasper your email address,
apparently he just remembered it when you told
Annie what it was after the shoot. I can't imagine
how, it's not as if it's particularly distinctive.
Your mother x

As if I didn't think I could feel any more livid, Jasper then MESSAGES me!

JASPER: Hi. It's Jasper. Sorry for getting you in trouble with your mum.

ME: HOW DID YOU GET THIS NUMBER?

JASPER: Oh. Sorry. From your mum.

I throw my phone down in frustration, let out a wild scream, then run up to my bedroom, strip to my boxers and cocoon myself under my duvet. I've had enough of this day. If I'm here, nothing can hurt me. Nothing else exists. I pretend it's just me and I know nothing of life outside of this duvet cocoon. It's comforting and I wish I could stay here for ever.

27

Of course, in reality, if I stayed under my duvet for ever, the school would eventually ring my mum and that would just be one more thing to disappoint her. But by the end of half-term, and several pep talks from Ruby ("All guys are bastards!") and Sam ("You don't need a man, Freddie!") I'm at least able to shower and get dressed and just about able to drag myself to school with the aim of keeping out of Zach's way as much as I can.

First thing in English is just about fine. Ruby and I devise a plan to arrive early, so we're able to swap seats and sit at a table together, leaving Zach and Calvin to enjoy a lying, cheating table all of their own.

"It was one stupid, drunken moment, I fully regret it, and I'm not back dating Lottie," Calvin says as he passes Ruby with his folders.

"What you do is entirely your business, Calvin," Ruby replies.

"Rubes—"

"Thank you, Calvin, goodbye!" she chirps.

"Argh!" And he stomps back to sit at the desk with Zach, who is acting like he doesn't have a care in the world.

Ruby and I make a huge effort during English to answer lots of questions and appear upbeat and generally good at life by occasionally appearing to share a joke, sipping from small bottles of Evian and sporadically laughing, and so on. We maintain this during morning break (another potential area of dread, should I have to witness Zach and Harrison together), helped by Sam, who arrives (as planned) with a tub of hummus and some carrot sticks, because nothing says, "I am over you, I'm happy, and I don't care!" more than eating mushed-up chickpeas with raw vegetables. It's such a miserable snack, you would *have* to be totally loving life to be able to endure it. (I also secretly eat a Twix and a grab bag of ready salted Hula Hoops while locked in a cubicle in the boys' toilets.)

But it's the *Grease* rehearsal at lunchtime that nearly breaks my resolve. I'd prepared myself to be busy, and I arrive with armfuls of the last items from the props list, as well as checklists for all the individual characters. Basically anything and everything to ensure I have lots to do and don't need to even *look* at Zach. The trouble is, eventually I do look. Zach and Harrison are sitting by themselves in a corner of the drama studio *peeling hard-boiled eggs for each other.* It's the tenderness and intimacy of this bizarre ritual that gets to me. It's a little moment of togetherness, something they both care about – *protein*. I never had a thing like that with Zach. I mean, I never had anything with Zach, as it turns out. I want to peel someone's egg for them. And I want them to peel one for me.

I stop myself because I can feel myself getting ridiculous. It's just an egg.

Ms Pearson (who is not aware of the drama), announces that this will be our final rehearsal in the studio before we decamp to the actual theatre. Today we're going to be running scenes back-to-back, with props, which results in my first interaction with Zach since the party.

"Hey," he says, approaching the props desk.

I look up at him. I am silent. *Powerful.*

"How are you?" he says.

I really want to scream in his stupid face, *How am I? How-the-fuck-am-I? I'll tell you – I'm humiliated and I feel totally used. And more than anything else, I really liked you, and I think you knew that, and even though I think you're an absolute tosser, I can't seem to stop myself from really liking you!* But I don't, I just look down at my papers and pretend to make an important note.

"Huh," Zach says. "Not talking to me, OK, cool. Where are the hubcaps?"

I don't look up (I can't, I'm raging, I want to commit a violent offence all over him), but vaguely wave my arm in the direction of the props table, where, to anyone who wasn't a self-obsessed dick, it would be obvious the props resided.

In the corner of my vision, I see Zach nod.

"I never said we were dating. Just a bit of fun, remember? I never said boyfriends. That's what you agreed to. Fun doesn't have to be exclusive. Plus, you knew I was getting over a bad break-up. . ."

I stare down hard at my notes.

Luckily, Ruby and Sam, who have agreed to be alert to potential Zach fuckery, arrive to save me.

"Freddie! Cafeteria trays?" Ruby trills, barging in front of Zach.

"Yep!" I say brightly. "We have trays. Will you be collecting trays for each character who requires one, or just your own?"

"I'll take the lot!" Ruby says, smiling widely.

"Righto, let me get them for you!"

It's a good way to take the sting out of Zach being there. But it does nothing to stop his horrible words churning around in my mind as rehearsals start. I know he said it was "fun". I know that. But I thought "fun" was the first step towards something more. Zach makes it sound like I got everything wrong, but that was what I was feeling, so how can it be wrong? And *did* I get everything wrong?

Zach and Lottie manage to play a scene where Danny and Sandy not only don't look at one another, but look actively murderous.

"I'm just not getting any love from him," Lottie complains, when Ms Pearson stops the scene again to give a note about the lack of chemistry.

"I'm not getting any love from *her*," Zach counters.

Lottie shakes her head. "I don't know, it feels like when Zach's with the *boys* there's lots of chemistry, almost . . . a sexual tension, maybe, but like, he loses it when he has lines with me. I mean, I guess that's a choice, but I'm not sure his portrayal really works?"

The rest of the cast are holding their breath. They all know what this is about.

Zach crosses his arms. "Are you criticizing my acting?"

"You keep looking at Doody, for some reason, when you're meant to be singing to me."

"No, I don't. And even if I was, you wouldn't even notice if you were properly immersed in your character!"

Lottie shrugs. "Just seems odd that Danny would sing all about love and look at Doody."

"OK, so," Zach says, giving her a really bitchy smile, "I don't know if you've ever heard of Stanislavski, or the theatre practitioner Uta Hagen, but I am actually channelling some pretty serious *method* here, I'm using a range of legitimate techniques to really understand the nuance of Danny, which includes some significant backstory to help add depth to the character."

"What backstory's that?" Lottie says. "That Danny noshed off Doody after a party during half-term?"

Zach throws down his script. "I can't work with this!"

"*This?*" Lottie screams. "You're referring to me as 'this'? Just take the note, Zach!"

"Focus on your own notes!" Zach retorts. "Particularly the ones in 'Summer Lovin'" – I'm pretty sure you're not hitting them!"

There's a collective gasp from the entire cast and crew.

"Do you know what?" Lottie sneers. "Screw you, and screw this production! I quit!"

There's another collective gasp, and a few shouts of, "Lottie! No!" as she storms out of the drama studio, slamming the door behind her.

"Drama queen, she'll be back." Zach shrugs.

Ms Pearson sighs. "We really don't have time for this. We need all the rehearsal time we can get."

I watch Jamil lean towards Kwame. "Should have started blocking it earlier, then!" he whispers.

I don't know what surprises me more – Kwame and Jamil suddenly being friendly enough to speak, or Jamil, the class clown, transforming into a bitchy theatre kid. I have no idea what's real or normal any more.

Priya raises her hand. "Actually, Ms Pearson, I think I probably know all of Sandy's lines . . . and most, if not all, of her blocking." She produces an entirely separate script, complete with Sandy's role highlighted and notes. "I always say it does no harm to be prepared for all eventualities." My god. Priya! The sly backstabber! The theatre kids really are all out for themselves!

The rehearsal resumes, but only after I have to watch Harrison fuss over Zach, squeeze his hand (like what just happened with Lottie might have been really upsetting for him), and have what looks like a hushed, gentle conversation. It hurts how Zach is so happy to be public with Harrison when he always shooed me away, didn't want anyone to see. I ask myself what's so special about him, but, of course, it's obvious. Harrison is good-looking, athletic, fit, confident, and, if you're into it, he's got a legendary penis. I'm nothing compared to him.

God, I feel like crap.

28

The Freddie Project may have inspired me to open the door to opportunity, but unfortunately the only thing rushing in now is humiliation and despair. As if I didn't already feel bad enough after the rehearsal, Mum announces that she's booked me a ticket for the cast and crew screening of the first episode of *Cherries*. I've been to these before for her other projects. They're not like red carpet premiere events. They're much smaller affairs, no public invited; it's just everyone involved in making the show, plus all the bigwigs from MegaFlix. Everyone will be so up each other's arses it'll be intolerable. There will be lots of backslapping and everyone will tell Jasper he's a "star" and the "New Asa Butterfield" and so on, while I skulk alone in the corner because no one at the party is able to identify with someone as unsuccessful and average-looking as me, so they have nothing to say.

I arrive at BAFTA with Mum, and everything is

exactly as I'd predicted ("Sarah! It's a hit! We're thrilled!" etc., etc.), and then we all head into the screening theatre and it suddenly gets a whole lot worse.

I'm sitting next to Jasper.

If I'd been hoping to just sit and wallow in self-pity and all the injustice of my life while I angrily watch the show, I'm now going to have to at least pretend to enjoy it, clap at the end, and inevitably tell Jasper, "Well done," or something. I can't be any more of a dick to him than I've already been. It's fine being a dick if you're confident you'll never see someone again, but somehow Jasper keeps popping up, making me feel even more foolish and ridiculous than I already naturally feel around him.

I don't have to like him. We don't have to be mates. I just need to not end tonight by giving him the impression I'm a total knob.

We nod at each other when I arrive, and luckily he's sitting next to his co-star and boyfriend, Connor, so they're happily chatting anyway like well-adjusted, successful teenagers, which makes me feel even more awful, but at least means I don't need to make small talk. I pretend to be sending messages on my phone, and make various exasperated sighs as I hammer out a really important and urgent email, which in my head is connected with the props for *Grease*, but in reality doesn't exist.

Finally the lights dim and the episode starts.

Cherries centres on a group of sixteen-year-olds who

all make a pact to lose their virginity before they go to uni. As such, the first episode is clearly playing for shock value (and maximum social media coverage): opening with a blow job in a school toilet, a subplot about someone having their water bottle spiked with Viagra and getting an uncontrollable boner in a maths class, and finally, Jasper's character having a wank. This final scene is the big one, and involves Jasper's on-screen mum coming home and walking up the stairs, unbeknown to Jasper, who is feverishly whacking off with his headphones on – a rookie error, and one, I feel, that would only ever be used for dramatic purposes in TV shows. We're all watching anyway, the audience is *loving* it, anticipating that Jasper is about to be caught by his mum, and then in a completely wild (and totally gross) climax (literally), the camera assumes his mum's point of view, she walks into his room and Jasper spaffs all over the lens, giving the impression he's just come all over his own mother – aka, every teenage boy's worst nightmare.

The audience roar – grossed out, ecstatic, utterly delighted, appalled and delirious with laughter and outrage in equal measure.

In the corner of my vision, Jasper is hunched over in his seat, head in his hands. I can hear him groaning.

The camera being covered in jizz fades to the blackout for the end of episode and the credits start rolling. There's immediate applause and whoops from the crowd.

Jasper sits back up and turns to me. "Mortifying!" he mouths.

I have to smile. And nod. I'm weirdly pleased he's feeling so awkward about it. He may be a superstar in the making, he may be one of the best-looking guys I think I'll ever meet, but some things are the same whoever you are.

As the lights come back up in the screening room, MegaFlix's "VP of Scripted Drama" (an American guy called Dallas Goodwin) takes the stage, bigs everyone up in that way that sounds so much better in an American accent, and announces that MegaFlix love the show so much they're already green-lighting the second season, which is going into production immediately. Understandably, everyone goes wild, and, you know, it is great news, I'm really pleased for Mum especially, although I can't help thinking she's probably known about this for a few weeks at least and that means she *could* have afforded the invisible braces for me, not these metal monstrosities that make me look even geekier than I already am. Anyway. Yay for everyone else's success and happiness.

There's a drinks reception in the upstairs bar afterwards. Jasper and Connor are whisked off by a publicist for press interviews and photos. Connor has his hand on the small of Jasper's back, guiding him out of the screening theatre in a protective, gentle way, and I'm reminded again that some people seem to have it all so easily, while some of us get very little and what we do get is bitterly fought for. But I don't want to be *that* person. I don't want to begrudge other people's happiness and grow into a vile old man who lives alone and bursts children's footballs when they accidentally come over his fence. So I go to the party, grab a drink, have a few canapés, totally do my best to not to look (and feel) like a spare part who has no real business being there except for being someone's son, *fail*, and end up sitting in the corner, once again trying to make it look like I'm dealing with something of critical importance on my phone. It's horrible. It's awkward. And all I can imagine is everyone else looking at me pityingly, knowing damn well I'm just scrolling the Instagram feeds of people who don't even follow me.

I'm ridiculously engrossed watching some dancing teenage boy point at various words on the screen (apparently, "girls who don't cheat are born in May, July, August and September..." Who knew? And how does *he* know? And why have 150K people watched this crap already?) when I hear, "Do you fancy getting some air?"

I look up. It's Jasper. I'm surprised, because this is *his* night, and surely he has way more important people to spend time with than me. Especially when he knows it's liable to end in me calling him some variation on "prick", although I've pretty much run out of slang terms for male genitalia to throw at him now. To be fair, he does look a bit nervous.

"I hate these things," he says, reading my mind. "I need to get out for ten minutes. Seriously, I can't be this nice to people for this long." He smirks. "It's really hard work pretending to be affable."

I laugh. I like that he's not as perfect as he comes across. "Sure."

We head out of the bar area, down the plush carpeted main stairs of BAFTA and out on to bustling Piccadilly. Jasper heads right and we walk into a church courtyard which is set back a little from the street. We settle on a bench, the car horns, traffic and shouts from people on a night out fading to a background hum.

"Pretty sure you're meant to be schmoozing press," I say.

"Are you going to grass me up to your mum?"

I snort and shake my head.

"Not being funny, but you're the only person in that room who doesn't want anything from me, and since you've already been *very* upfront about your feelings towards me, multiple times, I don't feel like I need to be on best behaviour since it won't make a scrap of difference anyway."

I nod. "Not enjoying yourself?"

"Hate it. It's all fake. Have to play the game, though." He turns towards me slightly. "Again, I'm sorry about wading in to all that Zach stuff in such a cack-handed manner. I'm not always very good at . . . combining the best words with the right feelings, if you get me?"

"I get you."

"And, um . . . I was, *am*, really, still pretty cut up about Zach myself. So, you being with him—"

"Which it turns out I wasn't."

"Sure, but . . . you *seeming* to be with him, that was . . . unpleasant for me."

I smirk at "unpleasant". It's such an understatement, if he's been feeling anything like I've been.

"You're laughing at me," he says.

"Only at your choice of words."

He tuts. "I already told you about that."

There's hurt in his voice. But I sense it's not about him thinking I was laughing – it's about Zach. It's about no one taking the Zach thing seriously, about them not understanding, and that's something I totally get. "Sorry," I say. "I'm not laughing. Tell me about you and Zach. Call me a masochist, but I think I need to hear it."

Jasper swallows and roughly scratches the back of his head. "OK, so, uh-huh, if you want to know. . . I . . . liked him, yeah? *Really* liked him. Before BYT, I'd never done anything with a boy. I mean, I knew I liked boys, and I wanted to, but, well, just 'cause you want something doesn't mean it'll happen."

"I get you, and just so you know, *hard same*." I put my hand up jokingly. "Total virgin here!"

"I wasn't a virgin, I'd had sex with a girl."

"OK, amazing." I nod, chastened. "How did. . . How

was... Was it... I mean, none of this is my business, but noted. Sex with girl. Big yay ... for that."

He blinks at me. "When I saw Zach on my first day at BYT, I couldn't believe I could fancy anyone that much. So, maybe it was the summer heat, maybe it was hormones, maybe it was just the thrill of being away from home on a course, and we're all in halls of residence together, so pretty much anything goes. Anyway, Zach and I got friendly very quickly, and I guess it was mainly him pushing it, but I was so, *so* happy to go along with it..."

I nod, because this is all sounding horribly familiar.

"Now, maybe it should have set alarm bells ringing when he asked if it was OK that we keep things casual, but it sounded so plausible—"

"He was nervous about getting too serious, too soon?"

"Huh. *Yeah.* You too?"

I nod. "Hard for him to ..."

"Take that leap!" we both chorus.

"The fucker." I shake my head.

"OK, so, hats off to him, he's got the lines, and we bought them. I guess, the thing is, I don't know about your school, Freddie, but he's kind of right, because at mine, two boys actually dating and being obviously affectionate with one another in public and very much being 'boyfriends' would cause a lot of chatter, and might change the dynamics of some of the friendships, and sure, that does make things harder, and it's tough enough when you don't even really know yourself who you are, without everyone else analysing your every move. I mean, I get the 'keeping it fun' thing to an extent." His leg is bouncing. "Did you think you were in love with him?"

I take an unsteady breath and nod.

Jasper nods too. "I was ... so convinced everything was building up to a long-term relationship, because I guess I'm an idiot like that, and then I walk in on him ... with another boy *in the costume store*, and, well... I probably don't need to spell out what they were doing."

"Ohhh," I sigh. "Also, that is pretty much exactly my experience."

He nods. "Well, it made me feel like absolute shit. Like, on some level he must have been laughing at me by going behind my back, knowing I would never do that to him. Stupid, naive, pathetically romantic when, hey, we're sixteen, right? So who wants romance at our age?" He meets my eyes.

"*I* want romance," I tell him, my voice quiet, unable to hide the sadness.

He raises his eyebrows. "Yeah?"

"Yeah. And that's exactly what I thought was happening with Zach too, because, I don't know, maybe I'm putting too much pressure on things being this mirror image of all the gay coming-of-age films I started secretly downloading about a year before I came out to Mum..."

Jasper chuckles an "I know what you mean" sort of

chuckle.

"I know I should know that outside of Hollywood gloss, 'perfect' doesn't exist," I continue. "And yet a big part of me still wants to stand on a busy street on Christmas Eve, snow gently falling, kissing a boy, with carol singers and a very big Christmas tree in the background, and he will say, 'All I want for Christmas . . . is you!', and I will smile, and as we kiss again, the camera tilts up into the falling snow as we fade to the end credits." I sigh. "Man, have we been conditioned to want this crap." I catch myself smiling wistfully, and wonder why the hell I'm pouring my heart out to a guy I literally couldn't stand just hours ago. Maybe it's just easier. There's nothing to lose because I've already shown him what a numpty I am, so I can't make it much worse.

Jasper laughs. "Fred, *I'm* part of the problem. I'm making telly that's not remotely like any sort of real life I've ever experienced. I'm complicit in this." He scuffs his boots on the ground a bit, chewing his lip. "What did you think of the show? Honestly."

"Yeah, it was totally unrealistic."

He nods.

"But everyone will lap it up."

"What did you think of me?" he asks.

I flick my eyes to him. "Good."

"Uh-huh."

I grin. "*Great* wanking."

"Ah!" He smiles. "Sure. Thank you. I . . . rehearsed a lot."

We both laugh.

"I went very method on that," he adds.

We sit in silence for a bit, just watching the people and buses go by on the street beyond the railings.

"Freddie? At that press event, I just need to say, when I asked you if you liked vinyl? I still beat myself up about that question, pretty much every night when I'm trying to get to sleep. Do you ever do that? Run through all the stupid shit you've ever said, so you end up keeping yourself awake with all the cringe?"

"Oh, god, *yes*. It's why I'm permanently knackered!"

"OK, good. So, just to confirm, I don't like vinyl. I'm not into vinyl. I don't do wheatgrass shots either, and my trousers always cover my ankles. *I'm not that person.*"

I laugh. "Noted and forgiven."

"I should probably get back," he says.

"Sure. I might stay here for a bit longer."

Jasper nods, stands up, and I think he's about to walk back when he turns to me again. "Thanks for the chat."

"Yeah, it was good."

He nods, still looking at me. "I hope you get over Zach. I hope it's not too painful at school. In my case, at least BYT ended and I never had to see him again."

"Until I turned up with him on set."

"Yeah. That was a brilliant day for me."

"Sorry."

Jasper smiles. "Be strong. I know he seems it, and I know *he* believes it, but he's not all that. And he's not the one."

"No?"

"If he's never going to give you clichéd lines in the snow, then he's not the one. You hold out for your dream romcom ending, Freddie."

I laugh. "Thanks, Jasper."

He nods and walks off towards the street.

"Hey? Jasper!" I shout.

He turns back.

"I'm glad this didn't end with me calling you a prick again!"

He gives me a thumbs up. "Me too!" He smirks. "You cock!"

"Wanker!"

We both laugh.

And he disappears into the crowd.

29

Zach and Harrison are busy spaffing their new-found love everywhere. At school the next day, they engage in a litany of sins, including but not limited to: holding hands in assembly, sharing a vending machine cup of hot chocolate, and literally recreating that scene from *Lady and the Tramp* where they slurp on the same piece of spaghetti, albeit for the sake of a jokey Instagram video, but still!

I, meanwhile, am trying to move on. You know what? It sucks that he would never do this with me, that I was never good enough for him, but, after talking to Jasper, I've got some perspective. Zach didn't think Jasper wasn't good enough for him either, which is mad, because if we're talking levels, let's be honest: Zach doesn't quite reach Jasper's hotness level. Jasper's the TV star. And it's not personal, but I just think Zach is self-obsessed and selfish and out for what he can get from other people.

It's our first run-through of Act One in the school

theatre this afternoon (we get off lessons to do it, which is more an indicator of how bad the school thinks the show is looking, rather than a sign of their commitment to the arts), and maybe it's the excitement of the move and the adrenaline from how close the show is now, but everyone is at loggerheads.

"I only did this show because of you!" Calvin is telling Ruby as I pass them backstage.

"Well, that's a lie! You did it for your Uni applications!" Ruby replies, walking away.

As I walk into the wings, Priya hurries past me, sobbing. Moments later, I see why: Lottie Stefani is back. And she is more powerful than ever. She stands in the wings, wrapped in some sort of fur-effect shawl, and I swear to god, if she could be languidly smoking a cigarette in a holder, she would be doing it.

"That fucking bitch!" Lottie hisses, to Kwame and Alice, who are both simpering around her like desperate PAs. "She'd rip the clothes off my still-warm dead body if she could!"

"She was straight in there, babe," Kwame says. "Had all the blocking down and everything."

"She'd push me down the fucking stairs if she thought she'd get to play Sandy!" Lottie replies. "Well, tough shit! The bitch is back!"

Kwame and Alice applaud.

"This show needs you, hun!" Kwame tells her.

"It needs you!" Alice repeats.

Lottie does a little flick of her head, shaking her hair around her shoulders. "I know."

I stifle a smile. Somewhere along the line, I've moved from rolling my eyes at all the theatre kid drama to absolutely loving it. It's like being trapped in an episode of *Riverdale*, and I cannot wait for the next gruesome, twisty, completely random instalment – just what I need to keep my mind from straying to Zach and Harrison.

"Ah, Freddie," a harassed-looking Ms Pearson says, walking into the wings. "I was looking for you. We need the hubcaps."

"OK, they're in the props store."

"It's fine, Zach said they were; he's gone to get them."

"Oh, how kind of him." I smile sweetly at Ms Pearson. "Ah! Lottie! You're back!" she says.

That sly little weasel! Gone to get them, has he? I know exactly what he's doing down there, and I know exactly who with. The props store is my domain. Not his. The rage boils over, and I stomp down there and fling the door open.

"Get out!" I tell Harrison as he and Zach spring apart from their horny, frantic groping. "Not you!" I say, pushing Zach back. I turn to Harrison. "This is *my* props store."

Harrison looks at me like I've totally lost the plot which, to be fair, I probably have. "Actually, Harrison," I say, "question for you!"

"Don't answer!" Zach says.

I ignore him and smile at Harrison. "When did you know about me and Zach? Oh, I know we were just some 'casual fun', like, no big deal, or anything, I mean, you knew me and him used to come down here quite a bit, right? Did you know that?"

"Ignore him," Zach repeats.

"No." Harrison shrugs. "But he explained it all after the party."

I nod, tight-lipped. "And you're OK with that?"

Harrison flicks his eyes to Zach then back to me. "So, like, I wasn't ready to come out yet, and Zach was left feeling insincere?"

"*Insecure*," Zach corrects him.

"*In-secure*. And he needed an outlet, right?" Harrison nods, sagely. "We all have emotional and physical needs."

"Do you even know what that means, Harrison?" I ask, unimpressed at him parroting excuses that Zach has blatantly fed him.

Harrison flicks his eyes to Zach again, then back to me. "No comment? Also, no one is perfect, Freddie. *We all make mistakes.* Forgive me. I mean, *him.* Forgive him."

I almost choke with indignation. Now I'm a 'mistake'? *Wow.* "Cool, thanks," I say. "Get out."

"Go on, it's fine," Zach tells Harrison, cocking his head towards the door.

This annoys me even more. They way they're looking out for each other, like I might be dangerous or something.

Everything about their smug little relationship sickens me.

Harrison leaves, shuts the door behind him, and then it's me and Zach, facing off.

"Ms Pearson couldn't find you, so she asked me to get the hubcaps," Zach says. "Not really the job of the cast, but—"

"Oh, shut up!" I snap at him.

To be fair, he does. And he looks really surprised that I've just spoken to him like that.

Well, now that I've got his attention. . .

"You know, I have resigned myself to having to watch you and Harrison be all loved-up around school, because I know you're essentially selfish and don't give a rat's arse about my feelings, as long as you're getting what you want. But this is *my* props store for the duration of this production, and you will not use it as a shag pad for your latest squeeze. Capeesh?"

I wish I hadn't used "capeesh" – it makes me sound like some Italian New York mobster. Zach opens his mouth to speak, but I don't let him.

"'Capeesh' was rhetorical!" I tell him, saving face somewhat. "Because I'm not asking if you understand, I don't care if you understand, I don't give a damn about anything to do with you any more. And I know this won't bother you in the slightest, but I want you to know: I really liked you, Zach. I know the official line was 'fun', but to me, it was more than that. You see, this was the first 'fun' I'd ever had. And I really liked it. And I really liked you. But you were sly, and you were sneaky, and you did what made you feel good, and you trampled all over what I might be feeling, and you could at least have been honest with me." I sigh. "Take the hubcaps and get out."

He stares at me for five solid seconds, and I cannot work out if it's pain or rage in his eyes. Then he grabs the hubcaps off the shelf and heads for the door.

My breathing gets jagged again. Really? Still no apology?

That's why I say it. Because I *know* it'll get to him, even if nothing else I've said has.

"Jasper was right about you."

He freezes at the door.

"You're really not all that. And you're definitely not 'the one'."

Despite my boiling rage, the words don't sound like I believe them. I *want* to believe it. I want it to be true. I just know that it isn't, quite.

Zach just stands there, staring at the door, breathing heavily. "You've been speaking to Jasper?"

"Yeah, I've been speaking to Jasper."

He hesitates, then walks out.

And I don't know how he does it, but somehow, I'm left feeling guilty.

30

"Oh my god, *Mum?*" I call, walking in through the front door, and spotting her case in the hall. "Are you actually home?"

"In the kitchen!" she shouts back. "And *funny.*"

I dump my rucksack in the hallway and stroll through towards the kitchen at the back of the house. "Yeah, I'm fine, don't worry," I say. "Left all alone, I've been on the hunt for a replacement guardian figure who can look after a lonely gay teen boy like me – let's just say, if you scroll through my phone and find 'Daddy' in the contacts, it's no one you've met!" I stop dead as I enter the kitchen.

"Hey," Jasper says, as if sitting at my kitchen table having a cup of tea with my mum is completely normal.

"That's nice, dear." Mum smiles. "No bad thing having an older male figure in your life, especially when your real father is so *unrelentingly useless.*"

I raise an eyebrow at Jasper, who I'm actually

quite pleased to see again. "See? No parental concern whatsoever!" I pause. "Hey."

Jasper laughs.

"I'm always concerned for you, Freddie," Mum says. "I think about you all the time. Here's a Twix to prove it." She indicates the chocolate bar on the table.

"Huh, I guess you do," I say, pulling up a chair and sitting down with them.

"Jasper and I were chatting through storyline ideas for season two."

"My character's finally getting a romance plot," Jasper explains.

"Cool," I nod, munching the Twix. "Does that mean you get a shagging scene?" I smirk at him.

"Don't give your mum ideas!" he says. "That closing scene of the first episode is bad enough – I'm never going to live it down."

"So, how's *Grease* going?" Mum asks me.

Jasper's eyes light up. "You're doing *Grease*? You didn't say!"

"Did I not say?" I chirp.

"You did not say."

"Funny that." I polish off the Twix. "Total mess. Even leaving aside the fact nobody really knows their lines, the dance routines aren't finished, the tension between Lottie (that's Harrison's ex, by the way), Zach and Harrison is *unbearable*. I mean, this is a production of *Grease* where

Sandy and Danny actively hate one another, so much so that she frequently 'accidentally' stamps on his feet and slaps his face with 'overenthusiastic' dance movements. And Danny and Doody are so bitchy to Sandy, like, constantly muttering snide little remarks during scenes."

"Sounds . . . unmissable," Jasper says.

I shrug. "Come if you want? I get a couple of comp tickets."

"That's a terrible idea," Jasper says, without missing a beat.

"Yes. You're right. Of course it is. It's terrible."

"Blatantly *awful*." Jasper laughs.

"I'm going to go and flail myself in punishment for such an insane suggestion."

"No need, since Jasper has a favour to ask," Mum says.

My eyes widen. A favour? From me? What could I possibly do for him?

"I'll leave you boys to it," Mum continues. "I'll be in my office, Fred. If the landline rings, I'm not here."

"Gotcha." I wait until Mum's left, then turn to Jasper, a slight nervousness in my stomach about what this could be, and why he thinks I, an awkward, serial messer-up of things, would be the obvious candidate to ask. "So, um . . . what is it?"

"I've got a self-tape I have to do for this American thing," he says.

"American 'thing'?"

"Just a stupid American movie."

I nearly choke. "Just a movie? Oh, small time!"

"Honestly, it's. . ."

"Who's making it?"

He swallows. "Warner Bros."

"Warner Bros!" I hoot. "Freakin' Warner Bros! Oh, yeah, it's nothing."

He scowls slightly at me.

"Anyway," I say. "Very nice, go on."

"I stayed at Connor's last night and I tried to do it with him, but. . ." He hesitates. "Well, I kind of feel I want to do it again, but it would be good if Connor didn't know that."

"Um . . . OK, I'm no actor. I'm not acting in *Grease*, I'm doing props. And even if I was in it, it's a school production, not Warner Bros! I can't act."

"Yeah, no, that's actually good for this. See," he sighs, "this will sound arrogant, but the self-tape is about me, *my* performance. You wouldn't even be in the shot, it's just your voice. Connor was good, but it was pulling focus from what I was doing, he was full-on going for it. I need someone a bit more . . . bland. No offence."

"Wow," I say. "*Bland*? I'm flattered."

"I didn't mean it badly. More like . . . reserved."

I roll my eyes at him. "It's fine, I've called you enough names, I think I can take 'bland'."

He smiles.

"OK, if you think I won't mess up your big chance.

Don't hate me when I'm crap, though, and the Americans are all, 'We would have cast you but we just can't get over the shitness of the guy you shot this with, so it's a no from us.'"

Jasper assures me I won't be shit (he hasn't seen me act, so this'll be priceless), and sets about unpacking an iPhone tripod from his rucksack, which I notice also contains a change of clothes and a washbag from his night with Connor. Wish I could have a nice romantic night with a boyfriend. It's good that Jasper's moved on. I'm hoping I get to that point too, ideally before middle age. A good start would probably be to stop feeling bad about upsetting Zach in the props store. He deserved it, didn't he?

"I told Zach what I thought of him," I say casually, as Jasper is distracted trying to clip his phone to the attachment on the tripod.

He looks up and smiles. "Yeah?"

"Uh-huh." I nod. "Told him he was selfish, among various other things."

"Good," Jasper says, going back to fiddling around with the tripod legs.

"How did you manage to get over him?"

His eyes meet mine.

I continue, "It's just . . . he still has this weird hold over me. I totally want to move on, forget about him, but even just telling him what a dick he was made me feel bad and like I should maybe hug it out with him instead. So how did you manage it?"

"I'm not sure I really have."

"Oh."

Jasper studies my face for a moment, then flicks his eyes back to the tripod.

"Let's do this," he says flatly.

"OK, cool."

I should have kept my mouth shut.

Jasper hands me the scene, printed out on two sides of A4, which I read through while he positions himself in front of a blank piece of wall and checks the camera angle. The movie is a romcom, where Jasper's character is the henpecked son of the UK prime minister, and, tired of all the demands of being in the public eye, and having to be the "perfect" son because of who his father is, he books on to an American summer camp, under an assumed identity, and ends up having the time of his life, helped by the fact he falls in love with an American boy who has no idea who he really is – something which, as Ruby might put it, will probably cause "conflict in Act Three".

In the scene for his self-tape, Jasper has to break the news to his PM father that he's booked to go on the summer camp, without asking permission first. Jasper hits record and we start to perform, until Jasper stops.

"OK, so. . ." he begins.

"I told you I was bad. Shall I fetch my mum and you could do it with her?"

"Fred—"

"Or we could try to reanimate a corpse from the graveyard? I think that might work better for you."

Jasper laughs. "You're performing the lines."

"Yeah, well, of course I am, it's a . . . performance?"

"OK, sure, yes, it is, but you're delivering them all way too big. I mean, that might be fine for stage, but for screen, you need to keep it really natural. Try your first line again."

"ARCHIE, I'M BUSY!"

"Too big."

"Archie, I'M BUSY!"

"Still too big."

"Archie, I am *busy*!"

"Weird emphasis."

"Archie, I'm busy!"

"Bring it down more."

"Archie! I'm . . . *eek! Eek!* Busy!" I squeak, doing a comedy mouse voice.

"Stop titting about."

"Archie, I'm busy."

"There you go," Jasper says.

I blink at him. "That was just my normal voice though."

"That's what we need."

"But I wasn't doing anything, I was just—"

"Being you, I know."

"That's not acting."

"That *is* acting. You're just being the role, you're not

forcing it, you're not playing at being someone else, it's real, natural. That was good."

I chew my lip. "So, you want me to just say the lines, like as if I'm just chatting to you now?"

He nods.

"But I should project for the camera, right?"

"No."

"Don't I sound boring, though?"

"OK, so again, this isn't about you."

I shake my head in mock outrage. "The arrogance."

"I know, but I'm an actor, I'm the bloody pinnacle of arrogance."

I do a big, theatrical sigh. I'm enjoying winding him up. I think it's because he's so successful and handsome, it's fun to tease him a bit. "It's fine, I get it."

He chuckles. "I'll try to make it up to you."

My eyes widen.

"Ready to go again?"

I nod. "Aaaand ACTION!" I grin.

He frowns. "Please don't."

I take a deep breath and compose myself.

"OK," he says, hitting record.

We do five takes in total, after which Jasper watches them all back, studying his phone screen intently, his face giving nothing away, until he eventually says, "Yep, that'll do." He slides his phone into his pocket. "Thank you, Freddie."

"No worries." I can't *believe* it's satisfactory, but, hey, turns out I've got no idea about much, so maybe it is.

"And if you happen to see Connor again, can we keep this quiet? It'll hurt his feelings if he knows I didn't use the takes he did with me."

I mime zipping my mouth shut, wishing I had a boyfriend who cared about *my* feelings like that. "How long have you two been together?"

"We're not."

"You're not?"

"I think . . . sorry, this is going to sound arrogant again—"

"I mean, I'm used to your appalling arrogance now, so. . ."

"Thank you, yes, well, I think Connor might possibly like to . . . be my . . . you know, but I'm so not in a place to . . . after Zach and everything. . . I'm. . ." He trails off and looks down at his trainers.

Scared about it happening again, having his heart broken by another boy? Zach's a bloody juggernaut, and we're the wreckage.

"Anyway, we're just friends, me and Connor." His eyes meet mine, and I get the sense he wants to say something, but he changes his mind and opts for something else. "Thanks for helping me out with the self-tape."

"I hope I haven't sabotaged your chances."

287

"You were good. Genuinely." He gives me a little smile, and I give him a little one back.

"All done, boys?" Mum says, appearing in the doorway.

I break Jasper's gaze and turn to her. "Yep."

"I ordered burgers from Roti Brothers in Crystal Palace – stay for dinner, Jasper, then we'll get you a car home, OK?"

"Great, thanks," he says, as she disappears towards the kitchen.

Half an hour later and we're sitting around the table, sinking our teeth into the most succulent cheeseburgers I've ever tasted. Jasper sheepishly asks if we can get an Instagram pic, since he's been strong-armed into having an account and desperately needs some content. I don't know whether it's the burger, or whether it's Jasper, but in the photo I'm grinning like an absolute loon, and I realize, for the first time in a long time, I'm having fun. I haven't once thought about how I'm a total mess and how I need to be saying yes to opportunities in order to salvage something from the wreckage of my life. Maybe it's because there are no stakes with Jasper. We both hated each other, so things can never get worse than that. And there's zero chance we'll ever end up together, since he's got model good looks and is about to become a huge, international movie star, and I've got a very forgettable face, wear a brace, and can't even get a bit part in the school show. But I don't feel remotely bad about that. It's actually very liberating. I can just be me.

31

Jasper messages me a few days later at the end of school:

> JASPER: Hey. My agent LOVED the self-tape,
> so I owe you one. How about food on the South
> Bank next week?

I'm well up for that. It sounds positively adult – in marked contrast to what is going on at after-school *Grease* rehearsals today. The cast were running the big hand jive routine, spacing it out now we're on the actual stage, and Lottie fell to the floor screaming, "My foot! My foot!" Everything stopped. Lottie took her jazz shoes off, and several small pebbles fell out. Cue accusations about how the stones got in her shoe, *who* would have put them there and *why*. For a moment, I was tempted to point out that sometimes stones do get into shoes, it's just a thing, but of course these are theatre kids, so everyone goes for maximum drama. We're all just waiting for an actual fatal "accident" really – some ropes get cut, a light crashes down on someone's head, or some scenery decapitates someone after being tampered with. Anyway, after I tell Jasper that sounds like a plan, and since he then asks me how the show is going, I take great pleasure in filling him in, in real time:

ME: Prime suspects in the shoe crime: Priya, Zach, Harrison. But what is the MOTIVE? Lottie says Priya is "an ambitious bitch who wouldn't think twice about causing temporary, or even permanent, disablement", while Zach hates Lottie / is intimidated by her talent (thus wants her DEAD, I kid you not!) and Harrison could be doing the bidding of either as he's (and I quote) "as easily manipulated as a three-year-old child".

JASPER: I am strangely invested in the outcome of this. Motive could be anyone's. Who had OPPORTUNITY?

ME: LOL, apparently not Zach or Harrison, as Harrison has just told everyone he was giving Zach a hand job in the ditch on top field at the relevant time. 😂

JASPER: Classy.

I laugh out loud. I'm loving the fact Jasper and I are united in disdain at what Zach and Harrison are getting up to. It feels like payback somehow, even if they know nothing of it, and I certainly feel better for having someone to share it with, someone who's been there and got the T-shirt, as it were.

"Glad you're having fun." Ruby grimaces as she pushes down one of the seats and flops next to me in the auditorium.

"Just updating Jasper on the day's events."

"So you two have found some common ground at last."

"Nothing more unifying than a common enemy!" I grin.

Ruby waves a wedge of typed A4 under my nose. "Then join me in lamenting this!" she says. "A ten-page essay from –" I follow her gaze to down stage left, where Calvin is standing, staring at her like a lost puppy "– *you know who*, detailing why I should give him another chance and how he definitely doesn't have feelings for Lottie. Ten pages! Although I can't seem to find an actual apology in it anywhere. Just a lot of guff about 'second chances' and, the old classic, 'everyone makes mistakes'." She laughs, contemptuously. "I mean, there's mistakes and then there's dry-humping someone on the floor while hungrily shoving your tongue in their mouth and muttering, 'I want you, baby!' mistakes."

"You sound so over him. Are you?"

Ruby shrugs. "Sure."

"But you really liked him."

"I did. But I like myself more, and he made me feel like crap, and I'm not prepared to be with someone who could make me feel that way. He did it once – what if he does it again? Doesn't matter how many grand-gesture apologies he makes, the 'what ifs' will always be there. Real life isn't a romcom where stupid boys suddenly mend their ways."

"I wish. You sound so definite, and strong, about it all, and I *want* to be like that, but every time I see Zach I just start to crumble." I lower my voice a bit. "Do you think Zach could be . . . magic?"

Ruby screws her face up. "*What?*"

"Like one of those mythical sirens, but a gay boy version, seemingly sweet and enchanting, but actually luring helpless lads to destruction and ruin?"

"No," Ruby says. "I just think he's a knob and you. . ." She looks at me sadly. "You feel like that's all you deserve; that you should be grateful for that somehow, when actually, you deserve the world, Freddie."

"Huh." I smile at her. 'Thanks, Rubes."

"Ask yourself this, Fred – *is Zach really what you want?*"

"I mean. . ."

"I know he's ridiculously good-looking. And I know he's a charmer. But you never seemed *relaxed* with him. Did you even talk about anything?"

"Of course we talked!"

"About anything important?"

I chew my lip.

"Everyone!" Ms Pearson shouts. "This is getting out of hand! I don't want to hear any more accusations. This is not how a professional production works!"

I turn to Ruby. "It literally is, though? The stories I could tell you from Mum's TV shows!"

Ruby chuckles.

"I want you all to take five, form a 'love circle' and reconnect with one another. There's no 'I' in 'team'!"

I mutter, "But there is in 'bunch of pricks'."

"I'm going to get some chamomile tea," Ms Pearson says, heading towards one of the exits.

I've never seen a "love circle" before, but it seems to involve the cast putting their arms across one another's shoulders and forming a huddle, while muttering various affirmations, like "Respect!" and "Trust!" and other words that simply don't apply to at least half the principal actors.

"Not taking part, Rubes?"

"Am I bollocks."

Probably also sensing that the exercise isn't for him, I see Zach picking his way through the auditorium. He seems to be making a beeline for me. "Oh *god*," I say.

"Want me to stay?" Ruby asks.

"Yep."

Ruby crosses her arms and observes Zach's approach

with such contempt it could curdle milk.

"Nice pic of you with my ex on Instagram," Zach says when he arrives. "Very cosy. Not at all hurtful."

"Oh, *please*," I say.

I see Ruby shaking her head and looking disapproving in the corner of my eye.

"Guess he's told you his version of events?"

"If by 'his version' you mean 'the truth', then, yes, he has."

Ruby nods, still not taking her eyes of him.

"One person's truth is another person's lie, though, innit?" Zach shrugs.

I stare at him. "Not in this case. And that doesn't make sense anyway. Truth is real. It's just hard to find it sometimes."

Zach crosses his arms "OK, I can see you've made up your mind. I'm the villain here, of course I am."

"Are you denying Jasper walked in on you with another boy at BYT?"

Ruby tuts and shakes her head again.

Zach stares at me, hard. "Well, you know everything, don't you? Or you think you do."

I raise my eyebrows.

"Anyway," he sighs. "I've been thinking about what you said to me in the props store, and I came to apologize. I thought I was clear about what I wanted, and I thought you understood that, but I get that you didn't, so I understand that my actions were hurtful. OK? I just wanted you to know that I'm sorry."

Huh. I glance at Zach, his eyes guarded but hopeful. "OK," I say.

"*Not* OK!" Ruby chimes in.

"This is between me and Freddie, so if he says it's OK, then it's OK, OK?" Zach snaps at her.

"Well, maybe it's *not* OK, on reflection," I add. I shouldn't be such a pushover. I don't want Zach. Even if he is now apologizing and has possibly grown as a person and people sometimes can be forgiven because... No, *shut up, Freddie! However much you like him, you like yourself more!*

"OK, well, whatever, change your mind, that's your prerogative." Zach glares at me, then digs his hands in his pockets. "Oh," he says, pulling one hand out, now holding a fun-sized Bounty bar. "Peace offering." He hands me the chocolate.

"Don't accept it," Ruby hisses.

I look at the Bounty bar.

"This is literally Eve and the apple all over again!" she continues. "Plus, it's a Bounty bar – the shittiest of all the fun-sized chocolates in the Celebrations tub. At least hold out for a Galaxy Caramel."

"Malteser, surely?" I suggest.

Zach tosses the Bounty to me and I instinctively catch it.

"Mates?" he says.

"Um..."

"Gotta say, Fred," he continues. "The way you spoke to me in the props store..." He blows out a breath and shakes his head. "You were impressive!"

"Was I?"

Ruby makes a squeaking sound in response, so I clear my throat and try again. "I mean, yeah, sure I was."

"You told it like it was. I have a lot of admiration for that."

"Good!" I say, really bloody pleased that finally he seems to have some respect for me.

"Too many people don't say what they mean and how they feel, and it doesn't get you anywhere. Like this lot." He gestures over his shoulder with his thumb, towards the "love circle" on stage. "If everyone just admitted why they hate each other – you know, the bitterness at the fact Lottie always gets a lead role because her dad paid for the theatre – then we could thrash it out and get on with it."

"Sure." I nod.

Zach smiles. "Didn't say in the props store, by the way, guess it was a bit too stressful, but nice braces!"

I instinctively clamp my mouth shut.

"I mean it," Zach says. He lowers his voice. "I kind of have a 'thing' for boys wearing braces."

He grins at Ruby, who scowls at him. "Loads of boys on Insta show off their braces. Maybe you should try it, Fred?" He laughs. "Gis a smile!"

"No, Zach! Just go, OK?"

"Mmmm," Zach replies, staring at my mouth.

"Oh my god," I mutter, covering my entire lower face with my hands.

A prickle of annoyance runs through me. I'm glad he's apologized; at least that means everything wasn't just in my head and I'm not actually delusional, but no way are we just switching back to chirpy flirting like that's in any way fine. It's hard, because I'm really paranoid about the braces (when the orthodontist asked if I had any questions, I wasn't sure I could really ask, "Will boys like me?" "Can I kiss boys still?" and "In the unlikely event it happens, is it fully safe to engage in intimate activities that are reminiscent of eating a banana?"), so it's nice to receive a compliment from Zach, but also, I do not want Zach to be thinking or saying that stuff about me because I'm still angry with him and he's a sly snake, and yet . . . and yet, there is some small part of me that just cannot be fully livid with him because maybe the whole thing was just a breakdown in communication about our differing expectations and for some messed-up reason I do find his slight cheekiness . . . not attractive, as such, but certainly not unattractive. Argh! I'm so weak! I deserve everything I get!

"Hi."

I look behind Zach's shoulder, and Harrison has arrived, somewhat stony-faced.

"Hi, Ruby. Hi, *Freddie*," he says. He glances at Zach. "What's happening?"

"Nothing's happening," Zach replies, possibly with a hint of irritation in his voice. "We're all cool, aren't we?"

I shrug.

Harrison glances at the fun-sized Bounty in my hands. "Where did you get that?"

"Zach gave it to me," I say.

Harrison nods. "Uh-huh." He turns to Zach again. "Can we talk?" And he heads back towards the stage.

"Better go and see what the wife wants!" Zach grins. "Good chat. Laters." He follows after Harrison, while Ruby dry heaves at his use of "the wife" and I'm left in a state of emotional confusion, trying to piece together if something is going on or not, watching as Zach and Harrison appear to have a fraught (but hushed) "debate" at the edge of the stage, which involves Harrison doing way more gesticulating than I ever saw him do as a straight boy, and culminates with Zach holding Harrison's shoulders and giving him a quick kiss on the end of his nose, which doesn't seem to placate Harrison much.

"All is not well in paradise," Ruby murmurs.

"Mmmm'kay!" Ms Pearson shouts, striding back in with a mug. "Let's go, Rydell High! Are you all feeling the love?! I said, ARE YOU ALL FEELING THE LOVE?!"

The cast give a semi-enthusiastic cheer, while I accidentally lock eyes with Zach, and he smiles and winks at me.

32

And then events come to light the next day, and I feel completely stupid for even entertaining a flicker of hope about Zach. I message Jasper to fill him in, because making it into a big, exciting, salacious scandal (which is what this is to everyone else) is the only way I can deal with it:

ME: Get ready for a major plot twist, Jasp!

JASPER: Here for it, Fred!

ME: Determined to catch the stone-in-shoe culprit, Lottie planted two Wi-Fi cams backstage after rehearsals.

JASPER: WTF?! Who has Wi-Fi cams? Why is this girl living in a CW teen show?!

ME: Linked them up via the theatre Wi-Fi and everything, footage uploads to cloud, blah blah. This is where it gets good.

JASPER: I'm excited!

ME: Footage doesn't capture the culprit.

JASPER: Oh.

ME: Footage DOES capture Zach kissing KWAME! WAAAAAAA!

JASPER: WAAAAAAAA!

ME: Harrison and Zach have split up. Harrison has quit Grease too. It's absolute CHAOS over here.

It's absolute chaos in my head too. I came so close to forgiving Zach yesterday. When he winked at me, the butterflies were right back in my stomach. I should have realized he's never going to change. I feel like the victim of a con who's just been scammed again. Too trusting. Ever hopeful.

JASPER: Still OK for South Bank later?

ME: Ohhhhh, yeeeeeeesssss!

JASPER: Cool. Let's make a promise though?

ME: ?

JASPER: No mention of Zach. Zach-free zone.

It's almost like Jasper knows how I'm really feeling about all this, despite the sensationalized tone of my previous texts. He knows it's eating me up. I smile and message him back:

ME: Who's Zach?

33

The street food market round the back of the Royal Festival Hall is buzzing. The whole courtyard is lit up with festoon lights, with food trucks and stalls under gazebos offering everything from beautifully fragrant curries and succulent-looking jerk chicken, to crepes and, my two weak spots, all manner of things with cheese, and *fresh doughnuts*. Jasper and I have a good look around, and I'm like a kid in a sweet shop, because *everything* looks great and smells so tasty, but there's Korean food, and Persian food, artisan hot dogs and tacos with every type of filling you could want, so how can you choose?

"Help," I mutter to him.

He laughs. "Is there anything you particularly love, food-wise?"

"I just love food really."

He laughs again. "But absolute favourites?"

"I mean, I love cheese."

"I was hoping you'd say that." He smiles. "Come with me."

We weave through the throngs of happy people, eventually reaching a food truck which serves something called raclette.

"I don't want to presume, but I think you'll like this," Jasper says.

My eyes widen as I see the puddles of oozing, melted cheese that are being dished out over the counter.

"My favourite is the maple bacon one," Jasper continues. "So it's garlic fried potatoes, cornichons, pickled red onion and maple bacon, topped with the melted raclette cheese, and—"

"Oh, yes." I nod. "That sounds like the one!"

Five minutes later and we each have a cardboard tray filled with goodies and topped with molten cheese, which we eat with little wooden forks as we weave our way back through the crowds, totally unable to concentrate on heading in any actual direction because we're both too focused on this cheese dream in front of us.

"Good, right?" Jasper says.

"Oh my god, Jasper. *Oh my god.*"

We meander along the side of the Festival Hall, then down some steps which lead to the riverside footpath. The restaurants and bars are packed, there are people hurrying along grasping tickets for the National Theatre and others just getting gently pissed with their mates, to the soundtrack of the buskers on the Golden Jubilee Bridge, or the guy playing bluesy jazz on his saxophone down by the BFI. I sometimes hate this city – when you see the inequality, and the poverty, and when you just want to shut yourself off from the world, that's when I hate it. But when it's like this, when I feel part of something bigger than me, when it's full of fun and energy and hope and love, like it is tonight, then I bloody adore London and I'm proud to call it home.

A group of teenagers with matching caps and rucksacks get called away by their teacher, vacating a bench in the process, which Jasper and I are able to nab just in time.

"So, how's the show?" Jasper asks at the exact same moment I say, "So, how's the show?"

We both laugh. "You first," Jasper says.

"Well, *Grease* is a total mess. Not the props, I should add, they're actually. . ." I kiss my fingers like a chef, making Jasper giggle. "But the cast? Jeez. When they're actually doing the routines, they're starting to look good, like, you can see it's going to look amazing under the lights and everything, but offstage? They cannot stand each other! It's a war zone, Jasper! And yet—"

"Still somehow exciting?"

I shrug. "Yeah, what's that about?"

"That's the magic of theatre!" Jasper smiles.

"I guess, maybe . . . it's weird, because I am *so* not that person, but I sit at the back watching everyone do their thing, and sometimes I just want. . . Ahh, well, it's stupid."

Jasper raises his eyebrows. "To be on the stage?"

"It looks like so much fun, that's all." I busy myself balancing a very large scoop of potato, bacon and cheese on my fork, being careful it reaches my mouth with zero incident en route. I can't believe I've just said this to him; I've never said that to anyone. Not Ruby, not Sam, definitely not Mum. It's not that I'm embarrassed, or that Ruby and Sam wouldn't understand, it's that . . . it's all connected to stuff I haven't ever talked about, and I'm not sure how, or if I even can, with *anyone*. "Um, so how are things with you?"

He doesn't reply, so I glance at him, mid-chew, and he's just looking at me. "If it's fun, why don't you pursue that?"

"It's not for me."

"Who says?"

"That is the general consensus."

"Whose consensus?"

"Just . . . *people*." I carry on eating, then look at him again when I can't stand the silence. He's looking back at me, a slightly amused look on his face. I sigh. "Do you really want to hear this?"

"Yeah," he says. "Yeah, I do. If you want to tell me."

"I did this show at primary school – mad, it was, *Les Mis*, we had this teacher who was way too optimistic about our abilities, but ... it was pretty bad. *I* was pretty bad. Actually, I was *really* bad."

"Who says?"

"Huh?"

"Who says you were so bad? That's a pretty harsh assessment to pass on, what, a ten-year-old?"

I nod. "Yeah, well, she tells it like it is."

"Who?" He frowns.

"My mum." I swallow. "Thing is, she *is* right."

Jasper eats for a bit, but I can tell his mind is ticking over. I probably shouldn't have said anything. I shouldn't borderline slag my mum off to someone she employs. Eventually, he asks the million-dollar question: "But what exactly went wrong?"

I swallow, then turn to him. His eyes are gentle, caring. Funny how it feels easier to talk about stuff like this with someone you don't really know that well. Jasper and I exist in such totally different universes, it's almost like I have nothing to prove, and therefore nothing to fear.

"I started crying," I tell him. "Sobbing. Uncontrollably. During my solo."

Jasper nods. "Stage fright?"

"No," I say, looking down at the ground.

Jasper doesn't say anything more, but I can sense him watching me, and somehow I get the feeling that he's ready to hear it, if I want to say it, but he's not going to force me.

"I looked out into the audience," I continue. "Big

mistake. I was able to see all the faces of everyone who came. Mum wasn't there." I swallow again. "Dad wasn't gonna be there because he and Mum were divorced now, and he had his new family, so that was that. I knew Mum had been working, and I knew she was gonna be rushing to get there in time for the show, but she promised me she'd make it and then . . . well, she didn't. I just wanted her to see me. I wanted to know I was as important as all her work stuff. That I was something . . . to someone. And I . . . I dunno, it just got to me and I started crying. And that's the moment she *does* flap through the doors at the back, takes one look at the stage, and sees me in floods of tears. And that's her one memory of the event." I sigh and sit back up. "I just wanted Mum to see my big moment. I wanted to make her proud. Because nothing I ever do does." I manage a tight smile. "So. That's the reason. Wow. Sorry to bring down this whole evening."

"Don't be silly," Jasper says. "Are you OK?"

I nod. "Yeah. I'm OK."

He studies my face for a moment, then nods, and we both go back to finishing off our food, me a little lighter for having finally shared that with someone.

"You know," Jasper says, after he's scraped the very final, tiniest morsel of cheese from the bottom of his tray, "you shouldn't let that stop you from doing theatre. If you love it, do it."

"Yeah, but when something you love ends up burning

you, it's hard, isn't it? You end up . . . not wanting to go there again."

Jasper bristles. "We promised we wouldn't—"

"This isn't about him."

"Kind of is, though, isn't it?"

He rolls his eyes at me and I smile.

"OK, sure," I say. "But I am crap at acting. Like, everything else aside. I did audition for *Grease*, I just didn't get in."

"But, Fred, *I* was crap. I had no idea when I started out, I just loved West End musicals. I had to practise. I went to youth theatre, I had singing lessons, dance classes, did an acting workshop through school. And gradually I got better. And so will you. And even if you don't, so what? You can love theatre at any level, it hasn't got to be that you're on TV or making movies. That's like saying you love tennis, but won't ever play unless you get to compete at Wimbledon."

I chew my lip a bit. He's right. I have always loved theatre. I pushed it away because of what happened with *Les Mis*, and, I think, in a wider sense because it felt like that whole world was Mum's thing, and I was never sure if I liked it for what it was, or out of some weird need to prove something to her. But I know now. Just being in rehearsals, and then even more so when we moved into the theatre, there's something electric about it. I don't think I'm ever going to be Jasper levels of brilliance, but maybe I can just enjoy it for whatever it is to me. Maybe that's enough. How does Jasper, who barely knows me, know me so well?

"And sometimes things do burn you," he continues, staring out across the Thames. "But, I think, you have to be proud of those scars. They're nothing to be ashamed of, or regret. And you can't let the fear of getting more scars stop you. I think they show you've lived. They're like . . . a testament. To a life full of adventure."

"Maybe I'll keep trying, then," I say.

He smiles and glances at me. "You do that."

"And, like, I agree. I'm up for adventure. At the start of this term, I made a vow. I wanted to find my 'thing', something that would make me less forgettable. I don't want to end up doing nothing and . . . I don't want to be one of those people who doesn't end up making a difference. Who doesn't have any impact. I'm not saying I have to be a big star like you, or become a politician and make sweeping changes, or discover the cure to cancer, but I want *something*. I want my thing. I even gave up doughnuts."

I go back to finishing the raclette.

Jasper frowns, an almost panicked look on his face. "Gave up doughnuts?"

I nod. "They're the old me. I'm trying to be more like other people. I'm trying to be more driven, stronger, focused. And I . . . I'm making progress. I think. I'm saying yes to stuff, where before I'd probably say no, or just say nothing."

"OK, look," Jasper says. "I think it's cool, it's just . . .

you know, I think all this self-improvement stuff can sometimes be good, I guess we all have things we'd like to work on, but . . . have you considered that, maybe, you're kind of OK as you are?"

"Right, that's . . . *hilarious*, Jasper, and I love that you said that, but come on. If that was the case, I wouldn't be in this mess."

"Is it a mess?"

"I feel like it's a mess."

"You haven't found your thing?"

"Mate, I can barely find my socks most mornings."

"Huh." Jasper sits back on the bench. "Thing is, your thing is your thing. By which I mean, you don't find *your* thing by trying to not be you."

I swallow down my final mouthful, stand up, take his tray too, walk over to the bin with them, throw them in, then return to the bench, mulling his words over. I flop back down. "No, you've lost me."

Jasper rolls his eyes like he maybe doesn't believe me, like I'm just playing dumb, but he goes in again. "You can't just look at everyone else and want to emulate their lives," he says. "Otherwise you'll be continually bouncing from, I don't know, being a chilled-out surfer dude who lives in a wooden shack in Newquay, to a high-flying city boy, to travelling the world in a camper van, to settling down and adopting a couple of kids, because all those things can be brilliant, and for those people, it's the right thing for them. But what's the right thing for *you*? Because it's not necessarily any of that. I think, if you want my opinion, and maybe you don't, in which case please ignore me, but I think if you truly want to find your thing, then I think you have to find the 'Freddie' who already exists, and I think. . ." He swallows and looks away. "And I think, dare I say it, I think you might have to start loving him a bit more, and realizing that *you* are *you*, and everyone else is everyone else, and no one ever, in the history of the world, ever did anything really remarkable by just following the pack and letting them dictate who you are." He glances at me again. "Here ends Jasper's bullshit lecture on life, thank you for coming."

"No, no, that was good," I sigh. "Something to think about." I love that he thinks that about me; that I'm OK as I am. I think Ruby was saying a similar thing the other day. I don't know if I believe either of them, but it makes me feel better about myself.

"Something to think about," Jasper agrees. He bends over and digs around in his rucksack, pulling out a small paper bag and handing it to me.

"What's this?"

"That, my friend, is a chocolate truffle doughnut from Crosstown Doughnuts. I was over at the production office in Soho, so I popped in on my way down here." He nods at the bag. "I remembered you loved doughnuts and at that point I didn't know that you don't do doughnuts these days, but just so you know, that little baby is filled with milk chocolate truffle mousse and topped with dark chocolate ganache, dusted with cocoa powder. But, I mean, if you don't want it, that's also cool."

"Jasper! Oh my god, this is like crack to me, you know that?"

"I wouldn't give it to you if it were crack," Jasper says. "But it's not. It's just a *really bloody delicious top-notch artisan doughnut*. You never had one before?"

I shake my head, and tentatively peer into the paper bag. "*Ohhhhh.*" I quickly close the bag again. "*Ohhhhhh.* Look at it!" I open the bag again. "*Oh, wow! Oh, boy!*" I look at him. "Are you having one?"

He scoops a second bag out of his rucksack. "'Course! This is their home-made raspberry jam one. A classic! Rolled in sugar and full of jammy goodness. Would you prefer this one?" I shake my head and he picks it out of the bag and takes a bite, the jam oozing out as he does so, and not just a meagre amount that you usually get in a supermarket doughnut. This doughnut is *rammed* with jam. It's everywhere. It's, like, eighty per cent jam.

Maybe Freddie is doughnuts. That's what I am. Maybe, like Jasper says, I just need to embrace that. There are worse things to be, so actually, I think I should embrace this doughnut, since the doughnut is me, and I am the doughnut.

I sink my teeth into it. Soft, luscious, decadent; I totally lose myself in sugar and chocolate truffle for about two minutes.

"Mm," Jasper says, dabbing at his mouth with a napkin. "Did you like it?"

"Jasper, I . . . I could *marry* it, that's how much I love it."

He laughs. "So!" And drums his palms on his thighs. "Do you fancy a walk along the river? We could head up past the National Theatre?"

I give him a small smile. "Yeah, that'd be great."

We amble along the Thames Path, soaking in the evening buzz, and I'm thinking how nice it's been to talk to Jasper, and how I don't want this evening to end. I want to stay here talking with him, because somehow, I'm enough for him, and it's nice, not feeling the pressure to impress, or be someone different, or be constantly worrying about whether I'm saying yes to life enough. With him, I've just been living it.

34

The wrong people hold you down.

But the right people lift you up.

And that's how I feel the next day. It's not that I feel invincible, exactly, but I have a sort of protective glow around me. It's almost as if all the normal grief, the doubts, the disappointments, can't hurt me so much. It's not just the high from being in the company of someone who likes me for me, either. Jasper's words are still bouncing around my head: *I should wear the scars of my past defeats proudly, not let them make me afraid of getting more* – after all, they're badges of honour: proof I lived. *Fearlessly.*

I'm not going to let the past dictate who I am any more. I'm not afraid.

By the time the technical rehearsal starts in the last period of the day, a sense of doom is hanging over the whole show. Ms Pearson has apparently made a last-ditch attempt to persuade Harrison not to quit, and while we all wait for him to "think about it" (apparently he was seen sitting outside the PE department, head in his hands, muttering, "Last year I was just a footballer and everything was simple. What is life?"), the cast are working through the scenes while the tech crew attempt to light the show, using a rounders post to stand in for Harrison, where needed.

"ARGH!" Kwame screams from the stage. "Miss! *He* keeps dancing in front of me!" He points at Zach.

"Does *he* not have a name?" Zach says, extending his arms like a drag queen.

"You literally pushed me out to be in the middle!"

"Dude, I'm the lead, get over it!" Zach replies.

"You're a *twat, get over it!*" Kwame counters, storming off the stage.

Miss Pearson puts her head in her hands from behind the lighting desk, just as Lottie shouts, "Sorry, could any remaining boys who *haven't* exchanged bodily fluids with Zach please form an orderly queue so we can put the final nail in the coffin of this production!"

Horrifically, a couple of confused year sevens start to line up.

"Lottie, I've pulled three boys at this school!" Zach protests. "Incidentally, that thing you used to do that you think Harrison likes? He doesn't."

Lottie screams again and storms offstage too, Ms Pearson hurries out of the auditorium, shoulders shaking like she might be sobbing, and then Kwame's voice comes sailing over all the mayhem, in the middle of a blazing row with one of the costume people.

"ASDA? I'm not wearing jeans from ASDA! I haven't spent *my entire life* working on perfecting this *ass* for it to be obscured by low-slung jeans from ASDA!"

Moments later, Ms Pearson returns, and announces that Harrison is definitely not going to be doing the show and so she either needs to recast the role or somehow amalgamate Doody's lines with some of the others. Dhruv immediately declines the latter suggestion, declaring it to be, "against the creator's wishes" and "a possible violation of the performance license". At this point, everyone else starts having a go at Zach, pointing out that all this is his fault, and Lottie claims "don't shit where you eat" is the first rule of professional theatre, and I find myself observing all this with this weird sense of calm, like *why are you all so hysterical?* And I guess it's part Freddie Project and part Jasper's advice, because before I know it, I'm standing up in the auditorium, and I shout towards the stage, "I'll do it!"

Everyone falls silent and looks out at me.

"Sorry, Freddie?" Ms Pearson says.

"I'll do it. I'll play Doody."

More stunned silence. But I don't know why. It seems like the natural solution. And I'm not the least bit scared.

"Really? There's choreography to learn, the songs. . ."

"I can do it."

Ms Pearson stares at me, then she must realize I'm serious because she clasps her hands together. "Freddie Bennett – you absolute *star*. You're on!"

Everyone starts applauding. Which is embarrassing. But I also love it. I catch Zach staring at me, a look on his face like he's only just seen me for the first time. And then he smiles and joins in the clapping too.

I realize, *shit*, I'm doing it. I'm really . . . doing it.

But I'm still not scared.

And if I'm going to embrace the madness, why not do loads of wild things all at once?

So immediately after everyone has leaped off the stage and run over to hug me, and Ms Pearson has gone off to put together a script with all the blocking for me, I do it. I send Jasper a text like we're long-time buddies now:

ME: Pizza night at mine this weekend? We're celebrating :)

And moments later he comes back with:

JASPER: What are we celebrating? (You had me at pizza.)

ME: I'm playing Doody in Grease. 🐷

JASPER: Freeeeeedieeee!!!!!! I love this news! Congratulations!

ME: I guess you inspired me. :)

JASPER: x

35

It's mad. Rehearsals are *insane*. I'm taken through the blocking at breakneck speed, having to learn exactly where Doody moves in every scene, as well as being slotted into all the dance numbers, properly learning the songs, and all the lines. I mean, I'd seen the show before and I've sat through many of the rehearsals so it's not totally new, but still I'm intensively coached, and Ruby and Sam spend every moment when we're *not* rehearsing going over the script with me, trying to make sure I'm word perfect. It's worth noting that any pretence of any of us doing A levels has gone out of the window at this point – but it doesn't matter. This is literally the most important thing in the world right now, and while I was sort of enjoying it before, doing the props, I am truly *loving* it now. I'm nervous, terrified really. Opening night is just days away, but it's a good kind of nerves, an exquisite sort of terror.

And I don't know if the adversity has somehow brought

all the cast together more, but the arguing has stopped and, dare I say it, we almost seem to be a bit of a team. Lottie even brought me a takeaway coffee while I was going over lines with the other guys. Kwame turned up with a bag of Haribo. Other kids are pointing at me in the corridor, like I'm a celebrity. The cast WhatsApp is alive with buzz about the show, and I'm in the middle of it. It's only Zach who's been quiet and withdrawn, like he's lost his sparkle a bit. Maybe splitting up with Harrison has hit him hard.

It's just as well I didn't build the evening up to Jasper as anything more than pizza, because I've barely got time to run home, shower and throw on some jeans and a hoodie after rehearsals on Friday before Jasper is at my front door. A huge smile spreads across my face when I see him. I hadn't quite realized how much I'd missed him, even in just a few days.

"I come bearing gifts," he says, reaching into his rucksack and pulling out one of those miniature bottles of champagne that you would normally see on an aeroplane.

"Uh-oh, with that baby we're going to get *so* drunk." I grin.

"I know, right? This is my mum for you. She gave it to me. I think she thought she was being both a 'cool mom' and also a responsible one."

I chuckle. "Come in."

He walks through into the hall, still rummaging around in his rucksack, and pulls out a massive bar of

Dairy Milk. "I also got this. Special offer in Tesco, so it was a no-brainer. Who doesn't love an entire kilogram of chocolate?"

"I need to warn you, I've ordered pizza and dessert from Mamma Dough, and the dessert is chocolate brownie."

"Death by chocolate, then?"

"There are worse ways to die."

We both laugh, and I take his coat and show him through to the lounge, while I grab two glasses for the champagne, then join him on the sofa.

"You should have brought thimbles," Jasper says as he pours us both a small glass. "Anyway –" he taps his glass against mine "– cheers. Nice to see you. And congratulations again on *Grease*."

"Maybe save the congratulations until the review comes out," I suggest. The school newspaper (which is technically an online blog with usually limited hits) has started being notoriously savage about school productions, since the committee realized that undermining, sarcastic pieces which completely destroy people get way more traffic and still aren't technically violating the school's code of conduct.

"You're going to be great. *I'll* review it! I'll put it on Twitter." He clears his throat and sweeps his hand in front of him, painting out the words. "Freddie Bennett lights up the stage with his sensational portrayal of Doody."

I laugh.

"Someone played Danny, it was OK," he continues.

I laugh harder and Jasper grins at me, pleased.

"You're not even coming to see it, are you? I mean, you can, I can still get you a ticket. . ." I flick my eyes to his and immediately feel stupid with how much needy hope there is in my voice, forgetting we'd already discussed how that was a bad idea anyway. And as if Jasper would have time. As if he wouldn't be on a night shoot, or busy learning lines for the next day, or going to some media party.

"Ah, well, I can't," he says, entirely predictably.

"That's OK."

"Is your mum going?" he asks.

I sigh. "Um . . . it's unclear. I told her about it, that I was in it now, I mean. She's pretty busy." I shrug. "I mean, it's fine, I get it. *Cherries* comes first – at least, it does if we want to keep the house – and, to be honest, if there's any danger I'm gonna screw it up, which there definitely is, then it's probably best she doesn't see it. I can't disappoint her again, I just can't."

Jasper nods.

"You filming, then?"

"Ah, *no*, actually."

I raise my eyebrows.

"I have something to tell you too." He gives me a little smile. "The execs at Warner Bros liked my self-tape – they're flying me over there to do a screen test."

"Jasper!" I squeal. "Oh my god! Oh my god, that's

awesome! Well done."

"You helped."

"I so didn't, not really, and I can't take any of this glory. Ahh, I'm ... I'm really happy for you." And I am, but I'm also sad, because if he gets the movie, he won't be in the UK for a huge chunk of time; maybe he'll decide to move over there permanently.

I don't know how he picks up on this, but he says: "You know I'll be back, right?"

"Sure!" I try to be extra perky.

"Because we need more pizza nights and that is way more important than some movie I probably won't get anyway because even though it's to play a sixteen-year-old, they'll give it to someone who's actually twenty-eight."

I laugh. "Yeah, what's that about? For ages I just thought that the world is full of people who are in their mid-twenties and still in high school. Like, did they fail that badly?"

"Everyone says they want real, that real's important, but if you give them real, they hate it. They don't want to see spots and weird proportions and unexpected erections; they want toned abs, clear skin, and kids who talk and think like they're in their thirties."

I snort and nod. "That would be a great name for a band."

"Huh?"

"Unexpected Erection."

He smirks and we both take a sip of champagne.

"And we do need more pizza nights," I say. "That would be nice." I glance at him and he smiles at me.

"Yeah." He holds my gaze for a moment, then goes to speak again, just as the doorbell goes.

There's a weird moment, where we've both heard it, but we're still just looking at each other.

"Pizza's here," I say quietly.

"Amazing."

I'm awful at choosing pizza; I can never decide, so to prevent what would literally be a sixty-minute umm-ing and ahh-ing session, I stayed up late last night considering my options and also sent Jasper the link to the menu in case he was the same. I picked the cured meat one, which comes topped with lashings of salami, Parma ham, mozzarella and chilli, and Jasper went for the "Beatrice" – which has butternut squash, feta, pine nuts and rosemary. I took the initiative, and also got us a garlic and rosemary bread to share, and I whack some mindless (but admittedly weird) show about a woman who dates dogs on the telly, and we settle down to eat.

Jasper frowns and gestures towards the TV. "I'm not understanding why exactly she dates dogs?"

"I know, we started it halfway through. I'm sensing she's had enough of human men."

"Hmm." Jasper chews on a pizza slice thoughtfully. "Maybe we should all find a Rover or Fido."

I casually eat some pizza, don't look at him, and say,

"Are you off guys, Jasper? I wouldn't blame you."

He chuckles. "I'm not 'off' them. I guess I just have to find the right one."

Interesting. Not so long ago, he told me he wasn't in a place where he was looking for a boyfriend, because of everything with Zach. So that's changed. And I feel a weird sparkle of excitement that I can't quite place.

I glance across at him and he's looking at me, a little smile on his lips.

"What's 'right', though?" I ask.

"I don't know," Jasper replies. "Just someone I can be myself around. Someone I can relax with." He stretches his legs out in front of him and yawns. "That's probably why that woman wants to date dogs – unconditional love. You can just sit around with them in your worst trackie bottoms having not showered, and you'll still be their favourite person. What about you? Have you got a perfect guy? Little list of things to check off? One of mine would be 'Loves pizza'!"

"Ooh, I'm in with a chance, then!" I joke before my brain can stop my mouth.

"You might be."

We both laugh, then both shut up.

Wow.

God.

He said I might be in with a chance.

He was joking. I was joking.

"How far do these dog dates go?" Jasper asks, looking at the TV again. "Does she kiss them? *More?*" An uneasy look passes over his face.

"Why would you put that image in my head, Jasper?!"

"Sorry."

"Oh, *god*. Do we need to call the RSPCA?"

"Maybe they just eat and chat."

"Chat?"

Jasper holds his hands in front of him like paws and pants with his tongue hanging out. "Woof! I really *wuff* you! I *wuff* you lots and lots!"

I do the paws as well. "I *wuff* you too!"

We both laugh again, then scoop up new slices. "Anyway," he says, picking up a stray cube of feta. "You were saying what you look for in a guy."

For some reason, this suddenly feels like a test. I can tell, because he's doing what I do: keeping it casual, distracting himself with eating pizza, and dropping in the big questions. Or at least, I think that's what he's doing. It's also possible I'm projecting all that on him and I've got this completely wrong.

"I don't know," I say. "I think it's like you said: someone I can be me around. If 'me' is in any way acceptable to anyone." I busy myself with a slice of Parma ham. See? Distracting myself while dropping the big questions.

"I think you're more than acceptable, Fred," Jasper says.

I'm still looking down into my pizza box. "Thanks.

You've never met me first thing in the morning having just crawled out of bed, but thanks."

Jasper laughs. "It's good you're not looking, because she's literally letting a Yorkshire terrier take a sausage slathered in peanut butter from her mouth and it's possibly the grossest thing I've ever seen and I want to gouge my eyes out and burn the memory from my brain."

I look at the TV. "Oh."

"You can't unsee it now. Why did you even put this on?"

"To get you in the mood, Jasper," I deadpan. "I thought it was more subtle than some porn site."

"You're outrageous."

"You love it."

"I do." He grins.

The brownies were delivered with the pizza (maximum laziness) but I convince Jasper that warming them in the oven will make them ultra-amazing, and he agrees as long as it's no longer than ten minutes, because "no one should have to wait that long for a brownie". I tell him I'll go and sort it in the kitchen, but he insists on coming through.

"Strawberries too?" I suggest.

"Um . . . yes?!"

"There's some in the fridge."

"Righto," he says, going to get them while I decant the brownies on to a tray and put them in the oven.

"Oooh," Jasper says, eyes all over the contents of our

fridge. "Squirty cream!"

"Mum hates that stuff. You want it? Let's have it!"

Jasper grins and takes the can, while I find a couple of plates in the cupboard.

"Aaaand," Jasper says, "how about we grate some of that chocolate I brought over everything too?"

"Or melt some?!"

"Oh my god, *yes*! YES!" Jasper claps his hands together in delight. "Can we do that in the microwave?"

"On a low setting, I think we can!"

I find a bowl and Jasper sets about breaking the chocolate into pieces ready for melting. I can see he's smiling as he works, then he looks up from the bowl. "Freddie?"

"Yeah?"

"I think this is my best day ever."

I can see in his face he means it, and it takes my breath away.

And then I smile, and almost laugh, because even though it's totally ridiculous, I think this is my best day ever too.

The doorbell goes and I roll my eyes. "No, we don't want to change energy company, sign up for a charity direct debit, or subscribe to an organic veg box!"

Jasper laughs and carries on breaking up chocolate as I head out of the kitchen and down the hall to the door to get rid of whoever it is.

"We need to talk," says Zach as I open the front door.

I'm stunned for a moment, then shake myself awake. "I'm busy right now."

"*Please.*" His eyes are pleading. And red. He's been crying.

I glance over my shoulder, the faint sound of Jasper humming contentedly to himself filtering through from the kitchen. "Can we do this tomorrow?"

"Five minutes? Please."

"Zach. . ."

"Three, then! God, just two. *Please.*" He wipes his eyes with the palms of his hands. "Please, Freddie."

I sigh in frustration. I don't want Zach to know Jasper's here, and I don't want Jasper to know Zach's turned up – it might put a dampener on the evening, or worse, it might look to Jasper that me and Zach are somehow still a thing. "Look. . . OK, two minutes, but. . ." I glance over my shoulder again. "We've got . . . people over, so let's. . ." I step out on to the path and guide him down towards the pavement, and behind the hedge that obscures the front of our house from the road. "What is it?"

"You know, um . . . I've had time to really think, and . . . I realize I owe you a huge apology, and I. . ."

I never seen him like this. Humble. Muttering. Lost, almost. Even so, this isn't the time.

"OK," I say. "You've already kind of done this. It's fine."

"It's not fine. And after everything with Harrison and Kwame. . . Honestly, I've taken a long, hard look at myself.

Like, what the hell am I doing? Freddie, I *am* sorry. Truly. I shouldn't have let this happen the way it did. I couldn't help how I felt about Harrison, but I could have helped not messing you about."

I eyeball him. "Not the first time you've done it, though, is it?"

He looks at the ground. "No. I messed up with Jasper too, and he didn't deserve it either. I knew how you felt about me, Fred. I *knew*, and I still let everything carry on. Can I say something, though?"

"Sure."

"My old school wasn't... It wasn't a very nice place, and it wasn't the sort of place you could just 'be gay' and not get abuse hurled at you. Everyone thinks London is this bastion of wonderfully liberal people, but I don't think that's true. A lot of my mates I grew up with, they were dating people since year eight, some of them. OK, really innocent at first, but it was so much easier for them. It's OK for straight people to date in school, it's expected. If I'd have ever done that, I'd get called 'batty boy' in the corridors, and far worse. It was bad enough anyway. Bad enough that I liked theatre – that was enough for a shit ton of bullying, but anything else?" He shakes his head sadly. "No way."

I let out a breath, because I get it.

"How are gay kids like us meant to do it?" he continues. "You must feel it too? Too scared to be yourself, too frightened to ask someone out in case they take offence 'cause they're not gay themselves, no LGBTQ+ society because your school doesn't want to upset some very vocal parents, too young for gay clubs and dating apps – so what do you do? I feel like I've been in limbo since I was twelve, and now I can finally be me—"

"You don't always know what to do?"

He nods. "Yeah. You *do* know."

"I know."

"I feel like I'm making all the mistakes I would have made if I'd been dating people since I was thirteen. Even if you're really just playing at being in a relationship, you're still feeling your way through it at least. You're finding out what it means to be with someone, to care about them, what it means to have someone else in your life like that. I feel like the straight kids all get a roadmap and a head start, and the queer kids get given a faulty compass and a dead leg so they have to limp their way to 'destination relationship' while blindfolded."

I sigh. That's exactly the feeling. The left behind, the not allowed to take part, the not invited to the party. And then, when you finally are, it's like everyone else has learned the steps to the latest dance craze without you, and you're just messing everything up, looking like an idiot on the sidelines, everyone wondering what the hell your problem is, why are you acting like that, *why are you so immature?*

–"At BYT over summer, and then when school started in September, I don't know what exactly happened," Zach says, "but I started grabbing hold of anyone I could, I guess . . . scared almost, in case it was all taken away again, but also, like I needed to prove to myself that the bullies were wrong. That I wasn't disgusting. That people would want to be with me. I don't know, but . . . you know when you post on Instagram, and one like is fine, but there's a buzz when you get loads? I guess . . . validation?"

I blow out a breath.

"I'm sorry, I knew that was a crass analogy as I was saying it."

"Likes don't have feelings."

Zach nods. "You're right. Sorry. It's just. . ." He swallows. "I'm not looking for a get-out-of-jail-free card. I'm just trying to explain where my head is. I guess casual and fun is fine, if you're both on board with that. But once deeper feelings get involved . . . see, somewhere along the line I forgot people have feelings. I think I . . . I barricaded myself in so much, because no one liked me at my old school, I was . . . I was so alone, Fred. No one cared about the bullying, I didn't have friends like you've got with Ruby and Sam, I didn't have. . . I didn't have anyone, it was just me, this . . . lonely gay kid, terrified of going into school each day, 'cause I didn't know what they'd do this time, who just thought no one would ever like him. I built walls to stop them hurting me. So my feelings wouldn't show. So I would care less. . ." A tear escapes down his cheek. "But that meant –" his voice is choked "– it meant I also stopped caring about other people. And after I left that place, I just got so focussed on what *I* needed – what I needed to sort my head out and prove them all wrong – that I wasn't worthless, that maybe, one day, I could be. . ."

"Loved?"

He nods, sadly, and swallows, looking down at the pavement. "But it's easy to get a messed up idea of what 'love' really is – especially when you've never been shown any. And then you crave it, so badly, like a drug, and you don't much care where you get it, you just need your fix. I used to care, I promise you, Fred, but they took him and they beat him, and they abused him, and they knocked everything out of him until nothing was left. And I don't want to be that person, Freddie, and I'm going to try not to be."

I put my arms around him. "Oh, Zach," I murmur. "Zach."

He holds me tight, face buried in my shoulder, while he sobs.

We stay like that for a few moments, until he untangles himself, steps back, and looks me straight in the eyes, his breathing jagged.

We're staring at one another.

"Freddie—"

I know what he's going to say. I shake my head. "*No,* Zach." And I mean it.

"OK, but I have to know, so just say it—"

333

"I just did. *No.*"

He nods. "No second chances?"

"It's not that. I've worked out what I want now. It just . . . took me a while."

He looks down at the ground. "Yeah, fair enough. I don't blame you. I wouldn't pick me either."

"Zach! I can't believe I'm saying this, after everything, but you actually do have plenty of . . . really nice qualities. And features. No, not 'features', that makes you sound like a house on Rightmove. Look, you and Harrison are great together. You need to say all this to him too. Try to make it better."

"He won't return my messages. Or calls."

"He's probably as confused as you are. Give him a break – he thought he was straight until you showed up!"

Zach looks back up and gives me a smile, wiping his eyes with his hands and sniffing. "Guess we're all just winging it."

"You're right about that."

"Thanks for not punching me."

"You don't deserve that, Zach."

"Matter of opinion." He sniffs again. "See you onstage, then."

He nods, turns and starts walking away, up the street.

He looks so . . . broken. So alone.

"Zach?"

He turns back, face illuminated by the orange of the

street lamp, and I see a flicker of hope that makes my heart break for him.

"What made you come and tell me this now?"

He stares at me for a moment. "Because you're a great guy, Freddie Bennett. You see the best in people and you give your heart, and that's brave. That's a brave thing to do and it deserves more respect than I've ever given you. You've saved *Grease*. And in a weird way, you've saved me too, I think."

I stare back at him, blinking in the cold night air, letting all that sink in for a moment. "If you . . . what I'm saying is, you're not alone. It's not like before. Come and . . . hang out sometime."

A smile spreads across his face. "Really? Even . . . Ruby and Sam hate me, don't they?"

"Yeah, they think you're a total knob," I concede. "But you're welcome to try and change their minds."

He swallows. "Thanks, Freddie. You don't have to. But I'd love that."

He stands, lost in thought for a moment, then shoves his hands in his pockets and heads up the street, disappearing into the shadows. I blow out a breath. I feel sorry for him.

I head back in through the open front door, heading down the hall towards the kitchen. "How's the chocolate coming on?" I shout.

I stop. Jasper's not in here.

"Jasper?!" I shout.

Maybe he's in the loo. The bowl of broken chocolate is still on the side, the brownies still in the oven, warming. I take them out and put them on the countertop. Jasper's still not back. I check the downstairs loo. He's not there. I check the lounge (also empty) and then, my heart starting to beat a little faster, run up to the bathroom. He isn't in there either.

"Jasper?!" I call again.

I run back down to the lounge. His rucksack has gone. Mouth dry, I dart into the hall – his coat has gone too.

"SHIT!" I mutter. "Fuck, fuck, fuck." He must have poked his head out of the door, and heard me and Zach talking, or maybe saw us hugging, and thought … that I still liked Zach? Or maybe, the truth is, *he* still likes Zach, and he's jealous. I don't know. But I know I need to sort this out. Fast.

I call him. He doesn't pick up.

I call five more times.

Nothing.

I message. Explain. Apologize.

Nothing.

Two hours later. . .

Nothing.

36

No one can completely disappear, of course. Jasper might not have responded to any of my calls or messages over the weekend, but by Monday morning there's a new Instagram post. He's sitting in one of the lounges at Heathrow, about to board a flight for LA. He doesn't mention what movie it is or anything, there's just a vague reference to a "meeting for an exciting project".

He's sitting with Connor.

They look pretty . . . *close*.

I try to tell myself that means nothing. Maybe Connor has a meeting out there too, or just fancied a trip to the States and this was a good excuse. Until my obsessive trawl of social media brings up an article from last week, alluding to the brewing off-camera romance between Jasper and Connor, including the line which puts the final nail in the coffin of my romantic dreams: *Despite the little glances, shared smiles and way they constantly finish each other's*

sentences, the pair maintain nothing is going on … but a
source close to the show tells a different story, and I would
place your bets on seeing a new TV power couple very shortly.

"Students of Rydell High, this is your five-minute
call!"

Ms Pearson's announcement brings me back to
reality. There're two hundred people out there, waiting
to be entertained. I give myself a once over in the mirror,
adjusting my fifties-style quiff and uniform white T-shirt
and leather jacket. Zach walks up behind me, places a hand
on my shoulder and grins. "Look at us!" he chuckles.

I force a smile. We look nothing like the characters
from the film. They were too old, and we're too young. We
look like babies playing dress-up.

"Break a leg, Fred," he says. "You can do this. And
we've all got your back if anything goes wrong."

I meet his eyes. I haven't quite forgiven him for how he
treated me – he made a choice, at the end of the day – but I
see what all the hate and bullying had done to him now, so
it's not anger. I understand him. "Thanks. You too."

"You got anyone in?" he asks.

I shake my head. "Mum's crazy busy with this massive
location shoot. But I'm cool with that – less pressure, right?"

"Right. My mum's booked a ticket for every single
show. It's too much."

I smile at him. It must be nice to have a parent who
cares that much.

"GO, RYDELL HIGH!" Zach shouts, to cheers from the rest of the changing room.

"Zach!" Ms Pearson hisses, poking her head around the door. "The audience can hear you!" She double-takes. "Jamil, *please* put some trousers on, I'm about to announce beginners."

Minutes later, I'm standing in the wings, absolutely bricking it. The lighting pre-set casts shafts of pink and blue light across the stage, with a gauze cloth hanging at the front, on to which is projected the logo for the show – just like they sometimes do in the West End. Props have been checked, costumes adjusted, the band are on standby, Miss Mills (the drama teacher, who has magnanimously agreed to be stage manager) is ticking off cast members as they arrive for the opening, and there's a hum of excited anticipation from the audience. It's the same magic you feel on Christmas Eve, that sense of a massive event to come, but for now, just for a few moments, a weird sense of calm before the storm . . . albeit with a dry mouth and adrenaline prickling and spiking through my veins.

Across in the opposite wing, I see Ruby blow me a kiss. I smile and blow one back. And just behind her, there's Sam, sharing a little kiss with Alice, who's holding both his hands and saying a few (doubtless reassuring) words to him before he goes on. *The right people lift you up.* I'm so stoked for him. Little, innocent Sam. Possibly not quite so "innocent" any more.

"Stand by," Miss Mills tells the cast. Then says, "LX cue one, stand by," into her headset. "Fly cue one, stand by; band stand by." She has a series of lights at her desk in the wings – currently they're all red. And then, in what feels like a wild leap into the unknown, she switches one of the lights to green and says in her headset, "LX cue one, go. Fly cue one, go." And we're off, the music starts, the gauze flies out, the lights come up, and Eugene, Patty and Miss Lynch walk on for the opening dialogue before we all run on in just a few moments. "Lights up on Act One, lights up on Act One," Miss Mills says into her headset. "Stand by, LX cue two."

I am suddenly only aware of my breathing – tight and jagged. I run through my lines one last time, the blocking, try to visualize how it will go, but now it's all mess and I can't remember the moves or the words in the right order, and there are people out there, and it's going to be like *Les Mis* all over again, and I'm going to look like an idiot all over again and . . . I look around frantically – is there a script? I just need to check it over again, I just need. . .

"Chill," Zach says, squeezing my shoulder. "You got this. And we've all got you."

"But I can't remember—"

"You will."

"I—"

"You *will*."

And all of a sudden it doesn't matter because it's time.

There's nothing I can do.

So I brace myself and run out on to the stage.

The first part of the show passes in a blur. Rydell High class of '59 reunion ... "Summer Nights"... but then it's my moment to sing "Those Magic Changes" – which is the thing I'm most nervous about. I've had a lot of rehearsal for this, it's not that I don't know the words, and I've been coached to within an inch of my life, so I think I sound OK too. It's just that I've never quite gelled with the song. It's always felt a bit stupid, like I'm just singing about how much I love a song. The intro starts, and Zach's standing next to me, and I catch a glimpse of Ruby and Sam in the wings, watching, and I suddenly think about everything that's happened this term, with them, with Jasper, with me. And it hits me. That's what the song is. It's not just about changing chords, it's how everything changes, it's about growing up, working things out, that weird place we're in, not kids any more, but not quite adults. It's painful, but it's also pretty special. Like Jasper said, you just can't let the painful bits get to you. So I sing it for him. And I sing it for Ruby, who's worked out she's happy by herself, and for Sam, who's worked out he isn't, and for Zach, who I think is still working it out. And for me, who's going to wear his battle scars with pride, and not let it get me down.

I only remember where I am when the applause starts. Not just that. The audience are on their feet. A standing-freakin'-ovation! I catch Zach's eye and he gives me a look that tells me I was good. And when I turn to walk off, Ruby and Sam are blowing huge, extravagant kisses to me from the wing.

No time to stop and think, though. "Greased Lightnin'" (which Dhruv aces, pumping the number with more energy than I ever saw in rehearsals)... Ruby gets big laughs and huge applause for "Look at Me, I'm Sandra Dee" ... people are in hysterics at Sam's portrayal of Eugene with a really high voice ... Zach and Lottie are actually *brilliant* as Danny and Sandy... "Born to Hand Jive" ... "Rock 'n Roll Party Queen"... and by the time we reach "We Go Together", I've relaxed, I'm really enjoying myself, I'm giving it everything I've got and the crowd are going wild for us. Honestly, it's the best feeling, I'm floating on air. We hit the button of the number, and the confetti cannons fire, and the audience leap to their feet, another standing ovation, whooping and cheering, my god, we did it, we actually did. *I* did it. The play-off music starts, and we all run into the wings, then take it in turns to run back on, take a bow centre stage, then join the line-up ready for group bows. When it's my turn, there's an extra loud cheer, and chants of "Fred-die! Fred-die!" and then once everyone is onstage, in a moment that's unrehearsed, the rest of the cast all turn to me and applaud, and the crowd go wild again.

That's when I look out into the audience and see my mum.

She made it?!

I can't believe she came. I can't believe she saw this.

And I know instinctively it's no accident. I feel the hand of Jasper in this. He knew how important having Mum here would be, he knew what it would mean to me, and he made it happen. Whether he did that before what happened at my house, or after, it doesn't matter. All I know is that Jasper is a good person. A kind person. A person who knows me better than anyone else, and not just knows me like he knows if I like gherkins on a McDonald's, or how many sugars I like in my coffee. He knows what I need. He did this and he didn't have to. He was thinking of me. And I'm so overwhelmed with gratitude, and regret, and also pride, that Mum came to this, and I've had such a great night, and I'm buzzing and knackered and elated and it's too much: I start crying.

I emerge into the theatre foyer freshly showered, to back slaps and people telling me, "Congratulations!" and "We heard you stepped in at the last minute – you were brilliant!"

Anisha and Molly, the two girls who didn't know who I was in the yearbook, approach me with the programme.

"Can you sign it, Freddie?" Anisha asks, pushing a pen in my hand. I grin and squiggle under my name, feeling like a proper star.

Even the headmaster and Mrs Mason, my head of year, stop chatting and both give me a thumbs up from over by the box office desk, Mrs Mason mouthing, "Well done, FREDDIE!", placing big emphasis on saying my correct name.

I push my way over to where Mum's standing by herself. "You were sensational." She beams. "I was really proud."

I look down at the floor. I'm embarrassed, but so chuffed. "Thanks. Thanks for coming."

"I owe you an apology. I should have said I was coming the moment you mentioned it. I put work first, I've always put work first, but I shouldn't have done."

"It's OK, Mum. I get it."

"No," she says. "And worse, it took a sixteen-year-old to bring that home to me." Mum meets my questioning eyes, then sighs. "Jasper."

I nod. "Uh-huh?" I swallow.

"After your dad walked out, I was so hell-bent on us being fine, I just focused on the telly stuff. I wanted us to be secure, Fred. We didn't – and we don't – need him. But somewhere in all that, I forgot what the whole point of that was. *You.* I'm sorry. Jasper told me the truth about *Les Mis*. He told me that you want me to be proud of you, Freddie. And I am. So proud. You're a funny, kind, sweet, good-looking—"

"Mum, seriously, too much, people are listening and—"

"I phoned the school and booked myself a *Grease* ticket right away." She looks me right in the eyes and smiles.

"You're one of the good guys. Like Jasper says."

My breath catches. "When, out of interest, when did he tell you that?"

Mum frowns a little, probably curious as to why it matters. "He called me on Sunday, literally before he boarded his flight to LA."

For a moment, my heart swells. He still did this, and thinks I'm a "good guy" after everything that happened. Which means, on some level, he's thinking about me, and even if nothing will ever happen, maybe we could still be mates.

"I really like him, Mum," I mutter.

"Of course you do, darling, he's fucking hot."

I laugh. "He's also a really nice guy."

"I *knew* you'd change your tune!"

I chew my lip. "He's seeing Connor, though."

"What makes you say that?" Her eyes suddenly seem to sparkle. "Did you read the article?"

"Yeah. It said 'a source close to the production' reckoned they were a thing." I shrug, trying to play it down in front of her.

She smiles. "That was me. I'm the source. And it's not true."

My eyes widen. "You're lying to the press now?"

"Jesus, do you understand anything about PR? It's not lying, per se. Do you know how hard it is to get people talking about stuff on social media, let alone in the newspapers? Especially with Jasper's complete lack of enthusiasm for it? You have to manufacture a little bit of hype sometimes."

I meet her eyes.

"He's free and single."

"You can't be sure."

"He literally told me."

I squint at her. "What? Why? *And when?*"

"The day after the cast and crew screening. I'm guessing in the hope it would get back to you. Did you hit it off that night, or something? I love it when teenagers think they're being subtle and cunning, when they're actually *so* obvious. Like when you spent all that time in your room when you were thirteen, 'playing Lego'."

I act like I didn't hear that last bit and focus on the (much more important!) first part. *He wanted me to know he was single.* And I give myself the hugest mental kick up the backside for messing things up, and my mother an even bigger one for only revealing this crucial information now.

"You didn't think to tell me?" I say.

"Fred, every time I mentioned Jasper you went off on one. I assumed you still hated him. I mean, you literally punched him in the face. Cardboard-speaking."

"Ugh!" I growl. "So he's not . . . with Connor?"

Mum shrugs. "Well, he *wasn't*. They've obviously now gone away together, and you know how it is, Fred, especially at your age. All those hormones crashing about, making you want to sleep with anything with a pulse. . ."

"This wasn't the reassurance I was looking for."

"Freddie!" It's Ms Pearson, holding a plastic beaker of wine, and already looking half cut. "Simply wonderful! Divine! You're a bloody *hero*!"

Mum gives me a little nudge in the side and smiles.

"Debbie Pearson." Ms Pearson extends her hand. "You must be Mum? Freddie saved the day!"

"I know. Isn't he the best?" Mum says.

Ms Pearson nods. "Reminds me of the time the third cover stepped in with zero rehearsal when I was performing in *Grease* in the WEST END." Ms Pearson laughs. "I don't know if Freddie mentioned I'm an actress?"

"Oh, right?" Mum says, as I watch her face glaze over, because this shit happens all the time.

"Mm, actually, I just signed with a new agent – Henrietta Stone Associates? Have you heard of them?"

"Oh, that's great." Mum smiles. "I'll . . . look out for you."

"They're really trying to get me some telly, so I'll ask them to send you a CV, shall I? I'm very good, aren't I, Fred?" She laughs, but I know this isn't a joke.

"Brilliant, yeah." I nod.

"Oh, *you*!" Ms Pearson says. "You're embarrassing me in front of your TV producer mum! What are you like?" She giggles. "No, but the headmaster just told me you're making this show for MegaFlix, and just to say, I'm only doing two days a week from next term to focus on my acting career again, so I'm totally available."

Mum nods.

"Oh, there's Mr Stefani – I'd better go and schmooze, we need new radio mics! Debbie Pearson!" she tells my mum again, as she walks off. "I'm on Spotlight!"

"Anyway!" Mum says brightly. "Talking of the show, I was reviewing the footage in the edit from the shoot you did and Zara Roland, our casting director, happened to be sitting in with me. She's currently shortlisting actors to come in for meetings for a new part in season two – it's this super geeky, nervous kind of boy, described in the script as 'the sort of kid who an anti-bullying charity would take on an Outward Bound weekend to build his self-esteem' and, don't take this the wrong way, but she saw you on-screen and wants you to come in."

"*What?!*"

"She thought you had the right look."

"Oh my god. Should I be pleased or offended?"

"Zara is great at spotting new talent, Freddie. She's top of her game. Auditions are on Friday, if you fancy it? No pressure."

It's a totally crazy idea. As if I stand any chance of getting it, when I'd be up against boys with way more experience and agents and everything. "What's the part exactly?"

Mum smiles at me. "It's to play Jasper's boyfriend."

I head out of school with Ruby and Sam. We're all too hyped to go back on the bus or in the car with our parents, and a half-hour stroll home is exactly what we need – especially because it'll give us time to chat about everything away from everyone else.

"Hey, Freddie!" Zach springs out of the exit and runs to catch up with us. "Hi. I've got news. I've been speaking to Mrs Mason, and she's agreed it, and . . . we're allowed to form an LGBTQ+ society at school. 'Cause maybe what we all need sometimes is just to talk to someone else who gets it, and won't judge, and just . . . yeah. So. If you wanna join. . ."

I smile at him. "That sounds awesome, Zach. Count me in."

"Cool. And Harrison's joining, Kwame . . . and I'll do posters, 'cause there'll be others. I mean, we're legion, right?"

I smirk at him. *"Expect us."*

Zach snaps his fingers. "That's the slogan right there! LGBTQ+ Society – *expect us!*" He laughs. "Well done again for tonight, you stole the show." He nods at the others. "Nice work, everyone. Pleasure being onstage with you."

He runs back inside, and I just hear, "Harrison? He said yes!" as the door closes behind him. I smile. Zach must have chatted to Harrison and things must be on their way back to being OK. I'm happy about that.

"So, guys," Sam says, once the coast is clear. "Just to get it out there, and I'm sure you've already guessed, I'm seeing Alice, in a girlfriend and boyfriend sort of way. We, um . . . hit it off during our extra Eugene and Patty rehearsals . . . you know, we started thinking, *how can we subvert expectations about these characters?* How can they be more than stereotypes? And Alice was like, 'What if they're having vast amounts of sex? And not just sex, but sometimes . . . *kinky* sex?' And I was like, 'OK, but I've never even had *standard* sex,' and Alice was all, 'Same!' so we took inspiration from this Stanislavski guy all the theatre kids are always going on about, and – long story short – we're basically at it like rabbits most of the time now."

"Wow," Ruby says.

"Wow, indeed," he replies. "It blows my tiny mind. We're making it official anyway, that's why I'm telling you. Oh, um . . . not the sex stuff. I only told you guys that."

"Meanwhile, in less sexually successful news, I have an update on the Jasper situation," I say, and I fill them in on what Mum told me.

"So what are you gonna do?" Ruby asks.

A smile spreads across my face. Once I would have given up. Once, I would have let Jasper go and admitted defeat.

But not now.

"I'm not sure," I admit. "I just know I'm not going to let life – or Jasper – slip away from me again, not without at least trying to do something about it. Not at least without trying to turn it back into a 'yes'."

37

I walk into the audition room and Mum introduces me to "the team" – which comprises two blokes from MegaFlix, both of whom are busy on their phones and only glance up occasionally in a blatant attempt to give the impression they have any interest in this; Oscar, this posh-boy director who must only be in his twenties; Rainbow (choppy pink-and-blue hair, and a tongue piercing), who is either someone's daughter on work experience, or, most likely, a runner; and Zara, the casting director, who is the only person who gives me a warm smile and the impression of wanting me to be there.

"I really enjoyed your background work on ep five," Zara says. "I definitely saw a little sparkle of something we could work with."

"Thanks," I say. "I didn't think I was very good, but, I mean—"

"OK," Zara says briskly. "So, did you have a chance to look at the sides?"

"Yeah."

"We're going to have you reading opposite Rainbow, she'll read Jasper's lines. So, if you want to take a seat and we'll get the camera ready?"

I nod and sit down opposite Rainbow while Zara fiddles about with a small camera on a tripod. "OK," she says. "Let's have a go."

I clear my throat, and try to channel the character of "Kit", who apparently is exactly like me, and I remember what Jasper told me when we were doing his self-tape, about how the trick was to just be myself, not try to act, so maybe no acting is actually required here?

"Kit," Rainbow says robotically, sounding bored. "I thought you'd gone."

"I'm still here," I reply, trying to keep my voice normal.

"I wanted to talk," Rainbow says, sounding like she can't be bothered.

I give it a pause, because I feel like that's something I would do. People saying they want to "talk" always strikes fear into my heart, so I'm readying myself, bracing for whatever it is.

But just as I'm doing that, Rainbow goes, "It's your line?"

And totally ruins the moment.

"I know," I tell her. I sigh and then do the line. "I'm listening."

"OK," says Oscar. "Can you give it a bit more? Kit's awkward, but he isn't a pothead, yah?"

"OK," I say. "So . . . more?"

"More." Oscar nods, without specifying what it actually is he wants more of. "Take it from 'I'm listening'."

I clear my throat. "I'm listening!"

"No." Oscar shakes his head. "Too. . ." He appears to grimace, then sighs, then screws his face up. "Your performance is . . . it feels *blue*, and I need it to be *orange*."

I stare at him.

"More *orange*," he repeats. "Yah?"

"OK?" I say. I glance at Mum, who just raises her eyebrows, like, "Can you do this or not? This isn't your high school show now."

Orange, I repeat in my mind. *Be more orange.* Does he mean more . . . citrusy? A bit . . . tangy? How would that even translate into delivering a line? "I'iiiiim . . . listening!" I chirp.

"Urgh!" Oscar says.

"Still not orange?" I ask.

"That was more neon pink," he says.

"Think about what's really being said in this scene," says one of the MegaFlix guys, without looking up from his phone. "It's you, it's him, there's history, there's backstory in bucketloads, there's all this baggage, this stuff, and you can't forget about that, it has to come through in every line, every facial expression, every atom of your being, do you know what I mean?"

"They haven't been sent the previous episodes though," Zara tells him, "so they don't actually know about that."

"Oops, my bad," the MegaFlix guy says, still not looking up.

"More David in *Schitt's Creek*," says the other MegaFlix guy, "but a teenage version, and not really David but more Asa Butterfield in *Sex Education*, but with a kind of Michael Cera vibe, but *Superbad* not *Arrested Development*, and gay, but not really *gay*."

I blink at him. This was a mistake. Thing is, I *get* this part, and I *get* this scene, because it's two boys, and they both like each other, it's just they can't say the words and express how they're feeling, and when I read it I felt *so seen*. I feel like I could do this, but the notes don't make any sense, and reading with Rainbow is hopeless because I can tell she doesn't really get it, hasn't been there – there's no sensitivity in her voice, she's just going through the motions.

"I fink, like, there's too many pauses?" says Rainbow, because apparently every fucker has opinion about my performance. "Like, he's not really a character who pauses much, yeah? Like, he's edgy, yeah? Like, on it?"

"Good note," says the first MegaFlix guy.

I can't do this, and I am literal nanoseconds from getting up and walking out, when the door opens behind me and Jasper walks in.

"Jasper!" the whole room coos, leaping up to shake his hand and hug him.

I just stare, open-mouthed, because he's meant to be in LA, and while I'd totally resolved to try to make amends with him, I was going to do that when he was back ... and since I wasn't expecting his return so soon, I haven't prepared anything. *Great.* He notices me staring, and says, "Long story," before turning to the execs and adding, "Shall we do this scene together, me and Freddie?"

Everyone readily agrees that would be excellent, and before I know it, I'm sitting opposite Jasper, who is weirdly acting like everything's cool and there's no issue between us, and we're ready to do the scene again.

"Kit, I thought you'd gone," he says in a way that's so natural it takes me a second to realize he's actually started the script, because it doesn't sound like something that's been written down and he's reading.

"...I'm still here!" I blurt out, because I've been knocked off guard now. But in the corner of my eye, I see Oscar nod, and so, maybe, that worked. Maybe it was "orange" enough.

"I wanted to talk," Jasper says softly, like he's saying it only to me and no one else is in the room.

It's so real, I just look straight into his eyes, and then swallow, and manage to say, "I'm listening," while an actual chill prickles through me. I go to speak again, then realize that's the end of my line, so don't.

Zara moves in my peripheral vision. "Guys, keep going, keep this feeling, but just ... just go with it, don't worry about the plot of the show, just improv whatever happens next, just talk," she whispers.

I'm still staring at Jasper.

And he's staring at me.

"I'm listening," I repeat.

He swallows and drops his eyes. "I'm ... so bad at this."

"Improvisation?" I frown.

He cracks a smile. *"Talking.* I've never been much good at it, *Kit."*

I remember I am Kit. "Well, *same,"* I say, because on that point, Kit and I are, in fact, identical.

"There's all this stuff that I often want to say, but I never quite can, or I get nervous about it," Jasper says. He looks at me again. "But I think ... sometimes, if you don't say those things, how does the other person know? Maybe they'll just think you're aloof, or. . ."

"A bit of a dick?"

There's laughter from the audition panel. Jasper chuckles too. "I was going to say 'cold' but, sure, 'a bit of a dick'."

"Huh, well, I'm the same, I ... I'm bad at saying stuff that's important to me too. Especially if I –" I go for it "– like someone." He looks at me and I hold his gaze – strong, firm, because I mean it.

"I like you too," Jasper says. He gives me a small, hopeful smile.

356

"At first, when we first met, I thought you were . . . *hot*." The word come out like a strangled cry. "But I also thought you were totally unnecessarily *rude*, quite frankly, when I spaffed that cream cheese jalapeño over you."

"Lovely and specific!" I hear Zara mutter as she makes a note.

"Anyway," I continue, "I basically assumed you hated me, so I . . . so, yeah. . ."

"And after that," Jasper cuts in, "I kicked myself that I'd been like that, and I kind of wanted to make a better impression. Ugh! Asking if you liked vinyl! Who even says that? An absolute bellend, that's who! I tried to make amends – attempted some humour . . . told your mum to tell you I had to take my top to the dry-cleaner's."

"*That* was humour?" I squint at him.

"I don't do jokes!" he pleads. "But then we got to know each other and. . . But the other night, when I saw you talking to . . . *Casanova*. . ."

I laugh. *That's* the name for Zach he's going with?

"When I saw you talking," he continues, "and you were doing it secretly, and it sounded so . . . intimate, and then you hugged, *for ages*, and I guess I just flipped, ran off. I thought you and me. . ."

"The stuff you saw, that was him explaining himself, and me realizing . . . that sometimes, when you've got the pressure of growing up as a queer kid – and you must know what that's like too – that everything can be so much harder,

357

and even when you seem like the confident and fun gay boy you're not, not really. I don't think Casanova is a bad guy. I think he's just so scared he won't be loved, he grabs hold of anything he can get. We did hug. It was 'I understand', nothing else."

Jasper sighs and looks down at his trainers. "Yeah. I get it."

"I called you. I messaged. I tried to explain."

"I needed some time. I guess I was scared too."

"OK, sure," I say. "But then, I didn't know if you were with Conn— I mean, that other guy, and, to be honest, I'm still not entirely sure, because. . ." I run my tongue over my lips. "You went on that . . . *holiday* with him recently?"

"Ohh," says Jasper. "No, no, no. He wanted to come to LA, wanted to try and get some meetings, that's all."

"OK . . . because the pic you posted looked—"

"Nothing's going on," Jasper confirms. He looks into my eyes and swallows. *"You're* the one that I want, Freddie."

I stare at him. Did I even hear him right? "What?" I mutter.

"You, Freddie," he says. "And I mean *you*. Not some version of yourself you're working on or trying to improve. Real, awkward, funny, sweet, kind, clumsy, shy, would-probably-rather-stay-in-and-watch-crap-telly-than-be-at-a-shit-party *you*. Don't get me wrong, I fully approve of saying yes to life, that's a good thing, a *great* thing. It's just. . . I also think, sometimes, it's OK to say no to life, and just *be*, just chill with someone you want to be with, cuddle up, do nothing, forget about the world and all your goals and hopes and dreams, and all the shit too, forget the whole thing, and just breathe. And do nothing."

I swallow a huge lump in my throat. He's using my name, not calling me Kit any more, so I think this is real. He means this. And yet, I still can't quite let myself believe it.

"But you're a star, Jasper," I say. "And I'm a mess. I'll mess up. I know it."

"It's OK," Jasper says, leaning forward and taking my hands. "No one is perfect, and life's not perfect, and we're not perfect. We're just . . . trying to work it all out, and if you're OK with that then I'm OK with that."

I can feel tears pricking at my eyes. "Oh my god, *yes*," I murmur, my throat tight. "And same. And I *will* mess up, again and again, so, huh, brace yourself."

"Assuming brace position!" Jasper grins.

"Please note your nearest exit may be behind you!" I add.

"Put on your own mask before helping others!" he replies.

We laugh and he leans closer towards me. "Can I?"

I nod, breathless, unbelieving.

And he kisses me.

I hear Mum clear her throat, then Zara gives us a clap. "Um . . . very good, boys."

But neither of us cares, we're so into the kiss, this is

all I want, and I never want it to end, because Jasper kisses like I have never been kissed by anyone, even in my best, most erotic dreams. He is soft, tender, gentle and yet strong, insistent, in control, passionate, deep, urgent, and I cannot get enough of him. . .

"OK! Thanks!" Mum says, dragging him off me. "We've seen all we need to see!" She gives me WTF eyes.

We both sit back in our chairs, staring at each other, desperate for round two.

"Some really exciting material you came up with there," one of the MegaFlix guys says eventually, breaking the spell.

I glance at him, and my cheeks start to flush with the realization we just did all that in front of the panel.

"Good job, we'll let you know," Zara says. "Nice to see you, Jasper. Thanks for stepping in. How was the casting?"

I turn back to Jasper, and he's looking at me, eyes sparkling, a cheeky grin on his face.

"Jasper?" Zara repeats.

"Huh?"

"How was the casting?"

"Oh!" he says, shaking himself and scratching the back of his head. "Terrible. They're hiring a twenty-nine-year-old."

"Hmm, yeah, because nothing says genuine teenager like massive pecs, stubble and a receding hairline," I add.

Jasper snorts.

"Right," Mum sighs. "Off you go. *Hi!* magazine are hosting a party for MegaFlix's new season tonight, if you fancy it? I'll ring ahead and make sure you're both on the guest list." She turns to me. "And I'll see you at home later, OK?" She cocks her head. "*Both* of you, I dare say."

I nod at her and turn to leave.

"Freddie?" she says.

I turn back.

"That was good. You did well."

"Thanks, Mum!" Two compliments in the space of a week. I think Mum's going soft on me.

38

Jasper and I walk out of the production office and straight into the early evening buzz of Soho, meandering down Wardour Street, past bars and restaurants already teeming with people.

"If they offer you the role, will you do it?" Jasper asks.

"I don't know. Maybe. I'd rather play the role of your off-screen boyfriend," I smile.

"Well, I'm offering you *that* part," he says.

"And I accept, thank you kindly."

He grins at me like a loon. I love that he can't contain his excitement either. "I sense you're actually not bothered about the TV show, though."

"Perceptive. Good boyfriend."

"How come?" he asks.

I meet his eyes and smile. "Because it can't all be about collecting big experiences, can it? I've done it, I was worried I was always on the sidelines, and this term, I haven't been.

I did *Grease*, I did the *Cherries* audition, I found you. Totally amazing. But, like you said, there's also magic in the ordinary, and sometimes it's OK to be on the sidelines, doing nothing, watching life go by. That's why I'm not bothered about the part. Because if I'm with you, whatever we're doing, even if it's nothing much, I'll be happy."

We come to halt on the street corner, and he pulls me into a doorway, out of the bustle of the street. "What you said in the casting," he says. "About me being some sort of star and you not being?"

"Oh. Yeah."

"First off, you should know I don't see things that way. I don't think I'm special just because I'm in a TV show. And anyway, it doesn't matter what experiences you have, you can have the most magical time in the world, but what does it really mean if you don't have someone to share it with?" He looks into my eyes. "I want you to be part of my life, Freddie. I want to share it with you. And I want you to share your life too. I want to meet your friends, I want you to show me the movies you enjoy, the food you can't get enough of (although I think I have an idea about that already), the music you dance around your kitchen to when you're home alone pretending you're a rock star playing Wembley, 'cause you do that too, right? And the dreams you've got, the things that still hurt you, the stuff you're scared of, all of it. Show me, Freddie. And I'll show you. And let's enjoy all these things together. I think it's better. Together."

I smile. "I'd really love that."

He smiles too, then narrows his eyes. "You want to go to the *Hi!* magazine party?"

"Sure."

He laughs. "Truthfully?"

"Not really."

"Good. Me neither." He reaches into his rucksack. "Plus, I already bought these. . ." He produces a bag with the Crosstown Doughnuts logo on it. "Tongan vanilla bean and yuzu and passionfruit, FYI. Who needs fancy canapés when you've got these?" He leans in and kisses me on the lips. "You ever been to the Sky Garden?"

I shake my head.

"It's on the forty-third floor of the Walkie-Talkie skyscraper. Floor-to-ceiling windows, with this awesome panoramic view over London from a huge atrium filled with palm trees. You can get food, and there're sometimes DJs, and even better, it's free to get in. The views are amazing. Jaw-dropping, Fred. Especially at night, with all the London lights, twinkling like crystals, reminding you . . . of how many more adventures are waiting. People. Places. Opportunities. Dreams. It's all waiting for you. *For us.* Fancy it?"

"Yes," I tell him. "I'd love that."

He smiles. "Come on, then," he says, taking my hand in his. "I'll show you."

Scholastic Children's Books Proudly Presents

You're the One That I Want

Book, music and lyrics by **Simon James Green**

Directed & choreographed by **Jenny Glencross & Linas Alsenas**

Set Design – **Liam Drane**

Sound Design – **Harriet Dunlea**

Lighting – **Rebecca Gillies**

Stage Manager – **Pete Matthews**

Deputy Stage Manager – **Jessica White**

Hair & make-up – **Jim, Uli & Erica at Gay's the Word**

Costume Supervisor – **Freddie at Kirkdale Bookshop**

Seamstress – **Sarah Counsell**

Props – **Matthew at Queer Lit**

Special Effects – **Liam & Gav at Waterstone's Gateshead and Tsam & Martha at Waterstone's Newcastle.**

Box Office & Front of House – **Bounce Marketing**

Simon James Green supplied by – **Joanna Moult at Skylark Literary**

Assistants to Mr Green – **Beau and Dolly**

Refreshments will be served in the library during the interval, courtesy of Lauren Fortune and the ladies of the W.I.

Noah Can't Even

"A riotous, real-feeling YA debut" – *The Guardian*

Poor Noah Grimes! His father disappeared years ago, his mother's Beyonce tribute act is an unacceptable embarrassment, and his beloved gran is no longer herself. He only has one friend, Harry, and school is... Well, it's pure hell. Why can't Noah be normal, like everyone else at school? Maybe if he struck up a romantic relationship with someone - maybe Sophie, who is perfect and lovely - he'd be seen in a different light? But Noah's plans are derailed when Harry kisses him at a party. That's when things go from bad to *utter chaos*.

NOAH CAN'T EVEN

SIMON JAMES GREEN

100% AWKWARD

Noah Could Never

Noah and Harry are now officially boyfriends, but is Noah ready for the difference? It's no help that French exchange students have descended on Little Fobbing - including sexy Pierre Victoire, who seems to have his eye on Harry! Meanwhile, Noah's paired up with a girl ... who is not even *French*. But that's not all: the police are monitoring Noah, and he can't tell if it's a) because his dad and secret half-brother, Eric, have made off with his gran's fake diamonds; b) because his PE teacher is receiving mysterious cash infusions from Russia; or c) because drag queen Bambi Sugapops is hiding out at Noah's house in the midst of a knock-down, bare-knuckled drag feud.

Will Noah ever catch a break?!

NOAH COULD NEVER
"SIDE-SPLITTING COMEDY"
THE GUARDIAN
SIMON JAMES GREEN

Alex In Wonderland

"Simon James Green is one of the most hilarious, heart-flippingly romantic, charmingly observant writers in the game right now." – Becky Albertalli, author of *Love, Simon*

In the town of Newsands, painfully shy Alex is abandoned by his two best friends for the summer. But he unexpectedly lands a part-time job at Wonderland, a run-down amusement arcade on the seafront, where he gets to know the other teen misfits who work there. Alex starts to come out of his shell, and even starts to develop feelings for co-worker Ben ... who, as Alex's bad luck would have it, has a girlfriend. Then as debtors close in on Wonderland and mysterious, threatening notes start to appear, Alex and his new friends take it on themselves to save their declining employer. But, like everything in Wonderland, nothing is quite what it seems...

Just shy of a boyfriend...

ALEX in WONDER LAND

"Hilarious and heart-flippingly romantic"

BECKY ALBERTALLI,
author of LOVE, SIMON

Simon James Green

Heartbreak Boys

At the start of summer, Jack and Nate find themselves dumped as their respective exes, Dylan and
Tariq, start up a new relationship together. Not only
that, their exes start posting pics on social media,
showing the whole world how fabulous their new
life together is! Jack and Nate are reeling. Not to be
outdone, they decide to create their own 'highlights
reel' and show their exes that they're having an even
better time. But between the depressing motorway
service station motels, damp campsites, and an
ultimate showdown with the exes, something epic
really is happening: Jack and Nate are learning to get
over their heartache and open themselves up to new
possibilities for love.

HEARTBREAK BOYS

NO VACANCY

SIMON JAMES GREEN

"One of the most
hilarious, romantic
writers in the game
right now."
BECKY ALBERTALLI,
author of
LOVE, SIMON

ABOUT SIMON

Simon James Green is the world's leading authority on awkward teenage boys*, mainly because he was one. He has written a number of desperately awkward young adult novels, including *Noah Can't Even* (longlisted for the Branford Boase); *Noah Could Never* (longlisted for nothing, despite it being a work of comic genius*); *Alex in Wonderland* (nominated for the Carnegie medal); and *Heartbreak Boys* (picked by *Attitude* magazine and Gay's the Word bookshop as one of the best LGBT novels of the year). 2020 also saw publication of Simon's debut picture book, *Llama Glamarama*, illustrated by Garry Parsons, and his first middle-grade book, *Life of Riley: Beginner's Luck* – so if dancing llamas or cursed ten-year-old boys are your thing, check them out.

www.simonjamesgreen.com

Twitter & Instagram: @simonjamesgreen

* probably